P9-CMW-805

BACKLASH

BACKLASH

CHRIS KNOPF

THE PERMANENT PRESS
Sag Harbor, NY 11963

For information, address:
    The Permanent Press
    4170 Noyac Road
    Sag Harbor, NY 11963
    www.thepermanentpress.com

Library of Congress Cataloging-in-Publication Data

    Knopf, Chris, author.
        Title: Back lash / Chris Knopf.
        Other titles: Backlash
        Description: Sag Harbor, NY : The Permanent Press, [2016]
        Series: A Sam Acquillo Hamptons mystery
        Identifiers: LCCN 2016002718
        ISBN 9781579624293 (hardcover)
        Subjects: LCSH: Acquillo, Sam (Fictitious character)—Fiction.
        GSAFD: Mystery fiction.
        Classification: LCC PS3611.N66 B32 2016 | DDC 813/.6—dc23
        LC record available at http://lccn.loc.gov/2016002718

Printed in the United States of America

CHAPTER ONE

It was obvious from the way the mechanic looked at the two guys walking into the bar that it wasn't going to be a regular night.

The mechanic liked his routines, always sitting in the same booth, near the back. He would arrive around five thirty when the booth was usually available. He faced the door, and most nights took very little interest in who came or went.

He always ordered a cheeseburger with a fried egg under the cheese, with lettuce and tomato on the side. A shot of Canadian whiskey and a draft beer, Miller High Life. He read the *Daily News*, folding it into quarters so he could hold the paper with one hand while eating his meal with the other.

He spoke with an accent people assumed was Italian based on the guy's name, though not from any part of Italy anybody knew. His clothes were fresh and clean, but a slight fragrance of petroleum products hung in his vicinity. A persistent dark stain along his right index finger was further proof that he spent the day fixing cars and trucks.

He always ate alone, and never said hello to the other regulars, most of whom were already at the bar when he arrived, their backs to the row of booths along the wall. Everyone was satisfied with this arrangement, settled into their own routines and free of forced social niceties. It was the reason the mechanic chose the bar to begin with. The patrons ignored his reticence, tolerant by way of utter indifference.

The place was a classic New York borough bar, though of an early vintage. Inside was a type of perpetual night, the few windows at the entryway small, with thick, translucent glass. The woodwork, a deep mahogany, soaked up what little natural light got through.

Above the woodwork was painted green plaster, covered here and there with framed covers of *Life* magazines, the most recent commemorating MacArthur's return to the Philippines. A threadbare carpet divided the bar from the wall of booths. Around the bar itself the floorboards were worn down to the naked wood. The foot rail was heavy, solid brass, shiny on top. The bartender often wondered why no enterprising thief had ripped it out, since it was the only thing of real value in the whole place.

The two guys who came in that night were new to the bar. They were young, about college age, though far from college material. It was the late seventies, but the aesthetic preferences of the fifties still clung to men in the Bronx who'd given allegiance to the principles of rebellion and social disharmony.

Black hair, combed back from the face, loose nylon jackets over blue jeans, black leather shoes. White leather driving gloves adorned with the logo of an Italian sports car. Cigarettes stuffed in T-shirt pockets under the jackets, nicotine stains on fingers and teeth attesting to their constant deployment.

They were both bigger than average, though one was bigger still. They took the two seats at the bar usually claimed by a set of cousins from the butcher shop who'd be showing up in about ten minutes. The violation bothered the bartender, but he also had an instinct for customer service, so he said, "What'll you have?" to the two young men with no betrayal of annoyance.

The men disappointed him further by ordering Southern Comfort on the rocks, a drink he considered sweetly effeminate, while acknowledging it packed a greater than average alcoholic punch. But he took it in stride and poured the drinks after wiping some dust off the little-used bottle. He also slid an ashtray in front of them as they lit up their Chesterfields.

That was when he noticed the mechanic looking over at the two young men. He still had the folded *Daily News* in his left hand, but his right was flat on the table and his gaze fixed in place. The two men didn't seem to notice, sipping their sugary liquor and speaking to each other in tones too low to easily make out the words.

The bartender's sister, who waited on the booths, asked the mechanic if he wanted another beer, which he always did after finishing his cheeseburger. And that night was no different, though it took him a moment to register that the waitress was standing there talking to him. Then, as if a spell was broken, he ordered the beer and went back to reading the *Daily News*.

The two young men at the bar asked for another round of Southern Comfort, this time doubles, joking that the drink glasses were all glass with no place to put any booze. The bartender was vaguely offended by this, but took the jibing in the spirit intended and gave each of them more than double the original portions. They toasted him and he nodded after wiping the bar clean and emptying out the ashtrays.

The cousins from the butcher shop came in on cue, and suffered a few moments confusion over the appropriation of their regular stools. The bartender jerked his head toward two seats at the other end of the bar, and the cousins lumbered on through, though not happily. After setting down their drinks, the bartender told them the first round was on the house, a gracious gesture deeply appreciated.

One of the two guys who'd commandeered the butchers' seats waved the bartender back in their direction. They asked if he had anything salty they could munch on, peanuts or beef jerky. When he said no, the smaller of the two said, "What kind of fucking bar doesn't have peanuts?" which caused the bigger one to swat him and say, "Shut up, douche bag. Plenty of fucking bars."

The bartender put menus in front of them and said they could have any of the appetizers half-price, as compensation for the missing peanuts. This seemed to please the two guys, as if they'd logged an important victory.

"You can take them gloves off if you want," he told them. "Be easier to eat."

"We like these gloves," said one of the guys. "Easier to wipe our noses."

The other guy thought this was pretty funny.

On the way to the kitchen, the bartender noticed the mechanic wasn't in his booth, though his partially consumed beer and the *Daily News* were still in place. He could see that the men's room door, usually open a crack, was closed, which explained things. When he came back from the kitchen, the mechanic was back in his seat, though still more interested in the two young guys at the bar than either his newspaper or the beer. He waved the bartender over to the booth.

"Did you know the back door to this place is locked?" the mechanic asked in his funny accent. "That's a safety hazard."

Since this amounted to a doubling of the words the mechanic had spoken to him over the years he'd been coming into the bar, it took the bartender a little by surprise.

"It ain't locked," he said to the mechanic. "And anyway, you the safety inspector?"

"No, just mentioning it. Seemed like it was locked."

"Only at the end of the night. Were you planning on catching a little air? We got a front door too."

The mechanic picked up his newspaper.

"Forget it," he said. "None of my business."

"That's all right, buddy. Enjoy the beer," said the bartender.

He went down the short, narrow hall to the back door and tried the knob. It didn't budge, though the dead bolt was released and another slide bolt near the top of the jamb was pulled into the open position.

"What the fuck," the bartender mumbled, making a mental note to go around back after closing time to see what the problem was.

He didn't own the place, but might as well have, since his aunt, the old widow of the original owner, entrusted him with everything. The pay wasn't fantastic, but she promised to sell it to him on the cheap someday, which he secretly found a little unsettling for reasons he hadn't bothered to figure out. But meanwhile, it gave him something to do, with plenty of freedom over how he did it, and it kept his sister from just rotting away in her apartment with her soap operas and tea-cups filled with Peppermint Schnapps.

Without much further thought about the door, he went back to serving drinks and plates of standard fare to the gradually increasing patronage.

At around seven P.M., the booths were full and seats at the bar became scarce. This was usually the cue for the mechanic to slip away, leaving behind a little pile of cash that precisely matched his tab, plus 15 percent for the bartender's sister. So it was notable that he still sat there, his beer glass empty and *Daily News* shoved off to the side.

The bartender kept an eye on him, without appearing to do so, while refilling glasses and clearing plates. That's why he saw the mechanic finally get up from the booth and walk slowly toward the back of the bar. In his peripheral vision, the bartender saw the two young guys also leave their seats, and move in the same direction.

The mechanic went into the men's room and closed the door. Moments later, the two guys reached the men's room and the bigger one tried the doorknob. The bartender moved closer to the wall phone next to the cash register, but kept his eyes on the two guys, which is how he saw the smaller one move as far away as the tight confines of the hallway would allow, and with a suddenness that seemed unnatural, bring up his right foot and smash it into the men's room door.

The bartender spun around and started dialing 911. He looked back in time to see both guys shouldering their way into the men's room. The low hum of conversation in the bar was overwhelmed by the crashing din coming from the back of the bar. Like a flock of birds startled by a sudden gunshot, the people in the bar jumped to their feet and fluttered toward the front entrance. One regular fell off his stool, but still managed a staggering retreat, with no look behind. The bartender's sister screamed.

The 911 dispatcher seemed unimpressed by the report of a bar fight. She made the bartender repeat his name, the name of the place, the address, and confirmation that no firearms were involved. This the bartender couldn't do, since the violent sounds coming from the men's room included everything from screeches to low thuds, more felt as vibrations from the floor as heard by ear.

The bartender grabbed a full bottle of single malt Scotch, instinctively picked for the expensive heft of the glass container, and ducked under the hinged access door. In the narrow hallway he could see only the nylon jackets of the two guys billowing around broad shoulders, animated by a windmill of repeated blows. He yelled, "Hey!" and took a swing with the bottle of Scotch, but the smaller guy had already begun to spin around, as if he had eyes in the back of his head, and with one gloved hand, caught the bottle mid-arc.

The guy grinned and the bartender heard a different kind of sound, this one from inside his own head. The world suddenly lost tangibility, and the floor seemed to slant upward, slapping him across the full of his back.

Jagged sparkles of light obscured his view of the tin ceiling. The noise in his head subsided, replaced by sounds of men grunting and huffing in hard labor, punctuated by steady, moist thumps.

And then all the sounds stopped. He tried to raise his head, but was thrown back by a foot to the sternum.

"Stay down," said one of the guys, his voice a determined rasp.

So he did. Closing his eyes and watching a pinwheel of tiny firecrackers, and feeling something warm and wet on his upper lip, realizing it was blood as it flowed over his right jaw and dripped down his neck.

He didn't hear them, but knew they'd left by the front door, since even in the delirium of the moment, it occurred to him that the back door was impassable, screwed shut as it surely was from the outside.

CHAPTER TWO

I spend a lot of time in an Adirondack chair perched above a breakwater looking out at the Little Peconic Bay. It's been a number of years since I started doing this in earnest, about the time I moved back into my dead parents' cottage in the North Sea area of Southampton, Long Island.

You'd think it would get tedious looking at the same body of water, and the opposite shore, a tree-covered coast with sandy hills and houses of its own etching the horizon. But with subtle variations in sunlight, wind, currents, and cloud cover, it turns out no two days are exactly the same. Maybe you wouldn't see these fine distinctions, but you probably wouldn't spend as much time as I do studying this particular body of water.

I like to drink while I'm doing all this looking, though only in the evening after I'm done working in my shop in the basement of the cottage. My dog, Eddie, is nearly always with me, and he'll watch the water as well, though he'd rather be chasing balls or seabirds, or other threats invisible to all but himself.

My girlfriend, Amanda Anselma, who lives next door, also puts in a lot of time in the Adirondack chairs, but she was at her house that evening when the tall man strode toward me across the lawn. I only knew he was there because Eddie

12

started barking, and I had to strain my neck to turn and watch his approach.

It was late September, though still warm enough to get away with a T-shirt and hoodie. The guy walking toward me wore a polyester jacket, which probably wasn't warm enough, since he had his hands shoved deep in the pockets. He was about six foot three, with a thin frame and equally thin grey hair that the wind unkindly whipped across his face.

Usually by that time of year, everyone on the East End was about as tan as they would get, though already starting to fade. The tall man, in contrast, was very pale, as if he'd seen little of the sun. Most of his height was in his legs and he was pigeon-toed, so the walk was more of a lope. The sun was just about to dive below the horizon, so you'd need sunglasses to look out at the bay, and the off-sea breeze didn't help, so the man had a pretty serious squint, though his eyes were fixed on me sitting in my chair.

Eddie ran up to him, welcoming but slightly wary. The man let a long arm drop down to give him a quick pat on the head, then kept walking.

"Sorry to bother you," he said. "I'm looking for Sam Acquillo."

"Not a bother. You found him."

He moved around to face the chair, which took the strain off my neck. He kept his bony hands in the pockets of the windbreaker.

"I'm Ray Osmund. This looks like a nice place to sit."

"I think it's the nicest place in the known universe, but I own it, so I'm probably biased."

"You weren't as hard to find as I thought you'd be," he said.

"I suppose that's true of everybody these days. All you need is a computer and a patient mind."

He looked at the empty Adirondack where Amanda usually sat. I tilted my head in that direction.

"Go ahead, take a seat," I said. "I've got beer in the house, unless you like straight vodka, in which case we'll need another glass."

"I took the pledge, so now it's strictly Diet Coke, though I'm all set for now, thanks."

I was glad to hear it, since I really didn't want to walk all the way back to the cottage. And I still got to make the offer.

"My sponsor is actually the reason I'm here," he said. "He was hoping I could find you. No, wait a minute. *I* was hoping I could find you, on his behalf."

People weren't usually looking for me. As far as I knew, I didn't owe anyone money. There was the possibility of a grudge, an itch for revenge, though Ray Osmund hardly looked the type to deliver the payback. There was very little anyone wanted from me, in a professional way, since custom wood-working usually came by way of a few known contractors. My former professional life, running a big R&D operation in the hydrocarbon-processing industry, was well behind me.

"Who would that be?" I asked. "Your sponsor."

"Marcelo Bonaventure. You probably knew him as Bonnie."

I told him that I'd known a Bonnie or two, but they were all women.

"It was a long time ago," said Ray. "You'd be forgiven for not remembering."

He was still standing in front of me, which was blocking the northwesterly breeze and the start of the sunset, the set-piece moment on the Little Peconic Bay. Unique every evening, but more important, perishable, never to be seen again in quite the same way.

"The other chair's still available," I said. "Take a load off."

He took a single long stride over to the chair and eased himself down. The chair was low to the ground, so his knees rose to an awkward elevation. I wondered about getting him back out again.

"How long ago is long?" I asked him.

"About forty years, give or take."

"That's long enough."

"Not even the same world, if you ask me. Might as well be another galaxy. And all in our short little lifetimes."

Now that he was turned full to the breeze, I could see his whole face. He had the type of fair complexion that resulted in millions of little age wrinkles, especially around the eyes, with crow's-feet that were more like the feathers of a tropical bird. Damaged capillaries blossomed on his cheeks and the tip of his nose.

"Forty years ago I was still trying to get my degree," I said. "The only thing I remember about those days was reconciling computational fluid dynamics with repeated blows to the head."

"I know. You were a boxer. I saw you fight."

My mind played the little movie it often did featuring images of the train ride down to New York from Cambridge with my gym bag and textbooks, the smelly locker room, getting my hands taped, and listening to the trainer counsel me against exposing my midsection. The smoky arena filled with men and women aroused with bloodlust and the prospect of a big win on their bets, rarely fulfilled. I wouldn't have remembered a younger Ray Osmund.

"How did I do?" I asked.

"You won. On points. You were faster than the other guy, but lacked the power to put him away."

That was a fair assessment of my boxing career in general. He likely didn't know the underlying issues, that the other guys were usually bigger and stronger, and I never stopped worrying about getting too close to a muscle-driven hook that would damage my brain, which was battered enough by the course work up at MIT.

"I hope I didn't lose you any money."

"That I don't remember. Though I didn't win much overall. Otherwise, I'd be sitting on my own waterfront lawn taking in the night."

"No credit to the fight game for that," I said. "It's inherited. My old man bought the land for 500 bucks and built the house out of scraps."

"Like I said. A different galaxy back then."

I took a pull from my aluminum tumbler before asking, "So what about Bonnie? What's he want?"

"A conversation."

"That's doable," I said. "Any idea about what?"

"He doesn't think you'll want to talk about it. That's why I said I'd find you and ask. He didn't think you'd even be around the area, so I already proved him wrong on that count."

"Even minor victories can feel good. Can you give me a headline? I'll talk to anybody, but I'm curious."

Osmund turned his head toward me, which caused the breeze to flutter his stringy hair back into his face. He withdrew a long-fingered hand from the pocket and pulled the hair out of the way.

"He doesn't want to talk about it, either, but I convinced him he should, if I made it easy for him."

"Okay. I'm listening."

"Your father."

I went back to looking at the water, and took a longer pull off the tumbler. The sunset had begun, a short-lived thing, but the first gold and fuchsia rays slicing up from the horizon held some promise. A clump of puffy clouds off to the east had already begun to glow from the underside, a preview of coming events.

"You're right," I said. "Not something I like talking about."

"I still think you might want to talk to Bonnie."

"Why's that?"

"He was there when it happened."

By "it" I knew what he meant. It was when my father was beaten to death in a men's room at the back of a bar in the Bronx. I didn't know which boxing match of mine Ray had seen, but it would have been around the same time. It might have been the exact same time, since I was about to board the train back to Boston when I thought to call my mother to tell her I was still intact and in reasonable command of my faculties. She was living in the cottage on the Little Peconic with my sister, whom she hadn't yet told that our father was in the morgue, or why he ended up there. That was unknown at that point, and had remained that way.

"Does he know who did it?" I asked Ray.

"That's what he wants to talk to you about."

Not everyone gets to live their adult lives orbiting a central mystery. If you do, you know about the gravitational pull, different from the celestial in that it waxes and wanes, often to the point of imperceptibility, though never entirely gone. In my case, it was the finality of death that complicated things. That he was gone forever was an irretrievable fact. So the biggest mystery was what might have happened between us if he'd lived on. I was enough of an empirical engineer to avoid speculation in the absence of tangible data. Though as I sat there in the Adirondack chair talking to Ray Osmund, obviously not empirical enough.

"Okay," I said. "I can do that. Now that he knows where I live."

"There's the problem," said Ray. "Bonnie's turning ninety this year. He's not going anywhere. And you won't get him on the phone, which is a waste of time anyway since he can't hear for beans. You got to go see him."

"So that's how it is," I said. "He's on the verge and wants to clear up a few things before he goes."

Ray shook his head.

"This is all my idea. I think it's a matter of his everlasting soul. He doesn't seem to care much about it, but in my opinion he saved mine. So I feel a duty to look after his whether he likes it or not."

"Part of the program?" I asked.

"Not exactly. Bonnie's not much of a believer. He likes telling me the only higher authority he ever bent to was his wife, and she's been dead for ten years. But he turned me to God anyway, whether he admits it or not. We all have our ways of approaching the issue. It's up to you, of course. But I think it's at least worth a trip to the Bronx and a few minutes talking to an old man. Can't hurt anything."

I wasn't so sure about that. He didn't know how I'd been spending the last forty years working through my own obsessions, preoccupations, and unmanageable behavior. Living with the unknowable had been its own type of mooring. What engineers call an operating condition, a set point upon which other assumptions relied.

"I'll think about it," I said.

Ray pulled an index card out of the pocket of his windbreaker and handed it to me. Written on it was Bonnie's full name, address, and phone number. He was in a place called Saint Anthony's, named after the patron saint of the elderly. I wondered how that sat with a skeptic like Marcelo Bonaventure. Probably hedging his bets.

"Don't think too long," said Ray. "Bonnie's working on a short tether."

He rose from the chair, unfolding his praying-mantis frame until he stood again before me. I stood up as well, and took his offered hand.

"I hear you," I said. "I'll go see him."

"He'll be expecting you," he said, then took his rangy, pigeon-toed stride across the lawn and around the cottage and disappeared, to my eyes at least, since by then I was back looking at the Little Peconic Bay where the sunset was in full bloom over calm seas, though the roiling tempest that defined my every waking hour had only just begun.

Chapter Three

Amanda Anselma had the type of green eyes that were actually green, in a pale, limpid way not unlike the sunlit Caribbean. That morning, I only saw one of those eyes, since the other was covered by thick auburn hair that rolled and cascaded over her face and down across the rumpled bedsheets.

I call it auburn, since that was the color when we met, back when I was first trying out the Adirondack chairs. It was still the same color, a sort of deep-stained mahogany that turned redder in the summer, contrasting nicely with her dark Italian skin, though she laid all the credit with her hairdresser. Whatever alchemy was responsible, I never tired of looking at her, day or night.

"What are you looking at?" she asked.

"I was watching you sleep."

"Sounds boring."

"It is, mostly. You're more interesting awake."

"I need to get up," she said. "I have work sites to sweep and carpenters to thrash."

Amanda owned a trove of aging houses in Southampton that she was steadily improving and selling at confiscatory prices. She was her own contractor, a role that seemed to suit her. I assumed her subs all liked her, though I knew for sure they respected her, in part because she wasn't beneath sweeping up sawdust or cracking heads whenever cracking was called for.

"I have to go to Saint Anthony's," I said.

She leaned back as if to get my face in clearer focus.

"Really. Finally ready to confess?"

"It's an old folks home. I'm paying a call on one of their oldest folks."

"Okay. No less a surprise."

"His name is Marcelo Bonaventure. They call him Bonnie, and he apparently knows something about my father's death."

This time she sat all the way up, the sheet pinched around her middle like a bath towel.

I told her about the visit from Ray Osmund and everything I remembered about the conversation. She listened with those green eyes a little wider than I was used to seeing.

"Holy cow," she said, when I was finished.

"At least god-sent, if you listen to Ray Osmund."

"You actually considered not doing this," she said.

I admitted I had. I made my living building custom wood-work and cabinetry, mostly for a local builder named Frank Entwhistle. What I liked about the work was it mostly took place in my shop in the basement of the cottage. Frank was easy to deal with, and usually gave me plenty of latitude to do the quality job he expected of me. I thought about the stack of designs he'd handed me as we watched his crew haul my latest contributions out of the basement. I was about to tell Amanda I had a tough deadline to meet, but honesty stopped me, since that really wasn't true.

"I'm not sure I really want to hear what Bonnie has to say. You're talking a long time ago and a lot of water under the bridge. What difference does it make now?"

She didn't like that.

"All the difference in the world. His death was one of the biggest things that ever happened in your life. You owe it to yourself. And your sister. And Allison."

She meant my daughter, who never knew her grandfather, which to me was a blessing. Allison's mother shared that view. One of the few things we managed to agree on.

"I guess that's true," I said. "Though we'd all be fine if Osmund had never come to call."

"Anyway, you said you'd see this Bonnie guy, so that's that."

"I did, and I will."

"And if you ask me, that decision was never in doubt," she added.

"Oh yeah?"

She almost looked disdainful.

"I know you, Sam Acquillo. Whatever reluctance you might have about opening old wounds, or even thinking about this stuff, there's one thing you never resist."

"What?"

She gently tapped on my forehead.

WHEN I phoned Amanda from the car on the way into the city, she asked if they knew I was coming. I said no, of course not. I never called ahead, and why bother when you're calling on a ninety-year-old guy in a nursing home?

"Maybe he'd like to spruce himself up. Get his hearing aids serviced."

"I'll call you on the way back. Tell you what he said."

"You better. And I'll want details."

"You're unusually keen on this."

"I am. I get that way when I think you're working against your better interests."

"What's so interesting?"

She took a moment to respond.

"Your dad might have been a son of a bitch, but at least you had one. I never knew mine. I could have. We lived in the same town, but my mother never told me who he was. And now she's dead too. There's nothing else for me to know."

So there was my answer. It really wasn't Allison and my sister I owed this to. It was Amanda. And in her wisdom, she knew that would make all the difference.

SAINT ANTHONY's looked as old as the saint himself. It was in a reasonably tidy section of the North Bronx, where it smelled like an old town, but there were lots of trees and the sidewalks were swept clean and the people on the streets more bustling than sinister. My father once had an apartment not far from there where I'd often stay for short visits, especially in the summer when I was off school. The rest of the time I was out on Oak Point with my mother and sister, where my father had established us as year-round residents. The story was he wanted us to grow up away from the dinge and dangers of the Bronx, not an unfair proposition given the times, though I never entirely bought that line. I'm certain my mother didn't either, though we were happier to see him drive off Sunday nights than see him show up on Fridays, exhausted and grease covered after a hard week on the job.

I'd probably walked by that old folks home plenty of times without knowing what it was. Around six stories high, made of brick, and enclosed by a tall cyclone fence, it could have been anything in a neighborhood of brick row houses, flat-roofed storefronts, and ancient industrial lofts.

I parked my car at the curb and pushed the button on a squawk box mounted to the fence. A female voice squawked back.

"Can I help you?"

"I'm here to see a resident named Marcelo Bonaventure. If I got the right place."

The voice came back a few moments later.

"The purpose of the visit?"

"Just a visit. I'm an old friend."

"And your name?"

"Sam Acquillo."

"We don't have you on our list of approved visitors."

"Just tell him I'm here. He'll want to see me."

At least I hoped he would, now that I'd driven all the way there.

"Approval needs to be obtained in advance."

Man, I said to myself. Nothing's easy.

"Is Ray Osmund on that list?" I asked.

She said he was absolutely on the list.

"Then call him and ask if I'm okay. I know he wants me here."

To her credit, she must have done just that, because a few minutes later the gate buzzed and I could push it open. I walked up a steep flight of concrete steps and through the tall double doors, oak-framed and covered in the accumulated nicks and scrapes of long, hard service.

Inside was a narrow foyer with a twelve-foot-high ceiling and a little table that served as the home's reception desk. A woman about the size of a third-grader sat there looking unsure whether to greet me or dial the cops.

"Mr. Bonaventure never mentioned you," she said.

"I thought we called him Bonnie," I said.

That was the right thing to say. It made her give up a smile.

"We do. His old friends anyway. You need to sign in and write your name on this."

She handed me a stick-on name tag.

"So you knew him in the day?" I asked.

"Drank at his bar, if that's what you mean. Fun place, what I remember of it."

"You also take the pledge?"

"Twenty-three years, two months, a week, and three days." She checked a big clock on the wall. "And about twelve hours, depending on when I found my bed."

"Is that the deal here? All AA?"

"It's part of the deal. You looking for a meeting?"

"Just with Bonnie, if that's okay."

"If it's okay with Ray, it's okay with me."

She picked up the phone, the only thing modern enough to prove we weren't still in the twentieth century, and tapped in a few numbers. She asked someone named Flora to come out and escort me up to Mr. Bonaventure on the fourth floor.

"You can wait here," she told me, so I sat in one of two matching wooden chairs. It was strangely comfortable, worn smooth by eons of waiting family and friends.

"Whatever happened to Bonnie's bar?" I asked her.

"He sold it to a couple of dolts who redid the inside and brought in a bunch of potted plants. Closed in a month. I think it's a Laundromat now, but I haven't been over there in years. No reason to. What's your connection?"

"I sort of lived around here as a kid," I said. "Bonnie knew my dad."

"That puts him in a pretty big crowd."

Flora was a delicate Latina in plain clothes just snug enough to show there was a shapely girl underneath. Her handshake was deliberate, though cautious.

"Mr. Aqui-yo?" she asked, looking at my name tag.

"Close. We pronounce the *l*'s. Think quill, like a porcupine. It's Italian."

"Certainly. Acquillo," she said, getting it right. "Follow me."

She led me down a long hall as poorly lit as the foyer with ceilings just as high. Then we took an elevator that probably once needed an operator. I braced myself for what was to come, but didn't have to. The elevator opened up on a large open space that would have done honor to a real estate brochure. Natural light flooded in from the tall double-hung windows, softly absorbed by soothing, but hip colors on the walls, furniture, and floors. Plants grew in profusion and a yellow Labrador made the rounds unattended. The wintry-haired clientele were all neatly dressed in regular clothes, and mostly sat in chrome and leather chairs and overstuffed sofas. The caregivers were distinguishable only by their younger age. A single TV was off in a far corner with the sound turned off.

At least that's what I thought, until I was close enough to see the TV watchers were wearing earphones.

Flora guided me through the room, turning a few heads and quieting conversations. That's when I noticed a missing virtue. Not many visitors. I looked for longing in the eyes of the aged, but only saw a covert curiosity.

We found Bonnie in a small reading room off the main area. He sat with his back to the window, posture straight, hands in his lap, with a book open on the table in front of him. He looked up as we approached, his tired eyes greeting Flora.

"Señor Bonnie, this is Mr. Acquillo," she said to him.

He looked familiar, though it might have been a manufactured memory. We'd last spoken forty years ago, so the vast breadth of time had doubtlessly warped both of us, and our memories, into the unrecognizable.

I remembered him as a handsome man, and he still was, in a reserved, circumspect way. His full head of short hair was black back then, and now as fine and white as fresh snow. The skin on his hands was translucent, crazed with tiny purple veins, and mottled, but his handshake was firm and decisive.

I wondered how the tattoo he got in the navy was holding up, hidden as it was by his long-sleeved shirt.

"Looks like Osmund made good on his promise," he said, as I sat down across from him and Flora made a silent retreat.

His voice was hoarse and the Bronx lay heavily on his accent, though a version you'd rarely hear today. As if he was imitating a character in an old gangster movie, reminding me that my father's generation really did speak that way. Though not my father, who'd grown up speaking French in Montreal, and was thus the master of his own distinctive pronunciations.

"He's pretty persuasive," I said.

"Pain in the ass, if you ask me."

"I guess you'd know. Not a bad place you got here," I added, looking around at the book-lined walls.

"The nuns do it up right, you gotta admit."

I had a jolt of yearning for a cigarette, most likely to give me something to do as I searched for my conversational footing. But I'd given up the habit more than a year before, and the nuns wouldn't allow it anyway.

"I asked the lady downstairs what happened to your bar, and she wasn't sure, only that you'd sold it awhile ago."

He nodded, with his lips puckered, as if still mulling the decision.

"Made good money off that place. Not too many guys can say that."

"I was only there the one time, a few days after it happened," I said. "You remember?"

"Yeah. I remember. Made the mistake of telling Osmund about it."

"You don't have to talk about this if you don't want to, Bonnie. I'm only here because my girlfriend leaned on me. You know how that is."

"I do. Had a wife and a sister with strong opinions on what I should or should not be doing. They're both dead, but I still have them women yakkin' away in my head."

I felt a little bad representing Amanda as anything like a nag, since she was anything but. Though it served to establish a scrap of common ground.

"Ray said you were there when it happened."

"I was always there. I was the bartender."

I acknowledged that.

"So what do you want to know?" he asked. "If anything."

"Who did it."

He had a steady nod going, which I realized was more an elderly tic than sign of agreement.

"I'm not sure. But I had my suspicions. Sorry if that disappoints you."

"Sort of. Tell me how it went down."

He told the story in a steady, relentless way that made me think he'd told it before. Maybe only to Ray Osmund, I couldn't tell. But it wasn't that different from what I was told by the cops at the time, when I stuck around and made a pest out of myself and risked my academic standing by blowing off two weeks of course work. One new piece of information was Bonnie's description of the two punks who did the deed. He seemed secure on that part of the memory, so I wrote it all down, though I knew eyewitness testimony was notoriously suspect, even without the forty-year interval.

He'd never seen the two guys before, and didn't know their names, but he was sure they were connected to organized crime by their arrogant and presumptuous manner. And the way they dressed and combed their hair. In those days, it was more important to signal your affiliation to the mob business than hide from the authorities, so I understood what he was saying.

"I counted myself lucky that the protection boys left us alone," he said. "My uncles who sold me the place knew a lot of people. Our name in Italy was Bonaventura. That don't mean the occasional wise guy wouldn't come in for a few drinks on the house, usually with some doll he was hiding from his old lady. We'd accommodate."

I'd always assumed my father had screwed up somehow with professional criminals. Even if it was just a rude remark or nasty look, two things he dispensed indiscriminately. So this was no great revelation.

"Did you hear anything afterward, any chatter on the street?" I asked.

"Not exactly. What I heard was worse."

"Oh."

"This is the point."

"Why something's still eating at you?" I asked.

"Didn't say that."

"Ray Osmund implied."

"He did, did he?"

"Or maybe I just inferred."

He adjusted himself slightly in his straight-backed chair, which suited his erect posture.

"It's about your old man," he said. "Once you start down this path, you might wish you hadn't."

I felt the rumble of irritation start somewhere deep in my insides, as if that's where the subconscious was actually lodged and not in the brain where it's supposed to be.

"If you're trying to protect me, Bonnie, you can knock it off. I've done a few things since we talked that day in your bar, and none of them involved dodging difficult news."

"Tough guy, eh? I guess. You could take a punch, you proved that."

"So spill it, or I'll tell Ray Osmund your everlasting soul's got an expiration date."

"Love that guy, but what a fuckin' buttinsky."

"Fine," I said, and got up to leave. I figured I could find my way out without Flora.

"Okay already," he said, as forcefully as his ancient croak would allow. "Sit down."

I sat.

"The day after, a cop comes around. Only it wasn't our regular beat cop, but a captain, somebody I'd never seen before. I told him everything I knew and gave descriptions of the two guys and all that. Told him how the back door was screwed shut, indicating some advance planning. He wrote it all down, but didn't seem all that interested in particulars. When I asked him what the chances were of catching those guys he sort of got up in my face, as if I was the one in Dutch. Then he told me the thing."

"What thing?"

He took a pause, then said, "That those punks had done a service to society. That if anybody needed killin', it was André Acquillo. He said don't get all hepped up on catchin' no killers. And sorry about my nose, which them bastards broke."

"Really."

"Osmund wanted me to tell you and you wanted to know. So there you go. Can't say I didn't warn you."

And he was right. He tried to warn me, but I had to ignore my better instincts, and like my pigheaded old man, I got exactly what I deserved.

CHAPTER FOUR

At issue was a missing pencil. In retrospect, it made the explosion even more preposterous, though at the time, I was still young enough to believe a missing pencil held some grave importance.

We were at the cottage on the Little Peconic. My father had built it himself, including hand-laying the cinder block foundation, running electrical and plumbing, and framing the walls.

There was a kitchen with an eating area and two bedrooms, one for my parents and the other shared by my sister and me. And the sunporch, which was almost as big as the rest of the house, serving as the receiver of summer breezes, and in winter a frigid living room.

My father was always bigger than me, and at that time he seemed to fill the little house, a thundering, French-inflected colossus. Whenever he was there, the kids would try to melt into secret crevices, but my mother had fewer places to hide, so she had to endure whatever came.

There was a shed at the back of the property tucked into a stand of oaks and cedar trees. It was big enough to garage his pickup, and leave space for a workshop and desk, where he kept a meticulous accounting of his mechanics business. At the heart of that operation was an old-fashioned ledger book, where he would pencil in trial balances, prospective income, and expenses anticipated in coming months, which were reversed out when the final billing came in. Consistent with the discipline he applied to the books, there was a specific type of pencil favored for the initial entries. A number three of a certain style that was crisp enough for clear numbering, but easy to erase.

One Saturday, when he went to work on the bookkeeping, the pencils were gone. Our first warning was a bellow coming from the shed, audible inside the cottage despite the long stretch of yard. When he left the shed, you had the sense of the air between the buildings being compressed by the force of rage coming toward us. We were in the kitchen, and I saw my mother grip the edge of the counter and stare down into the sink. My sister's eyes darted from where my mother stood at the window facing the shed, and then she bolted from her seat and ran outside.

To the rear was an aluminum screen door. The latch was never easy to maneuver, and that day proved far too recalcitrant for my father's urgency. After a brief agitated wrangling, he stood back and kicked the latch hard enough to bend the door frame clear of the catch, then grabbed the destroyed aluminum frame and ripped it off the hinges.

My mother stood by the counter, looking down. I was in my seat at the breakfast table when he came into the kitchen, screaming, "*Les crayons! Où est cet hostie des crayons!*"

"I don't know, André," said my mother, also in French. "I have no idea what you're talking about."

He then delivered a detailed description of the pencils, their crucial importance to his work, which in turn was vital to the survival of our family, who clearly had no appreciation for the sacrifices he'd made for us, who were so reckless and irresponsible as to willfully disregard his tireless effort to sustain our miserable, ungrateful lives. All at a volume that caused my mother's cup of tea on the kitchen table to rattle in its saucer.

My mother told him again, in her soft voice, that she had no knowledge of the pencils, or of their disappearance. Then he shifted his florid face toward me.

"No, André," she said, following his gaze. "He knows nothing of your pencils."

His voice dropped into a near whisper, which was far more terrifying than the animal roar.

"You are playing with the pencils," he said. I shook my head. "You have gone into my office and disturbed my work. I have told you this is never to be."

"No, André," said my mother. "We never go near your work."

That was when, without looking away from me, he backhanded her. She made a little "oh" and spun away, holding her cheek. I stood up and brought the kitchen table with me, catapulting the breakfast plates into the air and causing my father to step back out of the way. I was small for my age, but more than half my mother's height at that time, so by getting between her and my father, just inside the overturned table, I created a clear boundary.

He took the table by the edge and threw it behind him, the tips of the legs catching and ripping the kitchen curtains off the window. I tried to grow a few more inches and balled my fists.

My father stood motionless, his chest heaving, his eyes filled with fury. I said something in English. I don't remember what, or anything after my father's huge, labor-ravaged hand flashed toward me, with the words, *"Tu es un petit cochon."*

I PICKED up my daughter at the train station in Southampton Village. Along with her boyfriend, Nathan, a curly-headed, scrawny little guy who nevertheless carried both their bags.

He was prone to generosity, and Allison provided plenty of opportunity to give the impulse full expression. Though he still managed to have a backbone, another quality necessary in Allison's boyfriends.

They were visiting before flying to France for a long stay at her mother's house in Provence. It was rare for Allison to take so much time off from her graphic arts clients, but she still wasn't 100 percent after a bad beating suffered the year before, and she wanted her mother and stepfather to get a good dose of her boyfriend. I thought this was a good idea. There was a lot more to Nathan than met the eye, and I'd seen him in some of the toughest circumstances imaginable.

I gave her a hug and took over luggage-hauling duties, stowing everything in the old Grand Prix's vast cavern of a trunk. Nathan rode up front with me so Allison could ride in the back with Eddie, whose lavish greeting bordered on the unseemly.

We made the smallest of small talk on the fifteen-minute drive up to Oak Point, focusing on the train ride and their success at avoiding changing trains midstream. We compared the overall experience with the bus, an alternative method for reaching the Hamptons without a car, and agreed we liked the train better.

"After you're settled come out to the patio," said Amanda, when we arrived at her house. "Refreshments await."

Allison and Nathan would be staying in one of Amanda's sublime bedroom suites, a pleasant alternative to the accommodations at my cottage next door. I established a spot on the patio that allowed an uninterrupted view of the bay. It was late in the afternoon, but there was at least one sailboat still out on the water, racing the waning light into one of the harbors on the North Fork. With a blanket of pillowy clouds lying on the western horizon, the sunset promised to be a bit of a bust, but the rest of the sky was clear, and the old summer-style south-southwesterly breeze blew in some soft warm air.

Eddie was first out of the house, carrying a Big Dog biscuit in his mouth. His deal with Amanda meant he could have at least two a night, but they had to be consumed away from the fine rugs and furniture. I could eat anywhere I wanted, but I also preferred the patio, where you could procure tasty hors d'oeuvres from Amanda's outdoor refrigerator.

Thus engaged, the two of us waited for the rest of the crew. Amanda was the first out.

"You haven't told Allison about your chat with Mr. Bonaventure," she said, as she eased into the lounge chair next to mine.

"I haven't. How'd you know?"

"She would have asked my opinion," she said.

"And you'd tell her?"

"You know what I'd tell her."

Amanda and Allison were good friends. I don't know how that happened. It certainly wasn't engineered by me, if you could ever engineer such a thing. Maybe the burdens of dealing with me had furnished common cause. They also shared a general disinterest in other people, which strangely formed a basis for mutual attraction. Whatever the reason, I was deeply grateful.

After Allison and Nathan joined us, we made it into the dark hours without broaching any meaningful subjects, fraught or otherwise. So I'd nearly managed to put off thoughts of Bonnie the bartender when Amanda gave my calf a little nudge with her sandaled toed. I looked at her.

"What."

She lifted her eyebrows and jerked her head at Allison.

"Go ahead."

"Christ."

"Your father has some interesting news," she said to my daughter, making further delay impossible.

"What," said Allison.

"It's not that interesting."

"Let her be the judge of that," said Amanda.

It wasn't like Amanda to put me in a corner, since that would violate one of the prohibited behaviors long adhered to by unspoken agreement. That she did anyway caused more surprise than irritation.

"I talked to a guy who witnessed your grandfather's murder." Allison's reaction proved Amanda's point.

"Holy shit. What did he say?"

So I told the whole story, beginning with my visit long ago to Bonnie's bar, to Ray Osmund finding me on Oak Point, to my subsequent conversation with Bonnie at the old folks home in the Bronx. I spared no detail, so I got through the story without prompting from Amanda. Allison listened with a vaguely shocked look on her face.

"What are you going to do?" she asked me.

I looked at Amanda and got the answer.

"See it to the end," I said.

"Like you always do."

"Like I always do."

AFTER DROPPING Allison and Nathan off at the train station the next day, I drove over to see Ross Semple. He was the Southampton Town chief of police and a long-term associate of mine. Meaning he'd had me arrested a few times, grilled me more times than that, and at least once asked my help with an official police matter. So you wouldn't call us friends, though I've had friends I trusted less and few I held in higher, albeit grudging, regard.

First I had to get through Janet Orlovsky, the department gatekeeper who commanded her post behind a glass window off the reception area. I told her I needed to ask Ross a favor.

"He said something like 'beneficial acceptance of liberty vendor,'" she told me, after ringing Ross on the internal phone line.

"*Beneficium accipere libertatem est vendere,*" I said. "It means something like 'only chumps ask for favors.'"

"How do you people know this crap?"

"They teach that crap in school. Somebody has to learn it."

"He wants you to go on back," she said, buzzing me in.

He met me halfway, in the middle of an open squad room. The cops and administrators barely acknowledged my presence, since I'd been through there a lot in recent times. Ross stuck out his hand, his arm straight at the elbow, assuring the most awkward possible handshake. Awkward was Ross's forte.

"You know they prosecute police chiefs for doling out favors," he said.

"I just need some information. Free to the public if I had the time."

"So I'm a time-saver, am I?"

He wrestled a pack of Marlboros out of his pocket and lit up, a behavior entirely outside police department rules and one nobody in Town management had thought it worth enforcing with the chief.

"Haven't determined that yet."

He motioned for me to lead us back to his office.

"Lay on, MacDuff."

The office more resembled a warehouse for storing undifferentiated stacks of paper. Ross climbed over the smaller mounds to reach his desk and I cleared a space for myself on a visitor's chair.

"You've got my curiosity, Sam," he said, settling in. "Not easy to do."

"I wouldn't say that. I think you're a very curious man."

"Suspicion isn't the same as curiosity. So what's up?"

I told him the same story I'd told my family when we were sitting on Amanda's patio. With all the details intact, a first for a conversation with Ross Semple, which always required at least some defensive withholding. He listened like he always did, with care and suspicion. If not curiosity.

"This must be a little strange for you," he said.

"More than a little."

"Too bad the bartender couldn't tell you more. It's pretty thin gruel."

"I know. What do you think I should do?"

"What you're doing. Talking to me. I know a cop in the Bronx who works cold cases. Not the squad leader, but one of the obsessive types who live and breathe the stuff. Little touched in the head, in my opinion, but in service of a noble cause."

"Sounds like the right guy."

"Not a guy. Madelyn Wollencroft. Ran her own under-cover team for years till getting shot in the throat. Took some of the charm out of the job. Reassigned to administrative duty in records, which turned into a thing for cold cases."

"So you like her."

"Didn't say that. But if I give her a call, she'll talk to you. Professional courtesy if nothing else. Save you the trouble of clawing through the bureaucracy. Though don't expect them to put people on your father's case. Cold is a relative term, and forty years is pretty chilly."

"That's fine," I said. "No question there're worthier causes than this one."

"Doesn't sound like you."

I had to agree with him.

"This one's different," I said.

"Care too much?" he asked.

"Care too little."

AFTER VISITING Ross Semple I stopped off at the marina on Hawk Pond to check on my boat, the *Carpe Mañana*, a heavy-displacement performance cruiser I'd bought from my friend Burton Lewis with a settlement check from my old cor-poration. It was berthed next to another friend, Paul Hodges, a full-time liveaboard who was usually around, being mostly retired from running his greasy-spoon fish joint up in Sag Harbor.

Since he saw a lot more of her than I did, Hodges had developed proprietary feelings toward the *Carpe Mañana*, which was good for keeping her shipshape, if you could get past the meddling.

"I had to retie her again," he said by way of greeting. "Tide keeps changing. More than usual. Must be the global warming."

"Undoubtedly," I said. "Shrinking ice caps throw the earth off its axis."

"You're lucky the stern didn't crunch right into the dock," he said.

"I'm lucky you're keeping an eye on her."

He looked up at the sky.

"Goin' out? Wind's up."

I had to admit I wasn't.

"I need to go into the city for a bit. I was wondering if you're still selling that old Jeep."

We both looked across the parking lot at where the twenty-year-old Cherokee was parked next to the barrier hedge.

"I guess so, since it's still sittin' over there takin' up space."

"Consider it sold if I can take it today on loan and do the paperwork when I get back."

"You drive a hard bargain."

"I can't see lugging a '67 Grand Prix around New York City. And for some reason, Amanda's a little touchy about me using her Audi."

"What's doing in the city?"

I gave him the headline. He'd heard some of my father's story before, so didn't ask for details.

"Tell Amanda I'm around if she needs anything," he said. "Like somebody to test drive that little scooter of hers."

I left the Grand Prix in the marina parking lot and drove the Jeep to my cottage. It had a load of miles, but ran fine, as I knew it would, given Hodges's diligent maintenance and repair. After I threw an overnight bag in the back, I wrote a note to Amanda and stuck it to her front door.

"Heading for the Bronx. Please feed Eddie some real food along with the olives and prosciutto. Will call when I know where I'm staying."

As an entirely independent and self-sufficient woman, any word about being careful or noting who she should call in an emergency would have been insulting. Same with Eddie. All he needed was a pat on the head. I also asked him to keep an eye on Amanda, a request I could trust him to keep to himself.

CHAPTER FIVE

I broke with custom and called Madelyn Wollencroft from the car on the way into the city. Semple had made contact, which seemed to work as promised. She told me to come by in the afternoon, and gave me the address and her cell phone number, which guaranteed I could reach her if things got goofed up. Her voice sounded full of grit, though the tone was distracted, as if she were reading something while we talked.

I first checked into the hotel, which Amanda had pulled off the Internet. She said it was an independent operation, which I appreciated, and probably not a complete fleabag, which wouldn't have mattered provided there weren't any actual fleas. Turned out it was an old place some enterprising local had turned into his version of hipster chic, meaning the lights were too low and they'd gone Bauhaus, saving on decorations. At least it was clean and you didn't need to supply your own shampoo.

Most important, the room had a safe and a coffee maker, a balcony just wide enough to fit a sideways chair, and a table to put your drink on.

Wollencroft's office was in a precinct station that housed a Bronx homicide squad. I didn't recognize much about the area since it was outside my old neighborhood, and well past the boundaries of ancient memory. The two-story building had a peaked roof and white stucco exterior. The visitors' parking lot was behind a tall cyclone fence, but the gate popped up as soon as I approached.

Instead of a snarling Janet Orlovsky, the receptionist behind bulletproof glass was a friendly, fat blonde woman who looked relieved to see someone come through the door and interrupt her typing chores. She phoned up Wollencroft and offered me a chair to wait in.

I heard a buzz and Lieutenant Wollencroft walked through a security door. She was a slender woman in a dark blue summer suit over an open-necked blouse. The plastic surgeons had done a good job with her throat, though an informed eye could see an unnatural white line running from just below her jaw to the top of her collarbone.

She didn't offer to shake hands and neither did I.

"I don't have a lot of time," she said, her voice even more hoarse in person.

Her brunette hair was straight and cut in a line across her forehead, which contributed to the overall angularity of her face, with high cheekbones and sharp jawline, an edginess that seemed informed by her general demeanor. Her skin was a reddish tan, and free of makeup, though dark circles hung below weary brown eyes.

"I don't need a lot. This is what I got."

I handed her the facts I knew of the case printed on a piece of office paper. The name, dates, places, brief description of the event, and even briefer descriptions of the assailants. She looked at it, then gestured for me to follow her. We were buzzed back behind the glass and I followed Wollencroft down a stark hallway to her office, which was more of a conference room, with a metal table supporting neat stacks of files and loose papers and two walls lined with file cabinets, on one side interrupted by a desktop computer. The other wall was half corkboard covered in photographs, mug shots, newspaper clippings, and 8½ × 11 printouts, and half whiteboard, covered itself with words, numbers, and diagrams in a variety of colors.

We sat at the table and she continued studying my fact sheet.

"I guess you see a lot of these requests," I said.

She looked at me.

"Less than you'd think."

"Families?"

"Other cops, mostly. Working their pet cases."

"At their discretion?"

"Usually. Sometimes reporters get the bug. They're the worst."

"Too nosy?"

"Too quick to pull political strings. They assume we won't cooperate. It's annoying."

"I try to avoid annoying," I said, but she didn't respond.

"The first trick will be finding the case number," she said, rolling over to the computer. "I've been cataloging the archives whenever I get a chance, but it's tedious business."

"I'm not big on tedium either."

"So just sit there and amuse yourself while I look."

Since just sitting still and amusing myself was an impossibility, I diverted my mind to calculating the dimensions of an entertainment center I owed Frank Entwhistle. I reminded myself to establish the size of the TV screen, since modern preferences seem to run toward the scale of your average Jumbotron.

"Found it," said Wollencroft, with a light tap on the desk. "You're lucky."

"I wouldn't think such a thing could get lost."

"That's because you don't know the filing skills of the average homicide detective. Let's go."

She led me to a stairwell and up to the second story, then to a room full of uniformed cops and administrators. She walked to the back and knocked on the glass door to the captain's private office. A grey-haired, white-shirted guy with oily skin and black eyes let us in.

"I need the key," said Wollencroft. The captain pulled a small wad of keys out of a desk drawer and handed it to her. He looked at me like you would a vagrant with questionable hygiene.

"Reporter?" he asked.

"Civilian. Doing research on a cold case."

"Anything I should know about?" he asked.

"Only if you want to spend an hour getting briefed."

"I don't."

"Okay."

I followed her again as we climbed another set of stairs she said led to the attic.

"It would've taken less than an hour," I said.

"Five minutes would have been too much. We like to perpetuate the fiction that he's chronically overtaxed."

She flicked on the lights and under the tall open rafters was a big cage that reminded me of how they store expensive tools on a plant floor. Inside were rows of heavy-duty shelves holding crates, bins, and bankers' boxes in a range of styles based on their vintage. As we moved down one of the rows, Wollencroft grabbed a rolling ladder, which she used to reach the bankers' box in question. She yanked it out and handed it down to me.

I held the box as she slid open the drawer and leafed through it, eventually pulling out a brown accordion file about three inches thick.

"Another bit of luck," she said. "It was actually here."

She carried the file back to her captain's office, handed in the keys, and signed a ledger with the case number, her name, and the time and date.

"You'd think with all the security nothing would get lost," I said, as we walked back to her office.

"Forty years is plenty of time to lose anything."

Wollencroft dropped the file on her big table and pulled out a disorganized stack of papers. She seemed to find a key report, and ran a long fingernail along the text as she read.

Then she pulled a small notebook out of her suit jacket and wrote some things down. I stayed silent throughout, trying to avoid annoying.

"So what do you think?" I finally asked.

"Not much here," she said. "Your father fixed trucks?"

"Cars and trucks. And oil burners. Professionally, though he could fix anything."

"My father only fixed martinis. I took down the names of the investigating officers, but it looks like the only word they knew was 'none.'"

"And probably retired."

"Oh, yeah. Long time ago. Doesn't mean they're dead. Why're you into this now, anyway?" she asked, though without much interest.

"Ross didn't tell you?"

"He just said he owed you a favor."

"He did? I wish I'd known that. I'd 've used it better."

"Better than working on André Acquillo?"

"I might have some old parking tickets."

She tapped the long nail of her index finger on the report.

"You're using up a favor with me too. By way of Ross Semple, whose favor bank isn't limitless."

"A lot of favors flying around. Maybe we can start an exchange. Get a taste off every transaction."

"He also said you're a wiseass."

"That sounds more like it," I said. "Can I get copies of that file?"

"No. You can write down what you want and put everything back in the folder. I'll find an admin who can tell us about the investigating detectives. If you try to take anything, I'll arrest you and the prosecutor will do me a favor and toss your wiseass in jail."

She looked at me with those tired eyes.

"Sorry," I said. "It's a mental problem. No disrespect."

"I'll only help you if you want the help," she said.

"I want the help. I need it. I'll take down all the information in there, then I'll come see you again, okay?"

She left me alone with the file. I had a little notebook of my own that was already filled with other stuff, like architectural dimensions and grocery lists, but it was adequate to the task, since there wasn't that much to write down.

Everything was on carbon copies. The responding officer described the scene to include a team of paramedics who'd beaten him to the bar. He listed one deceased white male, the injured Marcelo Bonaventure, and his hysterical sister. He didn't do much else but secure the scene and make everybody wait for the detectives.

The detectives were Gerald Fitzsimmons and Ben Woo. Fitzsimmons described the scene with more detail, mostly involving Bonnie's testimony. The description of the murder was drearily familiar, only this time written in the formal, acronym- and number-laden cop parlance. Bonnie didn't give up any of the names of the patrons who fled, whom he probably knew would have no interest in bearing witness. So that was a missing piece.

A CSI had typed out another report, describing the items taken as evidence, including the assailants' drink glasses, plates, and utensils. He took fingerprints off my dead father, along with some of his blood, which he noted later in rough handwriting was type B.

Then I saw the photographs. Flash-lit five-by-seven color prints taken from several angles. He lay facedown, one arm tucked under his body, the other crammed unnaturally against the toilet. I remembered the madras shirt and khaki pants, thinning dark hair, and oversized nose. There wasn't much else to recognize, given all the blood.

I patted at my shirt pocket for the cigarettes I'd given up, surprising myself more for the way my hand shook. I took a breath and slipped the photos back in the folder.

Listed among my father's possessions—besides a thin wallet with a driver's license and a few bucks (no credit cards or tickets from the dry cleaner), the wrist watch his Italian father had brought from Viareggio, a ring of car keys, and a razor-sharp jackknife—was a crucifix with the name of a church stamped on the back: "The Mother of Divine Providence."

Another report described a phone interview with my mother, who'd refused to come to the Bronx to identify the body. She didn't add much but their full names and immigration history, their kids' names, his address in the Bronx, his education level (École secondaire Cavelier-De LaSalle in Montreal), profession, relatives in the United States (none), and thoughts on who might have done the deed (none).

The identification was handled by an employee of his named Donald Duxbury. I wrote down his address. On the same report was my father's criminal record (none), known associates with criminal records (none), known associates with no criminal records (one).

I stopped there and wrote down the name, Rozele Mikutavičienė, her age, and profession, noted as "domestic."

I'd nearly exhausted the information when Wollencroft walked in the office.

"One of your detectives is dead," she said. "The other's living out on Breezy Point, assuming Sandy didn't take his house and we just haven't updated the address."

"Thanks for that," I said. "It was good of you to look."

"After I called you a wiseass?"

"Interesting reading."

"You saw photos?"

I nodded.

"Are you full time on cold cases?" I asked.

"Nine thousand and eighty-two," she said.

"Cold cases?"

"Unsolved murders since 1985, so it doesn't even include your father."

"Any leads?" I asked. It nearly got the smile I was hoping for.

"No. No leads. That stuff on the corkboard? I made it all up."

"I've got a real one," I said.

"From the file? Really."

"They found a crucifix among my father's belongings. He wouldn't be caught dead with a crucifix."

"And yet he was," said Wollencroft.

"Exactly. Ever heard of a Catholic church called The Mother of Divine Providence?"

"No, but I'm Episcopalian. I'm sure we can find a Catholic somewhere in the building." She did the next best thing and looked it up on her computer. "It's up north near Mount Vernon. Big church. Doesn't mean anybody goes there."

"Name of the priest?"

She told me and I wrote it in my notebook.

"The bartender who was there that night figured the killers for punks from one of the families in town," I said. "Anywhere I can look up the local punk history?"

She went back to her computer, then spun it around so I could see a page on a website where you could buy a book called *Bronx Brotherhood: The Life and Times of Leon Pagliero.*

"Only one family that mattered. It's good information," she said.

"You know that?"

I looked closer at the web page. "Tyler Vaughn was the author," she said, reading my intent. "I've known him since we were kids."

"You're being very helpful," I said.

"It's involuntary. Connecting dots is all I do."

"You knew Ross when he worked homicide?"

She looked ready to dodge the question, but then nodded. "He's the one that got me fired."

She could see that threw me a little, so she said, "Off undercover. Said it was bad for my health. I couldn't speak at that point, so there was no use arguing."

"Ross can have strong opinions."

"He was probably right. That job has a shelf life. Didn't make it easier to swallow. Sorry, bad joke."

"I've heard some stories about him as well," I said.

She looked over at her corkboard, as if some of the stories were written there.

"They're all true. It was a rough time. And the ones you've never heard are even worse. That job in the Hamptons was fair recompense."

"Didn't turn out all that cushy, if that's what you mean."

"It's not, but I hear you." She stood up from the workstation and took off her suit jacket. The blouse underneath was badly wrinkled and partially untucked. I looked away as she adjusted things before sitting back down again. "You got a plan here?"

"Do you have a phone number for that detective?" I asked.

She wrote it down on a scrap of paper and handed it to me. Gerald Fitzsimmons, and his address on Breezy Point.

"He goes by Fitzy, like most Fitzsimmonses," said Wollencroft. "He retired to his summer shack, but I'd call ahead and see if he's still out there. A lot of that place burned down during the storm."

"Can I tell him you gave me his name?"

"Sure, why not. He probably remembers busting me when I was undercover. It was embarrassing, but didn't have to be. He couldn't know at the time."

"Embarrassment can be a powerful thing."

She nearly smiled, for the second time.

"Fitzy's okay. He got over it. Anything else I can do for you?"

"I should do something for you, though I don't know what the hell it would be."

"Let me get back to work?"

"Roger that."

CHAPTER SIX

You got to Breezy Point, the last stop at the tip of the Rockaways, by crossing the Gil Hodges Bridge, named after the guy who managed the Mets to a World Series title. The other miracle associated with the place was nobody died in the hurricane and firestorm that nearly wiped it off the map.

I'd taken Wollencroft's advice and called Fitzy on my cell phone. He listened to my spiel, but said he'd call back to set a time for me to come over. I assumed the ten minutes that took was for a call to Wollencroft, and likely Ross Semple as well. The next conversation was a lot friendlier, and involved complicated directions for getting onto the point via security huts, day passes, and automated turnstiles. Breezy Point was one big co-op, a dense, tightly knit community that aggressively guarded its privacy. And for good reason. Where else could a retired cop or fireman live next to a beach with a view of the Manhattan skyline?

He told me his house was not only still standing, but one of the lucky ones to come through relatively unscathed.

"If you don't count my boat and the pickup I used to haul it on the trailer," he said. "Still looking for them things."

Since I was already holding the phone, I called Amanda, but she was up on the ridge of a new roof where it was too windy to have a decent conversation. Though I could hear the popping of pneumatic nailers in the background. The best I could do was tell her how to say, "Make sure you hit the rafters," in Spanish, hoping the windswept words wouldn't come out as an insult.

"*Gracias, mi vida,*" she said before hanging up.

It was a little after one P.M., a time I hoped would dodge the worst of the traffic. A good call, since the traffic through Queens and around JFK was still pretty congested.

Fitzy lived on the southeast corner of Breezy Point, barely a tiny block or two from the worst of the carnage. Breezy Point had evolved much like a medieval village, a packed warren of improvised cottages and bungalows, so congested and entangled that only narrow footpaths could squeeze between the structures. Add in the combustible building materials and hurricane winds, and flooding too deep for fire trucks to navigate, and it wasn't much of a surprise that more than 120 homes had burned to the ground in just a few hours.

Fitzy's good fortune was to be just outside the roiling flames, with a little yard around his house and room for a driveway. The roof had such a low pitch he could stand up there during the fire, spraying embers that fell on the shingles with a motor-operated power washer.

That afternoon, he was in the driveway washing down the successor to his missing truck. No boat trailer in sight.

It was a nice day, but cool, though all he wore was a white T-shirt stretched over a belly as big and round as a medicine ball, a pair of calf-length polyester athletic shorts, and bright orange Crocs. His red hair had turned mostly white but he still had it all, cut and coaxed into a military flat top.

"You're Acquillo," he said, reaching out the hand not holding the garden hose.

"Yeah. I appreciate your seeing me."

"Well, you know, I had a date with the queen, but she can take a rain check."

"She's old. Probably forget."

He went back to hosing down the truck, asking me to give him ten minutes to finish the job. I told him to take all the time he wanted, I was happy to hang around in the sun and enjoy the sea breeze that gave the point its name. I walked down to the ocean and counted a half-dozen giant freighters coming into port and nearly as many going the other way. Plenty of sailboats were out there as well, doing their best to avoid getting mowed down. Proving that even the waters around Greater New York City could prove perilous to the unwary.

When I got back to Fitzy's house, he was just finishing up. He waved for me to follow him into the house. It was like any ordinary guy's beach bungalow anywhere on the East Coast, comfortably cluttered and haphazard, adorned with mounted fish and lamps made of little lighthouses, anchors, and fake driftwood, with only a hint of sour mold smell, though that might have been my imagination. There was no evidence of a Mrs. Fitzy.

We dwelled in the kitchen only long enough to dish a few beers out of the fridge and then headed out to a tiny concrete patio with a view of the Verrazano Bridge peeking up over the rooftops.

I told him I was sorry to hear his partner, Ben Woo, had died.

"Yeah, me too. A good cop. You didn't see many Chinese on the force in those days. Still don't, I imagine. Too busy writing software or whatever the fuck they do now. How long you know Ross Semple?" he asked me, after wriggling his butt into a crumpled beach chair. I took another of the same.

"Since high school, though not what you'd call close friends."

"You and everybody else. Weird sucker, for certain."

"Anyway, thanks for talking to me," I said.

"Thank me when we're done talking. So this is about the André Acquillo thing."

"He was my father."

"Yeah, I got that. You know this was a hell of a long time ago."

"I do. I have notes from your original report, if that'll help."

"Thanks, but not necessary. I got copies of every report I ever wrote. CYA, baby. Cover your ass. You can't imagine the snake pit we worked in back in the day."

He took a long pull off his beer and belched with no reservation.

"So you reviewed it before I came."

"I did. Interesting case."

"And?"

"How badly do you want to know all this shit?"

This was one of those moments when I had to decide between rendering a four-hour discourse on the intricacies of my psychological constitution, with all its attendant misbe-haviors and intractable pathologies, most prominent of which was a Hamlet-grade ambivalence over this immediate project, or simply say, "Yeah, I want to know all this shit."

Which is what I said.

"Okay," said Fitzy. "You read the report? Okay, here's more. André's garage was the type of operation that lived off the overflow from the dealers and fleet garages around the Bronx. People told us he was good at the fixing part, but kept his crew small, two or three guys at a time max, so he couldn't handle contract work, since that was more a high volume, run-'em-in, run-'em-out deal. But it wasn't unheard of for him to take the occasional semi, or postal vehicle, or rental car, if the customer had a special problem, or just needed some extra help. You dig so far?"

I said I was keeping up. Easy, since I knew this already from memory. My father's operating philosophy was what he called "there's a right way and a wrong way." The right way for him was doing quality work, but on his own schedule, at a set price. The wrong way was what everyone else did, accord-ing to him. Fleet work didn't fit that model so well.

"One of the bigger fleets in town at that time were the garbage haulers," said Fitzy. "One company had a lock on the business, if you know what I mean. André did a fair amount of work for them guys. So there you go."

"Go where?"

Fitzy looked a little disappointed.

"You don't read the papers? Garbage hauling was one of the bad boys' premier industries back then. Working on their wagons put André in direct contact with certain individuals."

"Illegally?"

I continued to disappoint Fitzy.

"Did I say that? It's what they call the appearance of impropriety. Guilt by association. Though you won't find that in the file."

"It actually said he had no known associates with criminal records."

"True enough. According to the arrest records, there was a beef around an assault and battery right before he got killed, but the other party dropped the charges."

"That wasn't in there either."

"Before you ask me, no, I didn't think it worth putting in the file. I had enough paperwork without writing down a bunch of bullshit hunches."

We sat out on his patio for another hour, talking mostly about his adventures during Sandy, his feelings about policing in the twenty-first century, ("Being a cop is something I'm glad to have done. Not sure I'd do it these days."), and the current prospects for New York baseball, in particular the Mets, a subject I knew nothing about. He also told me about Madelyn Wollencroft.

"Comes from a fancy old family up in Connecticut. Went to Vassar or some place like that. Black sheep, no doubt. You'd be surprised by the different kinds of people who end up doing crazy undercover shit."

Knowing Ross Semple, it wouldn't surprise me a bit.

"She said you busted her once."

He grinned, clearly recovered from any embarrassment.

"Seein' her, you'd 've busted her on general principles. Oh man, fierce-lookin' broad. Had her on a Class D aggravated assault for taking down a john twice her size."

He would have gladly sat and jawed longer, but I wanted to get back up to the Bronx before the worst traffic hit, so I thanked him again and made to leave. After one more question.

"The bartender who witnessed the beating, Marcelo Bonaventure, said a senior cop in a white shirt visited his bar. The cop told him the killers had done a public service taking André out of the game. You wouldn't guess who'd that be, or why he'd say that kind of thing?"

For the first time, Fitzy seemed a little reluctant to speculate.

"Coulda been any lieutenant, or maybe the captain. Those guys are long gone, so we can't be asking them. Not a typical thing, either, for the brass to be calling on witnesses."

"Not a good thing, though."

"No," he said, more forthrightly. "Not a good thing at all."

Chapter Seven

Back when normal people could work on internal com-
bustion engines, one common maintenance chore was to set
the clearance between the rocker arm and push rod, a procedure called adjusting the valve lash. You usually knew this
was needed when the engine produced a lot of steady chatter,
like the sound of a miniature machine gun. A lot of click
and clack.

The shed in the backyard of the cottage had room for
one vehicle, but there was plenty of space to either side for an
assortment of old trucks and cars in various stages of repair,
from street legal to completely torn apart. I had a '55 Chevy
panel truck salvaged from a yard full of abandoned utility
vehicles that spent its time with me somewhere in the middle
range, swinging between disembowelment and marginally
functional.

I had it out on the road one day, going fast down Mon-
tauk Highway, when suddenly the whole truck was enveloped
in thick, grey smoke. It was so bad inside the cab I nearly
plowed into a tree when I pulled off the road. I jumped out,
fearing imminent explosion, but with the engine off, the smoke
quickly dissipated. I popped the hood and found the problem
immediately. An oil leak had sprung, spraying oil under high

pressure directly onto the red-hot exhaust manifold, essentially creating an effective smoke machine.

A friend of mine came by with a heavy rope and we towed the thing back to the cottage.

I don't remember if it was the cause of the leak, or simply collateral damage, but the head gasket was also blown. When I pulled the head, I discovered a few burnt valves and other wreckage understandable in an engine with more than 200,000 hard miles under questionable maintenance.

Rebuilding the head in my father's shed was out of the question, so I erected my own rickety structure with discarded construction material, providing a workbench and partial refuge from the elements. I also talked a guy out of a manual that could guide me through refurbishing the Chevy inline six.

None of this was particularly difficult if you had the discipline to keep track of the parts and reassembled everything in an orderly and conscientious fashion. The only outside help I needed was to shave down the surface of the head where it joined the engine block, giving the new head gasket half a chance at preserving a solid seal.

Once the engine was back in the truck, one of the finishing touches was to adjust the valve lash. This was where I made my mistake. I told my father the clearance on that particular engine was zero. The rocker arm and push rod traveled up and down in precise synchronicity, with no possibility of clicks or clacks. I thought this was a fine improvement on an engine in steady service since the 1920s, and thought he might agree.

"Is not zero clearance," he said.

I told him it was clearly expressed in the manual. Zero clearance. I offered to show it to him.

"*C'est imposible*," he said, his voice beginning to rise, along with my alarm. "I fix those engines every day for thirty years. There is no zero clearance."

"They're saying it has to be zero or the backlash can bend a rod."

He was on a creeper under a pickup in the shed, his legs sticking out. Now they were furiously kicking at the concrete floor as he scooted out from under. I backed up a step or two.

"You read this shit out of a book?" he yelled, rearing up to his full height. In his hand was a heavy monkey wrench, more a tool for cracking drainpipes free than for turning bolts on a car or truck. "You gonna tell me who sets valve lash for a living where to put the clearance? You think reading a book is how you do this work?"

He said a few more things in French that I don't remember, probably because I was too frozen in fear to easily translate. I think I might have apologized for whatever offense I'd given, though my attention was focused on the big wrench, which by now had started to rise in his hand. The door to the shed was about six feet away, and narrowed by the rear end of the pickup. I must have made the proper calculation, because I was already heading toward the gap when the wrench flew at my head. In my wake came a metallic crash as the wrench drove into the garden implements hung on the wall. But by then I was already in full flight across the lawn, aiming for the Little Peconic Bay nearly an acre away.

What I lacked in bulk, I made up in speed, so the snarling French profanity faded as I ran, though it was still behind me as I approached the water. Not that the temperature mattered, but it was summertime, so I had to dodge past families on beach blankets and under umbrellas, around children and dogs playing in the sand, to reach the water, where I dove in and started swimming as fast as my work boots and greasy clothes would allow.

My father couldn't swim. So my only challenge after making the deep water was to stay afloat while stripping off my shoes and clothing. I wasn't much of a swimmer either, being all wiry muscle with no fat, and as buoyant as a lead brick. But I was young, with bottomless endurance, and highly motivated.

Mourning the loss of the boots, acquired at great cost not long before, I used my flailing swim stroke to power out to a green channel marker that was anchored to the bay floor.

At nightfall, I crept ashore and slept in the woods wrapped in beach towels swiped off a clothing line. The next day I hid at the widow's house next door, an ornery woman who knew my father well and was prepared to clobber him with a crowbar should he discover my whereabouts. The day after that, he was back in the Bronx, and I was on my way Up Island to a boxing gym to sign up for my first lesson.

Aside from the handy alliteration, they call it fight/flight for good reason, since in the midst of the sensation it's very hard to tell the two apart. I'd had to pick the flight option as a kid, having no recourse. But now, at sixteen, aware of my native gifts of reflex and endurance, I felt ready to try out the alternative.

THE MORNING after visiting Fitzy, I caught Wollencroft at the entrance to her building. She had on an orange fleece above a short skirt and clogs on her feet, a marked reverse in formality. Her legs were paler than her face and hands, as if intentionally kept from the sun. But shapely and youthful enough to make me wonder how old she was.

"You're back," she said, holding the door for me. "That didn't take long."

"I talked to Fitzy. You might be interested in what he told me."

She let me follow her to a crummy little canteen where she made us both coffees from a single-serve machine. She took a Dark Roast, me a French Vanilla. But I drank it black to show her I wasn't that much of a sissy.

"Looks like he got over busting you," I said, when we got back to her office. I stayed standing so she'd know I wasn't planning to take up much of her time. "Said you were a scary-looking girl back then."

"Scary woman. The work required it," she said, as she arranged papers on her worktable. "I got rid of the tattoos, which was quite painful by the way. What else did he tell you?"

"That there were things about my father that didn't get into the file."

I described what he told me about my father's association with mobbed-up garbage haulers and the prior assault charge. She listened carefully, frowning.

"This job is hard enough," she said, "You'd think at least the official police files would be complete."

"Does this happen often?"

"Of course. Who's going to complain? Thousands of dead nobodies whose principal claim to fame was getting killed by unknown assailants."

"But they're important to you," I said.

"They are the most important. Unsolved murder is an affront to society. And believe it or not, we track a lot of them down. Sometimes all it takes is actually trying to do a proper job. This doesn't always make us popular with the detective units, but ask me if I care. You can sit down if you want."

"I know you're busy."

"I can talk for a few minutes. Drink my coffee."

She unzipped her fleece. Underneath was a button-down Oxford cloth shirt with an ink stain on the pocket. She leaned back in her chair when I took mine.

"What do you think the missing stuff means?" I asked her.

"What it looks like. Not a lot of enthusiasm for this case at the time."

"Why would that be?"

"Your guess is as good as mine. Literally, since I hear you're a good guesser."

"Who told you that?"

"Ross Semple. He told me not to be fooled by your easy charm."

"What charm?"

She took off the fleece and rolled up her sleeves. It caused me to notice her fingernails, which could have used some work.

"I'd be grateful for any help you can give," I said.

She nodded, though without as much commitment as I wanted. Then she said, "We solve a lot of these cases, but not most. Something as far back as the seventies, it's very rare."

"Do you keep the blood?" I asked, after a sudden thought.

"We should've, but that'd be at the medical examiner's."

"What about his clothes and the drink glasses and all that? You can still pull the DNA, right? I hear that cracks more cold cases than anything."

"All that other stuff is in a central property room. Or it's not. What you're talking about would mean opening up a formal investigation."

"You can do that if you want, right? You said you have a lot of discretion."

"Ross also told me you were persistent."

"I hear the same about you. We can start a club. The Charming Persistents."

"Persistent isn't the same as being a pain in the ass," she said.

"That's what the club is for. We bring greater understanding to people with this affliction. Anyway, you want to know why that cop in the white shirt paid a visit to Bonaventure. I can see it all over you."

"What I really want to know is who killed the sixteen-year-old girl with the expensive dental work and no sign of drug use or sexual conduct, wearing filthy secondhand clothes, found strangled at the bottom of a big rolling laundry basket behind a commercial cleaner. That one's only been cold for two years. Her friends are just starting college."

"But we can at least check for DNA."

She shooed me with her strong hands and unkempt nails.

"I've got your cell number," she said. "Give it a few days, and I'll see what I can do."

Before I left with the cracked mug of coffee still in my hand, I said, "Fitzy said you went to Vassar."

That annoyed her, in a weary sort of way.

"Wellesley, as if it matters."

"It does to me. My ex-wife went there. Her parents thought it would improve her marriage prospects."

"I guess that didn't work out."

"Not too well."

IT TOOK nearly an hour to get from Wollencroft's office to The Mother of Divine Providence Church in the north end of the Bronx. I saw it before I needed to search the map, a giant stone edifice rising above the ragged remains of an old retail area with as many empty lots as storefronts. Parking was easy, though it took some walking around to find the rectory, an even older building made of stucco and hulking slabs of over-painted trim. A wire mesh gate covered the front door, but it had an intercom, not unlike the one at Saint Anthony's. I wondered when the Catholic Church had slid behind electronic fortifications.

I pressed the buzzer, with no results. So I went back to the church and tried the towering front door, which was also locked. I circled the building looking for other entrances, finally discovering an unlocked door toward the back. I went in.

It was never easy to light the inside of old churches, with their solid stone walls and soaring arches. But the gloom within The Mother of Divine Providence was dense enough to cup in your hands. The door led into the transept and I walked slowly, half afraid I'd fall into an open crypt. Candles burned from a few big candle stands, which at least foretold the presence of earthly life. I stopped at the altar and crossed myself, not so much out of devotion, but in case I'd already been spotted. I wanted to establish my Catholic bona fides.

As my eyes adjusted to the dark, I searched the pews, but they were empty, as was the choir loft, pulpits, and the sedilia, a row of high-backed, heavily carved seating where backup priests and altar boys could hang out between their prescribed duties. I walked up to the altar to look for side doors into the sacristy. One of the doors was open, beyond which came faint sounds.

I made some obvious sounds myself before I walked through the door, though saying anything, like "hello" or "don't shoot," seemed more likely to startle. It didn't work, since the guy sitting at a low table jumped when I walked into the room.

"Sorry," I said.

"How did you get in here?" he asked, more puzzled than alarmed.

"Side door. It was open."

He was older than me and wore a black T-shirt and blue jeans.

"Did you have an appointment?" he asked.

"No, I just walked in."

"Confessions are heard between one and four on Saturdays, otherwise you'll need to call ahead."

"Not here to confess, just talk, if you have a moment."

I told him my name and stuck out my hand. He looked at it and I thought for a moment he wouldn't shake, but then he stood up and took my hand. His grip fit the rest of him. Big and meaty.

"Nelson Cleary," he said. "But you can call me Father."

"You're the priest?"

"That's what they keep telling me."

"I don't mean to intrude. I just have a question."

"You can't say 'just' in the same sentence with 'question.' In my work, questions are always complicated. Do you want to sit down?"

He pointed to his chair then unfolded another one leaning against the wall.

"Let's see if you're right," I said, taking a drawing of the crucifix, showing both sides, out of my pocket and putting it on the table. "What can you tell me about this?"

He looked at it, but kept his hands in his lap.

"Have I seen you at Mass?" he asked, looking back up at me.

"Sorry, no. I live out in Southampton. I used to kick around here as a kid when I visited my father, but he wasn't a religious guy."

"That puts him in the majority."

He picked up the paper.

"One of ours," he said. "It's a pity."

"What is?"

"There used to be a budget for confirmation gifts. A different time."

"Like some forty years ago?"

"At least. I've seen these on sale as collectors' items. An even greater pity. Have you lost it?"

"Not exactly. It's in a box somewhere in the caverns of a police property room."

Cleary tossed the paper back on the table.

"You're a policeman."

"Nah. I'm just a guy. My father was killed in a barroom brawl. The guys who did it got away. The crucifix was found at the scene. I knew it couldn't be his, so it was probably one of his killer's."

"How many were there?"

"Two. Can you tell me when it was given out?"

"Not without the real thing, even with the careful drawing. Is it yours?"

"Yeah. I'm an engineer. They used to teach us draftsmanship."

"What was your name again?"

"Sam Acquillo. My father was André Acquillo. French Canadian. He ran a repair shop in Eastchester. Fixed trucks, mostly. And furnaces."

I told him where and when he was killed, and the highlights of the story, including the visit from Ray Osmund and my subsequent meeting with Marcelo Bonaventure at Saint Anthony's.

"I know about Bonnie," he said. "He's probably heard more confessions than any priest in the city. A good man, I suspect, given how many of the parishioners ask me to pray for him."

"Must have worked. He's still in pretty good shape for an eighty-nine-year-old."

"But he doesn't know who committed the crime."

"Nobody does, not that they tried all that hard to find out."

"There was a lot of killing back then, I'm sorry to say."

"So you were around?"

This seemed to puzzle him.

"Very much so."

He stood up from his chair, telling me to stay put. He left by a door opposite the one leading to the altar and was gone for about five minutes. When he returned, he held a crucifix dangling from the end of a silver chain. He handed it to me.

"This is mine," he said. "I can't say it was the spark that lit my calling, but it must have had some impact."

The crucifix looked more worn down than the one in the file photo, which had gone unused for forty years, though I could still make out the stamped words on the back.

"This was my family's parish," he said, "though the rest of them are more of your father's ilk."

"I hope that's only partly true, for your family's sake."

"I'll let you be the judge of that." Rather than sitting back down, he leaned on a counter, not unlike one you'd find in an office kitchen. "I'll save you the trouble by telling you the Clearys are a pretty well-known family in the Bronx. If you're in the business of nosing around, you'll find that out soon enough."

"Thanks for that," I said. "I don't know how this is going to work out, but any thoughts you might have I'd appreciate."

He crossed his arms and smiled at some internal thought.

"My business is in saving souls, not tracking down killers. Even if I knew anything, I wouldn't be in a position to share. You understand."

"I do."

"Though I'm curious, you don't seem very enthusiastic about this yourself."

He had me there.

"Your business is also reading people, I bet. No, Father, I'm what you'd call exceedingly ambivalent. A lot of time has gone by, most of which I've spent trying to forget about the whole thing. If it wasn't for my daughter and girlfriend, I wouldn't even be here."

"But he was your father."

"Yeah, sort of. Biologically. I got his nose and rotten temperament, so I guess there's your proof. But even if I figured out who killed him, I'm not sure what I'd get out of it."

"Vengeance?"

"More like gratitude."

CHAPTER EIGHT

When I got back in my car I called Jackie Swaitkowski. She was a lawyer who gave free legal services to the down-and-out in the Hamptons, who were more plentiful than the press would have you think. She was also a friend of mine, who'd defended me in a murder case, though I had to pay her a dollar.

"How's that computer working?" I asked, when she answered the phone.

"As hard as I am. In other words, I'm too busy to look things up for you."

"You don't have to do it now."

"I don't ever have to do it. You need to buy your own computer. It's time."

Then she hung up on me.

I waited for a few minutes, then called her back.

"You're right," I said. "I'll do it as soon as I get back home."

"Where are you?"

I told her a version of the story I'd been telling people all over the state of New York, so it was concise, to the point, and apparently compelling.

"Wow. That's amazing," she said.

"Amazed enough to Google something for me?"

"Sure. I'm looking up 'Libraries in the Bronx.' This is where I'd go if I didn't have my laptop and needed to get online."

I asked her to find the closest one to my hotel.

"You're giving up too easily," she said, as she tapped on the keys. "That always makes me suspicious."

"Ever read a book called *Bronx Brotherhood: The Life and Times of Leon Pagliero*?" I asked.

"No, but I'll love hearing all about it after you do."

"It was written by a guy named Tyler Vaughn. His father was an ADA here in the Bronx."

"Wilson Vaughn. Very effective prosecutor in the Giuliani days. Don't know if he's still alive."

"I bet you could find out."

"I absolutely could find out. But the question is, will I?"

"That's a complicated question. Apparently they all are."

She gave me the address and phone number for the library and I wrote it down in my little pocket notebook.

"I'm glad you're doing this," she said.

"You've been talking to Amanda?"

"I haven't, but I know what she'd say. And you know she's right."

"She'd want you to find Wilson Vaughn."

"Impossible," she said, and hung up again.

I HAD to bribe the librarian to get access to one of the eight unoccupied workstations. I didn't have a library card, and she wouldn't take the hotel as a legitimate address. I asked if I could get a card if I donated one hundred bucks to the library. She said no. I could get a plaque with my name on it for 100K, but to get a card, I needed an actual address somewhere in the Bronx.

I asked her if she had a favorite charity and she told me she usually gave to the Lupus Foundation, since her father had lupus, even though he ended up dying of a heart attack.

I told her if I gave her a hundred-dollar bill, she could deposit it, then write a check to the Lupus Foundation. Then maybe I could get a library card.

A card was out of the question, but in return for my generosity, she'd unlock the computer at desk number five and I could have two hours of work time.

One hundred dollars isn't worth what it used to be, but it still has a certain utility.

Imposing on Jackie's distinctive skills with a computer wasn't just a convenience. There was no better way to get her engaged in a project like this, and no better person for the job. I had other reasons to stay clear of the things, including their addictive properties, ones to which I was particularly susceptible. A handiness with technology and penchant for problem-solving is what earned me my corporate job running R&D for an international hydrocarbon-processing operation. We made things like gasoline, jet fuel, and the kind of plastic that went into dashboards and kids' toys. The problems needing solving were infinite and the paths to resolution often well disguised. It took an obsessive focus and determination most found unsustainable. It helped to be aroused by the power of computing, and prone to sleepless hours welded to a CRT.

When I gave all that up, I wanted the exile to be permanent, but the digital forces of modernity were seductive and relentless. And Jackie was right. It was time.

"How do you get Google on this thing?" I asked the librarian.

She packed a lot of feeling in the look she gave me.

"Open the browser and type Google in the search window."

Browser? I started clicking on icons and something came up that looked a lot like the Internet. From there you just had to use that little window and lots of interesting stuff popped up. Piece of cake.

I stumbled around a little at first, but eventually called up a robust list of sources covering organized crime in the Bronx in the sixties and seventies, including mention of the book

Bronx Brotherhood: The Life and Times of Leon Pagliero. When I clicked on that it took me to a place where I could actually read the table of contents and a big chunk of the book itself.

I burned up a sizable portion of my two hours on the book before realizing I could buy it off the same website and have it shipped to my hotel. Though by then I'd already become familiar with the central narrative of the story—the pitting of a powerful mob boss against an aggressive and highly principled prosecutor named Wilson Vaughn, who also happened to be the author's father.

The last thing I did was look through the acknowledgments, which is where I saw the name Trevor Cleary at the top of the list, as a direct source and the author of several important books on the Paglieros and other mob families. And lower down the list his brother Robert, who was a city councilman representing the Bronx. As his father, William J. Cleary, had once been himself. No mention of Nelson, though I knew then why the Clearys were well known around town.

Also nothing about André Acquillo, the angry Canadian mechanic.

For no good reason I drove by my father's old apartment in the Edenwald section of the Bronx north of East 233RD Street. The street was still mostly lined with separate dwellings, though the few empty lots I knew as a kid were filled in, contributing to the feeling that time had compressed the neighborhood. People who lived there in those days were first- or second-generation Irish, Italians, European Jews, and the occasional African-American, who now seemed to predominate.

My father had the second floor of a three-story house, the tallest on the street, that you reached from a staircase along the outside wall. It was roomy enough to have two bedrooms and a living room with a big coffee table where he'd rebuild carburetors and starter motors while watching sports on TV.

A preference for the Yankees over the Mets was the only subject on which we found uneasy agreement, though having the Expos in the National League avoided the worst of the possible conflicts.

The last time I was in the apartment was a stopover on my first trip up to Cambridge after miraculously gaining admission to MIT. I'd taken some time off after high school to build up tuition money with my paltry earnings from the ring, a pursuit I had to maintain for three more years to make it to graduation. My father never asked me about my boxing career, much less saw any of the fights, so we never talked about it. I'd just show up once in a while, sometimes stay over, watch a little TV, then haul ass out of there.

That time I brought a big duffel bag with me, more than I needed for a single night. He asked me where I was going, so I told him.

"I never hear nothing about this college thing," he said.

"I only just got enough money to go," I told him.

"A place like that take a lot of money."

"Like I said."

I was able to divert the conversation by asking him about the scattered pieces of machinery on the coffee table. It gave him a chance to expound on the traitorous unreliability of a certain pairing of spindle and gear. While allowing himself to bask in the triumph of making the repairs anyway.

"But of course you know all this because you are MIT," he said.

"Haven't started yet. I'm sure gearing will enter the picture at some point."

He grunted at that, and we left the subject for a while, time enough to get through a dinner of packaged food dug out of the freezer. I don't know what we talked about, though our conversations usually involved me listening to his inveighing against the political situation in Québec Provence, the disingenuousness of customers and incompetence of the hired help.

So it startled me a little when on my way out the next morning he said, "So you're not going to shave?"

I felt my chin, which seemed pretty smooth.

"I did."

"You're not going to a college with those things on your face."

I felt around some more, then said, "Sideburns?"

"You look like a hippie."

"I don't look like a hippie," I said. "Hippies don't look anything like me. If there are any hippies anymore."

"You want people to take you seriously, you have to look like a serious person."

We were standing in a tight little area near the door to the staircase, a suggestion of a foyer. I was holding my duffel bag and a backpack.

"Lots of serious people have sideburns. Almost everybody has sideburns. The fucking president has sideburns."

"Fucking president? Where'd you get that mouth?"

"From you."

He reached out a long arm and gave my sternum a little poke.

"Watch what come out of there, that mouth."

I raised my duffel bag and backpack.

"I'm leaving now. I've got a train to catch."

"Not until you shave off those disgusting *rouflaquettes*."

A vast hollowness opened up within me, desperate and unfillable.

"I'm not going to do that."

He moved closer.

"You go to that school, you represent our family. Our name. I will not have the dishonor of a degenerate son."

"What the hell are you talking about? What family name? Dishonoring what, ten generations of Franco-Italian grease monkeys?"

He used both hands this time to shove me up against the door.

"You show respect or I will beat it into you," he said, along with something in French I knew to be insulting, though untranslatable.

I dropped the duffel bag and backpack and balled my fists. "Not this time," I said.

He had a few inches of height and reach on me, and a lot more weight, mostly made of muscle from jacking up front ends and slinging transmissions around the repair shop. There was little room in the foyer for me to set a stance, though I didn't need it for what I knew how to do. A surprise left jab to the gut followed by a right hook to the side of the head. A combination I'd used more than once to put away guys trained to stop that from happening. But instead, I let him shove me again.

"You want to take a shot at me?" he asked. "Go ahead, it'll be the last shot you take."

I opened my fists and dropped my hands. I kept my eyes on his own fists as I bent down and picked up the luggage.

"You have all the respect you deserve, *gros cochon.*"

It wasn't until I made it out the door and down the staircase that I stopped, expecting angry blows to fall from behind. I looked up the stairs and he was standing on the landing, the mumble from his lips too far away to hear, the look on his face too entangled to interpret.

And those were the last words we spoke to each other.

On the way back to the hotel I called my friend Randall Dodge, a cybergeek par excellence. Randall was a tall, skinny Shinnecock Indian I taught how to box just in time for him to avoid getting his ass kicked by a guy from Connecticut who'd come down for the Southampton powwow. This began a relationship that was hardly in decent balance, given all of Randall's help in matters of the digital universe.

When I told him I wanted to buy a computer he told me I was doing a fine impersonation of Sam Acquillo, whom

I'd obviously kidnapped and was holding for ransom. I gave him my specs: something easy to use, didn't break down, and would stay ahead of obsolescence for at least a few months.

"They don't make such a thing," he said.

"Just get close. And tell me where I can pick it up today. If I wait till tomorrow I'll change my mind. By the way, I'm in the Bronx."

He told me to pull over at a cross street and give him the address. A few minutes later he came back on the line and told me where to go.

"Guy works out of his house. Give it a few hours, then drive over there and ask for Strider. Tell him Rudyard sent you."

"Pseudonyms?"

"Gamer handles. Never actually met the dude."

"Then Strider could be a dog."

"So bring along a biscuit."

As it turned out, Strider wasn't a dog, rather a human girl. A slim little white woman with straight brown hair combed in a way that nearly covered her face. Her hands were dirty and nicked up like a carpenter's, not unlike Madelyn Wollencroft's. Yet clearly female, with boobs too big for her body, a fact made apparent by a tight red T-shirt that said, "Anarchists Disunite!" in large white letters.

Her house was a single-story, pale green building stuck behind another house, so apparently a converted garage. And it turned out not to be her house, but rather a loaner for the purpose of meeting me.

"I don't really do the hardware thing," she said. "But as a favor to Rudyard, why the fuck not."

"Why the fuck not indeed."

She handed me a flat, silver laptop, a shoulder bag to carry it in, and a large tote bag filled with boxes, cables, and what I assumed were ancillary devices.

"He said you were a smart person, but didn't know diddly about computers. I loaded the software he thought you'd need.

It's all pretty self-explanatory, but I put links to help sites in a folder on your desktop."

"I used to be systems administrator for the massively parallel mainframe array at Consolidated Global. Before they put me in charge of R&D. Société Commerciale Fontaine owns it all now, so maybe they moved it all to France."

She looked up at me through the stringy hair, allowing me to get a better look at her blue eyes and inordinately long lashes.

"Not too diddly. I've been inside Fontaine's administrative servers, but never cracked the big daddies, which are still in White Plains, by the way. Not that I really tried. Even so, nice security architecture."

"I'm sure it was built by the guys who took over for me."

She frowned.

"I don't like false modesty. It obscures the truth and insults my intelligence."

"Agreed. I'm totally hot shit, kid. Can't wait to reconfigure this amateur PC so it can actually do something."

"It's not a PC. Technically yeah, but not according to standard terminology."

"That's the first thing I'll fix."

I hauled all the gear out to the Jeep and drove it back to the hotel. Ten minutes after figuring out how to turn the thing on, I took the plunge. Contrary to commentary from my friends and family, I'd driven a few PCs, though usually with someone like Amanda nearby to grab the wheel. Strider's folder full of help-site links was hugely valuable, given that the prevailing approach of the software companies was akin to teaching a kid to swim by tossing him in a lake.

I sent her a whispered word of gratitude between the profanities.

Before my eyeballs wore out, I did a study of the Cleary family. Most of the information was on the old man, Councilman William J., who'd died a few years before the book was written. His own father had opened up one of the first

Chevy dealerships in Greater New York City, giving William J. the wherewithal to swallow up every GM dealership in the boroughs that competitive territories would allow.

His eldest son, Robert, obviously benefited from his father's wealth and notoriety, under the adage that name recognition by any means is always a good thing. He handily won his seat on the city council and was on his second term. Before that, he'd been an assistant prosecutor, his biggest case being part of the team that dismantled the Pagliero family business.

In addition to Trevor, who had a long career as a police reporter at *Newsday* and a column for a local paper in the Bronx before writing books on true crime, there were two other brothers who owned a plumbing business. Google offered up their website, which made for interesting reading, if you're interested in all the things plumbing contractors are capable of achieving.

All the brothers still lived in the Bronx.

Only Trevor had shared a personal e-mail address, so I wrote him, giving the barest sketch of the story and invoking the Tyler Vaughn book, and asked if I could pay him a visit. Imagining him also hunched over a computer somewhere, it didn't surprise me that he wrote back in a few minutes.

He gave me a few options of time and place, and I picked the closest of both.

I spent the rest of the evening sitting on the little balcony, staring out at the hotel's cramped parking lot and the ragged storefronts across the street, and longing for the Little Peconic Bay.

CHAPTER NINE

Madelyn Wollencroft woke me up at seven A.M. I didn't recognize the number on the little window on the face of my cell phone, so it took a moment to decide whether or not to answer.

"I'm heading over to the property room this morning," she said, after I croaked out a hello. "You can come if you want."

"I would. Do I have time to take a shower?"

"You can take a shower and perm your hair. I can't get there till about ten."

"What about checking the DNA?"

"Let's see what we find first."

She gave me directions and told me to stay in my car if I got there ahead of her.

"They might have acres of worthless junk, but it's easier to get into Fort Knox."

So I took my time getting ready, making up a vat of flavored coffee and messing around on the computer like the rest of the American population. It didn't make me feel more part of the tribe, except maybe for the hypnotic pull of the screen.

I told myself to quit now and go back to cigarettes. A safer habit.

THE CENTRAL property room was in a giant warehouse in a newly freshened-up industrial section of the Bronx—a big, plain box surrounded by a wall with a single discreet sign that boldly declared: "City of New York. Records."

I was there first, so I stayed in my car. Wollencroft showed up soon after in a plain, grey SUV with enough cargo space to fit my Cherokee. That day she wore a flannel shirt and khaki shorts, sunglasses, and sensible flats and her hair tucked up inside a baseball hat. She carried a crumpled canvas and leather briefcase slung over her shoulder.

"If they ask who you are, let me do the talking," she said.

No one did. After she signed in, an old guy at the counter scanned in Wollencroft's police ID and my driver's license, took our picture with a camera mounted to the wall, punched the case number she'd given him into a handheld device, and left us in the receiving room to wait.

"I bought the Vaughn book on the Paglieros," I said, as we sat down on a pair of molded plastic chairs arranged around a worktable.

"You can send it back," she said, pulling a copy out of her weathered briefcase and handing it to me.

"That was good of you."

She seemed unimpressed with her own largesse, but I took the book and stuck it in my new computer bag. We sat in silence until the property room guy came out a door next to the counter and put a large bin on the table. He handed us surgical gloves and masks and pointed up at the surveillance cameras on two walls and overhead.

"You know the drill," he said to Wollencroft, though he looked at me.

She stood up and snapped on her gloves and put on the mask, then carefully took the stuff out of the bin and laid it out on the table. I wasn't sure if seeing my father's bland wardrobe after forty years or the dried blood that covered it was more disturbing. Inside individual plastic bags were his wallet, the crucifix, and a set of car keys, including one stamped with a GM logo. This explained why I had to rekey the ignition switch on the Grand Prix when I found it in the shed behind the cottage.

"How come this stuff wasn't returned to my mother?"

"If no one asks, it all stays here," said Wollencroft.

The wallet held his driver's license, green card, a receipt from Pep Boys, a discount card from a restaurant—not Bonnie's place—and a note in French from a person named Rozele, who'd been identified in the file as an associate. The handwriting and spelling were poor, but it looked like a list of cleaning products and a few vegetables.

"Can I get a copy of this?" I asked Wollencroft.

She took out her smartphone and shot a photo of the note. "I'll e-mail it to you."

"What about the blood?" I asked.

She opened her hand to show me a clear plastic vial, which she then uncapped and using a sharp stainless steel tool, scraped a sample off my father's shirt. Then using separate vials, she scraped other bits off his pants and the bottoms of his shoes. She logged the scrapings on the form, stuck labels on the vials, and put them in her briefcase.

The drink glasses and silverware used by the killers were also there. She dabbed them with swabs moistened with something, and dropped them in separate vials, carefully labeled.

"Okay?" she asked me.

"Thanks. When do we get the results?"

"Two weeks if I walk it in. Six months if I don't."

"I choose the walk."

"Don't worry, I walk everything in. They love seeing me. Ha-ha."

After that she had her regular cases to work on, so she told me to get lost. I waved good-bye to the surveillance cameras and did as she asked.

It was two hours before my meeting with Trevor Cleary, but I went to the restaurant we'd agreed on anyway so I could play some more on the computer, though I ended up reading the Pagliero book instead. Though the lurid promotional copy on the cover promised a sensational, terrifying read, the text was actually crisp, unembroidered, and intelligent. The shape of the story was familiar even to me, uninterested as I was in gangster lore. Leon Pagliero followed the usual path from Sicily to initiation by the hoods who preceded him to his neighborhood, the steady rise through the ranks, cracking heads and terrorizing honest citizens, modernizing the trade as it moved from numbers and heists to drugs and white slavery, eventually taking his position as head of the dominant family in the Bronx.

As I started rereading the chapter that introduced the elder Vaughn, Trevor Cleary walked in the restaurant. I recognized him easily as the brother of Nelson, smaller but clearly stamped with the family's broad features and physical heft. His walk had a slight shuffle, though I didn't absorb that at the time. I waved him over.

"I recommend the turkey burger," he said, sitting down, "unless you've already eaten."

"Just coffee. Thanks for meeting me."

"You got me curious," he said, "which you might guess is a professional affliction. And I love these turkey burgers."

I held up the book.

"Interesting stuff," I said.

"So I'll save you the history lesson. It's all in there. I know because half of it came from me. Why don't you give me your story? I might take notes, if you don't mind. Another professional habit."

So I told him the story with more detail than I usually did, assuming his calling and notebook were up to a more complete narrative. He stopped me a few times to clarify, but otherwise looked at least as attentive to me as his cherished burger. I had the meatloaf.

"I don't remember everything in that book," he said, when I was finished, "but I don't think it mentions André Acquillo, or his garage."

"But it's plausible that my father worked on their garbage trucks."

"Sure, why not. Everybody used to know somebody connected with the mob. It was sort of the glory days, if you can call it that."

"Do you know anyone who might remember those days? Somebody in the garbage business?"

"Of course. I've spent my whole professional life on the police beat. I know every thug, hustler, and psychopath in the Bronx. Bailed more than one of them out of jail. Go to their kids' baptisms."

"Can you give me some names?"

He took a mighty bite of the turkey burger and licked his fingers before answering.

"No way in hell. They're confidential sources, for starters, and unlike you, I have to live in this town. Emphasis on live."

"But you can tell them I'm looking for information on André Acquillo," I said, "and they can contact me if they want."

He grinned at that, which is when I noticed only half his face got into the act. Explained the shuffle and why he ate his turkey burger single-handed.

"That was what I was about to suggest," he said, "though you'll always think it was your idea."

"I don't mind sharing credit. Here's my information," I said, writing it in my little notebook and ripping out the page.

"I'd like to get in the loop if you figure out what happened. It could be an article. Nothing wrong with a little quid pro quo?"

"*Something for something.* I get it. I also did my time in the Bronx."

"I guess I've destroyed your image of the heroic journalist," he said, pocketing the little piece of paper.

"I didn't have an image, and even if I did, heroics aren't what they're cracked up to be."

"A cynic after my own heart."

"I don't know about that either. Cynics tend to bore me. An easy way out of actually trying to learn what the world is all about. *Nil desperandum.*"

"What did you say you did for a living?"

"Cabinetmaker. Latin's a prerequisite."

"I'll try some out on the guy who fucked up my kitchen."

"*Culpae poenae par esto.*"

"Yeah, that too."

I DECIDED to spend the evening ignoring the computer, my father's murder, and thoughts about anything troubling of any kind for any reason. I achieved this by drinking the hotel's bitter coffee and reading the *New York Post* while sitting on the cramped balcony off my hotel room.

Amanda broke the tedium by giving me a call.

"So tell me you've cracked the case."

"Hardly. What about you?"

"I haven't cracked a thing, unless you include my poor nails, which look like I've been working in the potato fields."

"You've been working the Hamptons' construction business, which is overrunning the potato fields, so it's equivalent."

"I thought we weren't going to talk about disturbing things."

"Okay, so how's the dog?"

"I think he misses you, though it's hard to tell. How do dogs look when they pine?"

"They jump in the lap of the next person who'll let them."

"Then he's definitely pining. You *are* going to share with me at some point, I trust. At least so I know you aren't just tomcatting around."

"I will, when I have more to share. And I never learned how to tomcat. Probably arrested development."

"Just stay arrested, buddy. I know where you live."

"Remind Eddie he lives there too. Otherwise, you'll have to keep feeding him."

"As long as the fillet and foie gras hold out."

I felt a little ache when we hung up. I've learned late in life that being a loner and loving a person doesn't add up all that well. Another example of arrested development.

LATER THAT night the door to my hotel room opened. I'm not a great sleeper, so it wasn't unusual for me to be awake when that happened. Even in my alarm I noted how quiet it was—a soft click of the lock and a turn of the doorknob.

The hall light formed a silhouette of a man in baggy clothes. He moved carefully, adjusting to the gloom.

I threw a pillow at him. Not a great weapon, but the closest thing within reach. He reacted by firing off a muted round from a gun held in his right hand. I rolled off the bed as a few more bullets ripped into where I once was. He kicked the door closed, then there was a quiet moment as he moved into the room. I could hear him breathing, and muttering something unintelligible, though I'd guess profane.

I pulled myself up on my hands and knees, still on the other side of the bed, and waited. When I saw the faint outline of his legs, I leaped, lamenting as I did the stiffness of my aging joints.

"Motherfucker," he yelled, as I slammed hard against his knees. The gun went off again, but by then I was grabbing at his shirtfront and frantically trying to get a grip on the hand with the weapon. He was strong, but skinny, and I instantly registered the weight advantage. I gathered him up with two hands and slammed both of us to the floor.

"Motherfucking prick," he yelled, though with labored breath, feeling the pressure I was putting on his chest.

Still fighting blind, I could sense the hand with the gun trying to take aim. I grabbed his forearm and dug in my nails, and shook it like an enraged terrier. He cursed some more and fired off another shot. It felt like somebody'd just whacked me on the side with a baseball bat, but I kept the pressure on his forearm while getting my right fist into the action.

When his knee came up I was reminded that all I wore was a pair of boxer shorts. This changed the theater of conflict for a moment, as I risked letting go of his shirtfront and stood up to get my balls out of the way.

The unexpected tactic did what it often does, causing him to pause for a second in confusion, allowing me to hit him in the face the way I'd been taught to do. Straight in and without reserve.

As he tried to ward off the blows, I wrenched the gun out of his hand. A lot of squirming and fist flying followed, and I found myself back on my ass struggling to keep the gun away from his grasping hands. I realized I was reaching the end of my endurance, wishing for the clock to go back a few decades, when I could have unleashed the type of punch that would split a two-by-four. Instead I tucked the gun sideways into my gut and curled up in a ball. I took a few blows to the head, through which I heard someone pounding on the door.

"Security," a guy yelled. "What seems to be the problem?"

I stayed balled up as I listened to the balcony door open and sounds of the guy slipping through. I tried to get back on my feet so I could grab him by the shirttails, but I was too battered to move like I wanted to.

A moment later the door to the room opened and I knew I'd still get to be alive.

CHAPTER TEN

I wasn't the only gunshot victim in the emergency room. The other was in the process of dying despite the best efforts of the ER crew, so I had to wait an hour before the young doc could take a look at the wound on my side.

At the hotel, the security guard had wrapped up my midsection with an elastic thing he called an Israeli bandage, then drove me to the hospital. When I first arrived, they'd replaced the thing with two square pieces of gauze. After the doc said getting them off might sting a little, I told her stinging would be an improvement.

"Looks like it just grazed you," she said, after dabbing off some of the dried blood. "You're lucky."

"Luck being a relative thing."

"Did you shoot him back?" she asked, using her head to gesture toward a pair of plainclothesmen waiting patiently at the door to the ER. The security guard from the hotel was there as well, and they seemed to be having a nice chat.

"No, I was too busy curling up in a ball. I did get the gun, however."

"They want to talk to you as soon as we patch you up. It's not deep, but it's wide. Nothing to sew up. Antiseptic and gauze is really all we can do. You're going to be sore for a while, especially the ribs underneath. There could be a fracture. We'll do an x-ray to be sure. Bruising at a minimum."

"I got hit by a truck last year. Busted a couple ribs. I know what I'm in for."

"You have bad luck with ribs."

"Like I said, it's all relative."

The cops and security guard interviewed me in the nurse's canteen, so we all got to have coffee and little cups of fruit cocktail out of the fridge. I told them everything I could remember about the attack, which wasn't much, given the darkness and frantic nature of the occasion. The security guard, a round young Eastern European in a plain blue suit, couldn't offer much more, except to guess that the attacker was injured jumping from the second-story balcony, though able to make a run for it, disappearing into the surrounding neighborhood.

I'd given the security guard the gun, which I presumed was on its way to the crime lab, maybe the same one I hoped was lifting DNA off Bonnie's old cocktail glasses.

I told them my own DNA was in the system, along with my fingerprints and mug shots, to save them the trouble of asking for elimination samples. And no, I hadn't done time, unless you counted a few sleepovers at Southampton Town lockup.

As to why the guy wanted to shoot me, I was less forthcoming. I told them about digging around my father's murder of forty-some years ago, about talking to Bonnie and Ray Osmund, Madelyn Wollencroft and Fitzy Fitzsimmons, but not much on what I'd learned, however inconclusive. It's not that I didn't trust the cops, but I'd been around these things enough to know how easily you could lose control of your digging around when officialdom got involved. Even well intended, they could really gum up the works.

I planned to save the details for Wollencroft, whose interest in the project might take an upswing. Or so I hoped.

The guard drove me back to the hotel where they gave me a new room and some toiletries, since mine were now behind yellow crime-scene tape while the CSIs did their thing.

On the way, I had woken up Amanda to tell her what happened, opening with "I'm okay, not that big a deal." She didn't actually agree with that, but took it well enough. One of my favorite things about Amanda was her dislike of hysterics, a handy trait given the number of times I'd made those calls. Or maybe because of that. She wasn't exactly used to it, but it helped that we had a history of surviving the consequent fallout.

The worst part had been asking if Joe Sullivan could move in with her for a while. Sullivan was a friend of mine and a Southampton Town detective, who'd performed that duty before, and was just as happy hanging around Amanda's waterfront French Provincial as moping in his divorced guy's little apartment. She was less bothered by the implicit suggestion of threat than the intrusion on her private world, one she valued as much as I did my own. Luckily, she liked Sullivan, who was a very low impact guest. And she knew if she didn't agree, I'd come right home and give up on my father's murder, since I'd be too preoccupied with worry to get anything done.

"Just call me a lot," she said, reminding me I wasn't the only one who got to worry.

I can't say I slept all that well through what was left of the night, despite the painkillers they'd given me, and knowing that a fresh security guy was hanging around the hall outside my door. I was familiar with the aftershock from a surge of adrenaline, and the recognition that a bullet's trajectory is a mindless thing, that an inch or two determines how fate decides your survival. I got all that, and was ready for it.

What I wasn't prepared for was the sudden change in the composition of the project. What had been a history lesson, albeit fraught with unwanted associations, had become all too present. And while I hated the new affinity, I had to accept that my father and I actually did have something in common.

The same people wanted us dead.

WOLLENCROFT SHOWED up before noon with an easygoing, square-jawed young man she introduced as Jake Johnson, the homicide detective they usually assigned her when she had to visit the living when investigating the long-ago dead. He had a knuckle-breaker handshake, but I took it as enthusiasm more than machismo.

"I have to say this is unexpected," she said to me, as we settled around a table in the hotel's little breakfast room, mostly emptied of the morning trade.

"I was thinking the same thing," I said.

"Any ideas?" she asked.

I told them about meeting with Trevor Cleary and his offer to pass along my interest in André Acquillo's murder to people who might have been involved in the garbage business at the time, who might also be able to shed some light on André's death. So I didn't have any names, and assumed Cleary would cleave to confidentiality, preserving both journalistic ethics and his own ass.

"But it's a cinch word got to somebody who wasn't too happy with what you're doing," said Johnson, as he scratched around his curly blond hair, as if feeling for invasive species.

"Did you tell Cleary where you were staying?" Wollencroft asked.

"Sure. And gave him the room number. The only thing I didn't do was arrange for a little 'Welcome Killer' party."

"We'll have preliminary results from the lab by this afternoon," said Johnson. "We stopped there on the way so Madelyn could bring cookies and do her 'joke of the day' routine."

Wollencroft tapped his shoulder with her fist.

"They'd love me anyway," she said. "I'm nice."

"She's not nice. She just wants the lab to think she is," said Johnson, keeping his crooked grin in place and moving a little farther out of her reach.

"So what happens now?" I asked them.

"Well, you wanted an active investigation," said Wollencroft. "You just got one."

"Clever ploy."

"Jake gets the attempted hit, since I'm exclusively cold case girl, but we're a decent team. Meaning we see the lines, but don't get too hung up on who's crossing whose."

"First stop is Trevor Cleary," I said.

"Oh yeah," said Jake, emphasizing the point by downing the coffee in his oversized travel mug, refreshed already a few times at the hotel's expense.

"I agree," said Wollencroft. "And fuck those journalistic ethics."

"Like I said," Johnson added. "Not so nice."

It took some convincing to get them to let me tag along. At first they relied on the handy excuse that I'd recently been shot, and might want to rest up a bit like the doctors told me to do. I asserted smashed-up ribs were a routine thing for me, that working through the pain was a kind of sport.

Then they said civilians weren't usually invited along on police investigations, and I described my long history of interfering in law enforcement, promising to hang back, keep my mouth shut, and let them run the show.

"You wouldn't be seeing him if it weren't for me," I said. "What's the point of leaving me behind?"

"Ross warned me about this," said Wollencroft, but she relented and I got to ride in the backseat of Johnson's ancient, unmarked Crown Victoria, the last of a dying breed.

A woman with a face filled with trepidation answered the door after we climbed the outside stairs and rang the bell at

Trevor Cleary's house. It was packed in a dense row of little houses just like it, and the neighborhood was spare, but well cared for.

"Is your husband here, ma'am?" Johnson asked, holding out his police identification.

"We're not married. He calls me his partner, which makes it sound like we're running a law firm."

"Is he here? Can we talk to him please?"

"Sure." She turned and yelled back into the house. "Trev! People are here!"

"Can we come in?" Johnson asked.

"We'll let him decide that," she said, with a taut smile.

Cleary showed up soon after, wearing a grey sweat suit and suede slippers. It occurred to me that athletic wear on older people often makes them look older than they really are.

"Hey, Sam, what's up?" he said, ignoring my two companions.

Johnson and Wollencroft held up their IDs. Again, Johnson did the talking.

"At approximately one this morning, an unknown individual entered Mr. Acquillo's hotel room, armed with a semi-automatic handgun, with which he proceeded to shoot at Mr. Acquillo with the clear intention of doing harm."

He would have kept going, but Cleary rocked back on his heels and stopped him.

"Holy Christ, Sam, are you all right?"

"Grazed my side, but I'm still standing."

Cleary's face turned the color of his sweat suit, and his partner took him by the elbow.

"We're not big on excess stress around here," she told us.

She walked him back into the house, and before Cleary had a chance to make a formal invitation, we all followed. We sat in their diminutive living room, with Cleary taking the faux-leather Barcalounger.

"What she means is I had a stroke as a young man because of an embolus, a chunk of crap from a blood vessel that got stuck in my brain for a few hours. Nothing to do with stress."

"Everything has to do with stress," said his partner.

"I'm really sorry, Sam," said Cleary, "Fuckin' gumbas. Sorry about the slur. It just so pisses me off."

"I'm the only gumba here, far as I know," I said. "Been called worse."

"We're going to ask you, Mr. Cleary, who you spoke to the day before the assault," said Wollencroft.

Nobody bothered to pull out a pad and pencil to write down their names, since we all knew he wouldn't say.

"Confidential," said Cleary. "There's no constitutional amendment protecting journalists, but this doesn't rise to anything the DA would care about. Doesn't mean I'm not really sorry. Though I was only doing Sam a favor."

"That's how I look at it," I said. "I stuck my own neck out."

Wollencroft didn't approve of that and frowned at me before saying, "Would you have any thoughts on why Mr. Acquillo's interest in a forty-year-old unsolved murder would elicit this sort of response?"

Cleary shook his head.

"Absolutely none. I'm not breaking confidences to say nobody knew anything about it, or could give a rat's ass about trying to find out. I felt bad for Sam, that he'd be chasing down a very cold trail. I know what that's like."

"Somebody gave a rat's ass," I said.

He nodded, looking down at his belly, as if trying to better recall those conversations.

"I don't know," he said. "I'm baffled." Then he seemed to brighten. "And interested. Too bad about how we got here, but there might be a story after all."

Wollencroft looked disgusted, but Jake Johnson, despite the professional tone, held on to his sunny demeanor.

"We all got jobs to do, right?" he said. "A little cooperation goes a long way with us, Mr. Cleary. You tell us things, we tell you things, everybody wins."

"Aware of that, detective," said Cleary, not bothering to add he'd been a police reporter when Johnson was still shitting in his diapers.

"So, okay?" said Trevor's partner, getting up from her chair.

She managed to shoo us out of there after Johnson gave them his card and said to call any time day or night, complimented them on their house, and told Cleary he hoped he'd be feeling better soon, as if the stroke was a bad head cold.

I'm sure they felt the visit was a necessary waste of time, but it wasn't a waste for me. Sitting in the back of the Crown Vic, I heard a little chime on my cell phone. I looked at the screen and it said I had a text message.

From Trevor Cleary.

Talk to Orfio Pagliero. Didn't get the name from me.

I wasn't surprised. Guilt over the attack was probably something Cleary could easily shoulder. But we shared a common affliction, something far more powerful than regret.

Curiosity.

Chapter Eleven

I first looked him up in the Vaughn book. Orfio Pagliero was the only son of Leon, the founder of the family business, from which Orfio successfully resigned after his father died in prison. Vaughn believed such a thing was possible for several reasons, chief among them Orfio's steadfast refusal to even speak with law enforcement much less cooperate. By taking himself out of the fight for succession, he earned the gratitude of a crowd of aspirants, even though several would be dead before the matter was decided.

Finally, though firmly committed to leaving a life of crime, no one thought he was any less capable a criminal, with a reputation for ruthlessness only surpassed by his old man. The family decided to save all that blood and quietly move on with their lives.

I had no way of confirming any of this, but it was nice to know. I usually didn't get to read a profile of the people from whom I was planning to pry information.

Orfio's chosen line of presumably honest work was excavation, specializing in big and deep. Clients included builders of skyscrapers and sports arenas. His corporate motto was, "Hire people who know their ass from a hole in the ground."

I wondered how the branding people at my old company would feel about this. Probably just fine if the CEO was Orfio Pagliero.

I thought I'd wait until the next day to pay a call on Superior Earth Moving. Despite my bravado with the cops, my side was a symphony of burning agony and I needed the night to collect myself. I spent it trying to figure out how to breathe and clear my throat without whimpering, though the best distraction was a call from Amanda who told me Sullivan was back in his old digs on the first floor watching the ramp-up to post-season baseball and drinking his six-pack beer allotment. She said he brought her flowers.

"Flowers? Joe Sullivan?"

"He said he knew this was an inconvenience and appreciated my understanding. I won't state the obvious."

"That someone else you know has never brought you flowers?"

"You noted my lush garden and said something about carrying coals to Newcastle."

"You appreciate my pragmatism."

"I'll let Detective Sullivan respond to that."

I told her about our visit to Trevor Cleary, but left out the subsequent phone text. I never lied to Amanda, but often saw little value in full disclosure. Luckily she wasn't the type of woman who made unconditional sharing a prerequisite for romantic relationships, probably because she wasn't so eager to share everything herself.

"Thank him for me and tell him to keep his combat boots off the furniture."

She gave me a report on Eddie's well being, which she knew I'd want, and that was that. I could go back to sitting still and upright on the bed, which is how I woke in the morning, amazed that my sleeping self knew to stay put through the entire night.

The first thing that occurred to me as I sat there was the utter impossibility of succeeding with Trevor Cleary's suggestion. I'd never considered extracting information from a person with so little leverage. What I learned from the Vaughn book were strictly the facts as the author understood them. It said nothing about Orfio as a person, except to emphasize an unbreachable combination of toughness and reticence. He'd disavowed his relationship with the mob, so chances were good the family history wouldn't top his list of favorite conversational subjects.

And who was I? He knew nothing about me and not caring a rat's ass was an understatement. Would a man who'd stonewalled American law enforcement at every level—municipal, state, and federal—say anything to a complete stranger, aside from, "Get out of here or I'll have your viscera served to the sand crabs."

I'd never physically threatened anyone I didn't think richly deserved it, but that wasn't remotely in the cards here. Even in my prime, and far less prone to mature deliberation, I'd know that was folly.

So if I couldn't charm, beg, cajole, blackmail, intimidate, scam, thrash, or mind-read this guy, what was left?

E-mailing Jackie Swaitkowski:

This is Sam Acquillo. Do you read me?

I don't know who you are, but I have very powerful hacker friends who will burn your computer to the ground if you attempt to contact me again.

It's me. Randall set me up. You're my first e-mail. You should be honored. You hated your mother's schnauzer whom you thought had devil's eyes.

I can't believe you sent that in an e-mail. Now the whole world will know.

I need your help. I did what you said and got a computer. The least you could do is come out here and help move this thing along. Let me remind you, I paid you a dollar. In some places, that's real money.

I've already lost that dollar in Prudhoe Bay oil futures.

I can't help your reckless investment strategies. I'll text you my location. By the way, I've been shot. Just a flesh wound, though it was my flesh, which I deeply care about. My point: things are getting lively.

Shot? I assume you're kidding. I can only spare a couple days.

That's all it will take. Bring the Glock and your brain. And that outfit. You know the one I mean.

So that's the way it is.

Okay, bring Kevlar instead.

You will explain.

Wilco and out.

Getting dressed and out of the hotel room took an extra hour, but the fresh air was worth it. I'd located the site of my father's old shop and drove over there to see what they'd done with the lot.

Nothing. It didn't seem possible, but there it was, a painted-brick building in an industrial area near the Hutchinson River. It had two truck-sized bays, a door to the office, and a small parking area crammed with vehicles. He'd never had a sign, but now there was one above the bays that read José's Garage. Under that it said *Lo rompes, lo arreglamos.* Roughly, "You break 'em, we fix 'em."

I parked on the street and went into the office. The random parts, greasy stacks of papers, and dilapidated furniture had been replaced by a freshly painted room with a counter, waiting room chairs half occupied, and a magazine rack filled with *Car and Driver* and *Motor Trend* along with *Hola!*,

Autopista, and *La Voz Hispana.* On the walls were photos of tourist traps in the Dominican Republic and a tattered, faded Dominican flag behind a piece of plexiglass.

A dark-haired woman with a smile full of teeth held down the counter.

"What can we do for you?" she asked.

"You can let me say hello to the owner, if he's here."

"You can say hello to one of the owners right now," she said, sticking out her hand. I shook it. "The other owner is my husband, who's working on a set of brakes. Whatcha need?"

"My father used to own this place. Haven't been here in about forty years and thought I'd take a look."

"Really," she said, with a lot of gusto. "That's amazing. Who's your father?"

"André Acquillo. He's been dead since then. I'm sort of surprised the place is still here."

She looked around as if confirming that for herself.

"It is indeed. Don't know anyone named Acquillo. We bought it from José's Uncle Esteban, who had it for, like, thirty years? Maybe he knew your dad."

"Is he still around?"

Her smile gained a few more watts, which didn't seem possible.

"You're kidding me; Esteban will live forever. We love him. Crazy guy."

"Can you get in touch with him? See if he can talk to me?"

She told me she'd go get José, so I waited under the scrutiny of the waiting customers, who probably thought I was trying to jump the queue. José came in wiping his hands and grinning. I felt like I'd stumbled on the world's happiest couple.

"Sorry for the grease," he said, sticking out his hand.

"I grew up with grease," I said, taking it.

"Your dad had this place? That's amazing."

"Yeah, and your wife told me you took over for your Uncle Esteban. I'd love to have a chat with him."

"You won't say that after the chat. You get Esteban talking, he never stops."

"Fine by me."

"Acquillo?" he asked. "Don't remember that name."

I took out my driver's license as if to show him the spelling, though I wanted him to know I really was the son of the prior owner. He looked at it carefully with his wife looking over his shoulder.

"Aqui-yo?"

"Spanish speakers always make that mistake. It's Italian. We pronounce the *l*'s."

He went over to the phone on the counter and punched in a number.

"Hey, *tio*, I got a guy here in the shop whose father used to own the place. *Sí*. Acquillo." He spelled it and said to pronounce the *l*'s. "André Acquillo." He looked at me to confirm he got the first name right. I nodded. "His son Sam wants to talk to you. Yeah, he's here right now. I'm sure he can wait a few minutes." I nodded again. "You remember this André?" This time he nodded at me as he listened. "I think his son will be happy to hear that. You want anything to eat?" he added in Spanish. "Adelita has cold cuts in the back. Okay."

He hung up and told me Esteban would be over in about ten minutes. He warned me again the guy liked to talk.

"He used to work for your dad. Him and another mechanic bought it from your mother. He's excited about this, though he's always looking for something to get excited about. Especially since my aunt died. We like to say the cause was fatal *bochinche*."

"José," said Adelita, though without letting go of the smile.

I think it took less than ten minutes for Esteban to show up. He came through the door like there was a million-dollar check waiting for him inside. A lot shorter than his nephew, though the family resemblance was there, minus the hair. He wore a pair of bottle-bottom glasses and his grip rivaled Detective Johnson's.

"Sam Acquillo, come on, you don't remember me?"

I struggled to, but had to be honest that I didn't.

"That's okay," he said. "You didn't get into the bays that much. And I didn't look like this. Much more handsome, like José. Come on, let's go in the back."

He took me into a room I also struggled to remember, until it occurred to me that it was the old parts cage, back when mechanics kept a lot of stuff on hand. Now it was a combination kitchen and office, with a computer workstation, file cabinets, and a table for the family and crew to eat lunch. Like the waiting room, it was spotless and freshly painted a bright yellow.

"Look a little different, eh?" said Esteban. "The kids have really done it up nice. Everything modern. Me and Donny cleaned up the place after we took over, but nothing like this. They got a knack for customer service, and employee relations. It's different than in the day, but it's smart. They both got college degrees. Adelita's a sociologist, for Pete's sake. You want a soda or something?"

He got us both a Dr. Pepper out of the fridge.

"Was it Donny Duxbury?" I asked.

"Yeah. You remember him but not me? Not offended. Donny knew your dad better. You might've seen him at the apartment."

"No, I just got the name from a police report. You remember all that."

Esteban's cheerful face went grim.

"What a terrible thing. I'm sorry, I did forget. Must have pushed it out of my memory. We were happy to be able to buy the garage, but I wished for a better reason. Your mother, I gotta say, gave us a very good deal. She wanted nothing to do with the place. A lovely woman, your mother. Only talked to her once on the phone. Very polite, but had a kind voice. Very respectful. I remember that."

"Thanks for that. She was kind."

I didn't add that she was also bitter and withdrawn, as if retreating from the profound disappointments of her life into her own limbo, a staging area before passing into the next world about which she held no greater hope or expectation.

"Donny knew her from when they both lived in that apartment. He always said good things. Your dad was one of the smartest men I ever knew," he said, taking a turn that jolted me. "He could fix anything. Knew everything there was to know about cars and trucks, and anything that ran—clocks, washing machines, lawnmowers, radios, TVs. People don't fix things anymore. Something goes wrong, they throw it away and buy a new one. Your father would get right in the guts of those gadgets and operate like a surgeon. Made the parts himself if they weren't around. We had machine tools in the shop. Did the tricky jobs at night. I saw him make a gear for a pocket watch. Sat there with an eyeglass drilling out a little brass disk with a bit twisting between his fingers. Cursing away in French. He didn't think I knew what he was saying, but Spanish is not that different, if you listen carefully and you heard those words a few thousand times."

He stopped to take a sip of his soda, giving me an opening, but before I got a word in he said, "Could've ruled the world with that brain, if he hadn't been so mad at it."

"The world or his brain?" I asked.

Esteban grinned at that.

"Both, now that you mention it. Let me tell you something, I don't like speaking poorly of the dead, and I wouldn't anyway about André. He treated us fine, and equally, none of that spic stuff out of his mouth. Or anything like that. Maybe being French Canadian, I don't know. He sure liked to bitch about people, but it was equal opportunity."

"Tell me Donny Duxbury's still alive," I said.

Esteban squinted at me through the thick eyeglasses.

"Donny? Sure, he's still barking. Can't hear too good, but who can? His daughter got him his own place behind their house. Can't see, either. Like, completely blind, but his brain's still good. Nother smart one, only more into history and scientific things. Listens to books all day. I bring him the CDs from the library. Makes me listen with him. Right now we're on a Normandy kick. Just got off the beaches and heading into France. He'll be glad for the visit. I think he's sick of me. Just kidding. We're like a duet. Can't break up the act. I used to drive him around till they took away my license. Not the cops, my kids. Said I can't see the nose in front of my face, how'm I supposed to drive? Can't say they're wrong, but don't tell them I said that."

I listened to more about his partnership with Duxbury, which led into several conversational tributaries, before bringing things back to where I wanted.

"So Esteban, any thoughts on my father's murder? Any ideas?"

He stopped talking long enough to think about it.

"Like I said, André was a smart guy, but he loved to fight with people. Not so much real fights, but arguments. You couldn't count how many people the man pissed off in a day. Nobody stood out to me at the time, I remember that. Donny's the one who talked to the cops, but he and I agreed there was nothing going on that could lead to such a thing. They said the guys who did it were mobbed-up. That could be true. But we didn't have anything to do with those people."

"Garbage trucks?" I asked, as lightly as I could.

Esteban laughed.

"Oh, my Lord, André cursed at those things. Stunk like holy hell. Couldn't get them out of here fast enough."

"I heard the mob was big in the garbage business."

He agreed.

"Sure, but we just fixed an occasional truck. It wasn't a big business, and usually for this one guy André knew. Don't remember his name, but honestly, nothing about any wise guys ever came up. If the guy was hooked in, we never talked about it."

"Maybe Donny knows."

"Maybe he does. Let's go see him."

Chapter Twelve

I was somewhere between ten and twelve years old. Old enough to catch a football, but still too small and awkward to catch everything thrown at me.

It was me, my father, and one of his friends. We were out in the street, the only area wide and deep enough to effectively toss a football, the few cars parked at the curb acting as inanimate defensive players. The initial rotation was my father to the friend, the friend to me, me to my father. This worked pretty well, since my spiral lacked velocity, but was fairly precise, thus effortless for an adult to catch.

We got into a nice rhythm, and in the quiet of the afternoon, all you heard were hands on the pigskin football, a steady slap, slap, slap.

After a long time of this, probably due to the emerging monotony, the friend took the ball from my father, then sent it back to him. Which meant I had to take my father's throw. Which I did, though there was something different about the texture of the experience. Faster, tighter, and more precise. In response, my throw to the friend was more robust, and he bobbled it up in the air before securing the catch.

"Hey, Johnny Unitas," said the friend, "you gonna break my hands."

He was smiling, so I smiled back, proud of the toss.

He threw one to my father, who threw one to me, this time even faster and tougher to hold on to. I caught it in the crook of my arm, and held it against my body. It stung, and I wondered how I managed to hold the ball. I lobbed the next one to the friend.

His throw to my father was an adult thing, a much more advanced form of the act. People forget a football is mostly inflated air, so it's hard and tends to bounce. Which is what it did, right out of my father's hands. He scrambled after the loose ball, digging it out from underneath a parked car.

Then a rocket-propelled missile was heading my way.

Time slowed, as it does in these situations, and I was quick enough to get my body in front of the speeding ball, though I had to leap up to meet the trajectory, which caused me to lose control over my hands, ending in my fumbling the catch.

I ran after the football, bouncing erratically as they do, so focused on retrieval that I didn't notice my father running up behind me until I had the football in hand and was about to throw it to the friend.

Instead, my father hip checked me to the ground, slapped the ball out of my hands in a way that allowed him to catch it, turn, and deliver a ferocious spiraling bullet into the arms of his friend.

The friend caught it, laughed, and threw it back to my father with the same measure of vigor and accuracy. I was out of this game, watching the ball zip back and forth between the adults.

But then the friend threw it to me, and once in possession, I took a beat to ponder the next play. My father was walking away from me, heading to his former spot, and I yelled, "Hey!"

As he turned, casually, I threw the ball with everything I had directly at his face. He reared back when the football hit, grasping at his nose, and I just stood there and said, "Sorry. I'm not as good at this as you guys are."

My father used the sleeve of his shirt to wipe the blood running from his nose off his upper lip, then picked up the football and threw it at where I was once standing, but though small and young, I was also fast, and by now I was heading down the street, wondering where I was going to spend that night, without my sleeping bag, toothbrush, or change of clothes.

As soon as I saw him, I knew the friend in the football catch was Donny Duxbury.

He didn't have much of a chin, and his eyes stared into nothingness. At least two days of grey stubble covered his face and his clothes hung loose and disheveled on his tall frame, as if they belonged to someone else. Esteban gently slapped a paper bag at his midriff, and Donny seized it without looking away from dead air.

"Ham and cheese, lettuce and mayo, no tomato," said Esteban. "And the junior Acquillo, which I also promised you."

Donny's house was a garage converted so long ago its original purpose was completely obscured. It was musty, but clean enough and well tended. A striped orange and white cat sat on a side table, watching me move through the main area. Also on the table were a stack of audiobooks, a compact CD player, and a set of headphones. A fan was running on the kitchen counter, an antique model with an art nouveau base and a stylish cage through which you could easily pass a hand.

Esteban took his forearm and raised it so we could shake.

"What's he look like?" Donny asked Esteban.

"Like his old man only smaller and without the gut."

He put his hand on my head.

"Still got all your hair. Wish I could say the same," he said, running his other hand over the bald pate.

He walked a few steps over to his easy chair and Esteban brought two chairs for us from the kitchen. Donny held the unopened paper bag in his lap. The cat kept its eyes on me.

"I'm glad you let me visit," I said. "Esteban and I have been going over old times."

"How's your mother?"

"She died. I moved into their place on the Little Peconic. Been there ever since."

"Retired?"

"Fired."

"Not laid off?"

"No. I punched the company's chief counsel in the nose."

"You *are* André's son."

"He didn't exactly deserve it, but it saved them from paying me severance."

Esteban asked me what job I got fired from, and I told them, which led to describing my time at MIT and the brief boxing career that funded it. They seemed to enjoy the story, which wasn't my purpose, but at least for Donny, the vision of André's scruffy little kid making his way through college and into corporate life was probably a pleasure. So I kept going and told them how I'd lost my wife, the big house in the suburbs and all my money, before finding honest work as a cabinetmaker. And getting a little chunk of dough out of the company after all, from a class action lawsuit I had nothing to do with, which I immediately converted into a sailboat.

"So things turned out okay in the end," said Esteban.

"Yeah. A friend of mine once said the trick is staying alive long enough for your luck to change."

"I concur with that," said Donny. "It's my luck to go blind so I could get an education."

"By now, you oughta be a PhD," said Esteban.

Donny put the paper bag on the side table and its place in his lap was immediately taken by the cat.

"Sam's actually here looking into André's murder," said Esteban, causing Donny to cast his sightless eyes in my direction. "I don't know much about it. We thought maybe you would."

"Some think it was a mob hit," I said. "The Mafia controlled the garbage business in those days, and you guys fixed garbage trucks, so that's the only link we have. Esteban said you knew the guy who brought in the trucks. We're hoping you remember him."

Donny stroked the cat, who raised itself up to meet the caress.

"Richie Scamporino," he said. "He went to trade school with Donny Junior. And yeah, he was connected, but not made. A punk, we'd call those guys, not in the way the word means today. Ran errands. Probably kicked some ass, but I wouldn't know about that. Brought us the trucks as a favor to Junior, which would piss me off. You don't ever let a punk do you a favor, cause there's always a little string attached to it, and you don't want it pulled. I tried to explain that to André, but he'd brush me off. Richie always paid on the spot, top money. Cash. The only problem for André was the damned smell."

Esteban smiled, "See, like I told you."

The gush of fresh information made me a little light-headed, which might have amped up my pulse rate, and consequently, the pain in my side. Out of reflex, I touched the bandage.

"You okay, Sam?" Esteban asked.

"Sore ribs. Fell in my hotel room. Is Richie around any-where?" I asked Donny.

He shook his head.

"No idea. Haven't heard from him since we bought the garage. About the same time Junior took off with his mother for California. Don't hear much from her, either. Lucky for us, those trucks stopped showing up. Didn't want any more of that, especially when we owned the place. Another chunk of good luck."

Esteban looked at me, as if to confirm that I was getting what I needed. I nodded.

"Sorry I can't remember anything else," said Donny. "I got to admit, Sam, after seeing André in the morgue all bashed up and pasty-looking, I wasn't too eager to get involved. Maybe that looks like cowardice, but there was nothing I could do to bring him back, and I had a family to worry about, even though my wife hated me and my son was out of control. At least I had my daughter, thank the Lord, who stuck with me. Rozele had to find another place to live, and Tasenka was just a little kid. It was a lot all at once."

"Rozele Mikutavičienė?" I asked.

He repeated the name, with the proper pronunciation.

"Of course you didn't know her," said Donny. "I didn't think you would. She's dead too."

"Her name was on the police report. It said she was a domestic."

"Right. Cleaned houses. Including André's apartment. That's how they met."

I must have looked confused, like Esteban, who asked Donny what he meant.

"You didn't know her either," Donny said to Esteban. "Not something André wanted to advertise. He was a private guy. You know that."

"Rozele cleaned his apartment," I said. "So who was Tasenka?"

Donny moved his head toward the kitchen, a second before the cat jumped up on the counter and knocked into a stack of dishes on the drainboard. Esteban and I followed his gaze, at least one of us surprised that the cat had slipped away from Donny's lap.

"Her daughter. Their daughter. Hers and André's. Your half sister. Sorry, you asked."

THERE'S NO better distraction from sudden shocks to the nervous system than a bracing visit from Jackie Swaitkowski.

I'd made it back to my hotel room after leaving Esteban and Donny Duxbury to their assault of the German Fatherland with my engines of denial, avoidance, and rationalization at full throttle. So the extent of my internal deliberation was a repeating loop of Donny's words, in particular the name Tasenka and "half sister."

I found Jackie pacing around the hotel lobby holding a smartphone stuck to her ear, the other hand scrunching around her electric ball of frizzy hair.

"I told you not to have any contact whatsoever with your accuser," she was saying into the phone. "And no, beating the snot out of him is not legal in the state of New York, even if he really deserved it. You're just handing the ADA another reason to stick your sorry ass in a deep, dark cell."

Jackie worked for a law firm that provided free legal services to the poor and disadvantaged, which she often referred to as the wretched refuse. Only to me, who'd once been the beneficiary of her professional skills. It cost me that dollar, since she hadn't yet transitioned into snatching needy defendants from the jaws of criminal justice, some of whom were actually innocent. Her only experience up to that point was clearing titles, obtaining setback variances, and closing on houses. But it gave her a taste.

When she saw me, she raised a finger and nodded, listened for a few moments, then told her client he could enjoy his stay in Southampton Town lockup for the next few days, giving him an opportunity to reflect on his choices in life, and perhaps emerge with an invigorated commitment to behavior that won't guarantee his next residence would be the state penitentiary.

"Knucklehead," she said to me, as she hit the end button.

"Good advice," I said. "Penitentiary is from the Latin, *paenitentia*, meaning 'of penance.'"

"I'm sure my client would find that comforting. You weren't really shot, were you?"

"I actually was."

"So how's the bullet hole?"

"Not a hole. More of a trench. And I've had worse."

"Let's get some coffee and you can tell me all about it."

And so I did, after rustling up a fresh pot from the surly overweight women cleaning up in the kitchen. I was as polite and deferential as I could make myself, though it didn't help.

This took a long time, because I knew Jackie would want the details, her chaotic nature belying a very deliberative, meticulous mind. She tapped notes into a tablet device as I talked, only faltering when I told her the sister thing I'd learned from the retired mechanics, Donny and Esteban.

"Holy shit."

"That's one way of putting it."

"What are you going to do?"

"Go home to Oak Point and play with my dog. After apologizing for dragging you out here."

"You can't do that."

"Yeah, I can. None of this was my idea. I know you and Amanda have some cockeyed notion that digging up long-buried bags of misery and regret is somehow therapeutic. It's not. It just means you find other reasons to feel shitty. The only therapy I need is what I already have. A view of the Little Peconic, and a place to put down my drink. I'm fine with that."

"That's not what I mean," she said. "It's too late. Now they know who you are, which means they know where you live, and where your friends and family live. Five seconds on Google and they'll know what you're capable of. This has got to be dealt with, or it'll never go away."

"Gee, thanks, Jackie. That's exactly what I wanted to hear."

"You know I'm right."

As I felt my carefully constructed edifice of avoidance and denial crumble around me, I knew she was. She stared at me until I copped to it.

"Okay, so Orfio Pagliero. What do we do?"

"I have no idea. But that can wait until we find Tasenka."

"No. Absolutely not. And get that look off your face."

We spent the next hour or so tossing around options and approaches, finally settling on the one that probably made the least sense.

"Let's drive over there and drop in on him," she said.

"Sounds good."

"Give me your room key. I'll change into the outfit."

CHAPTER THIRTEEN

Superior Earth Moving was in the far reaches of the East Bronx. Headquarters was in a pair of mobile office trailers surrounded by a herd of giant mechanical critters confined behind a tall cyclone fence. You could drive right up to the trailers and knock on the door, which we did.

Jackie had a little trouble walking over the gravel that covered the parking area in her high heels, which worked great with the form-fitting skirt and silk blouse. There was nothing particularly revealing about the outfit, but I'd seen it hush restaurants and clear barstools enough to know its unique properties. Nudging her way toward forty, Jackie had shed the softening vestiges of youth, leaving only lean curves and a bearing that was defiantly all woman.

We'd never had anything like romantic feelings for one another, but I could still notice what was obvious to every other straight male on the planet.

The guy who answered the door being one of them. He was slight, slim, and handsome, with a nice head of dyed hair more tightly curled than mine and the kind of horn-rimmed glasses you'd see on the engineering professors at MIT. Before I could ask if Orfio Pagliero was around, Jackie stuck out her hand and said, "Mr. Pagliero. I'm attorney Jacqueline

Swaitkowski. We're very sorry to bother you, but we're facing an urgent legal matter and hope the Sons of Italy might be engaged to help."

He shoved the glasses up on his forehead and asked if we had identification. We showed him our driver's licenses and Jackie pulled out one of her "Officer of the Court" business cards that opened more doors than Publishers Clearing House.

"I don't normally work on the OSIA's business during business hours," he said, his voice a soft baritone that made me think of Tony Bennett.

"I understand," said Jackie, "but we're under some time pressure. Ten minutes is all we need."

"That's about all I have." He took us into a small conference room with a folding table and chairs. "Acquillo," he said to me. "Are you with the OSIA?"

"No, sir," I said. "But I admire what you do."

That didn't seem to impress him, but he sat down with his arms folded to listen.

"Here's the thing," said Jackie. "Mr. Acquillo has recently learned of a significant inheritance from his Uncle Francisco Acquillo who died at nearly one hundred last year in Viareggio. It's a strange matter, in that the beneficiaries are required to be descended from the Acquillos who immigrated to North America, but cannot exceed fifty years of age. Don't ask me why, but it means Sam's daughter qualifies, as does his half sister, born out of wedlock to Sam's father forty-some years ago. So you can see the urgency. We need to find this young lady now. A lot of money is at stake."

I nodded along as if I knew exactly what she was talking about, even though I truly didn't.

"The last time Sam knew her whereabouts she went by Tasenka Mikutavičienė, surname of her Lithuanian mother, Rozele, now deceased. We were wondering if someone attached to the OSIA might have some guidance on how to proceed."

Orfio gently nodded as she spoke, and then sat quietly, I hoped not trying to decide how to have two intruders incorporated into the main by-products of his excavation business. Fresh dirt and big holes in the ground.

"This is a noble thing you are doing, and of course we will do all we can to help," he said. "I'm not sure what form that could take, but we have people who specialize in immigrant affairs, and they're always eager to lend a hand."

Jackie smiled at me, pleased as punch, though not for the reason Orfio assumed.

"Now comes the more delicate part," said Jackie, turning back to him. My mood, briefly buoyed by the unexpected turn of events, suddenly sank. "You probably don't know that Tasenka's father, André, was murdered nearly forty years ago. In his efforts to locate his lost half sister, Sam has been making inquiries with various people who lived in and around their old Bronx neighborhood. But then last night he was attacked in his hotel room, injured by a bullet that could have hit his heart. So now, in addition to the looming deadline, we have concerns over Sam's safety. Would you have any thoughts on that?"

I learned a lot watching my father work on cars and trucks, even though he made no effort to directly teach me anything. One thing was to resist the temptation to torque a bolt past the point where it was comfortably snugged into place. All it took was one extra turn to twist off the head, with potentially dire consequences.

Inside my head, I heard the snap.

Orfio looked down at Jackie's card.

"Miss Swaitkowski is it?" he asked. She nodded. "You might be unaware that the Bronx is blessed with a very effective police force," he said, in a voice that lowered the temperature in the conference room by about one hundred degrees. "I know many of the leadership personally. I will absolutely be contacting them to share your story, and if I learn anything that may aid in your pursuit, you will be the first to know. You and Mr. Acquillo. Is that satisfactory?"

"We couldn't ask for more," she said, rising from her seat. I didn't hesitate to follow suit. He walked us to the door to the trailer.

"What sort of law do you practice, Miss Swaitkowski?" he asked her.

"I'm a defense attorney," she said. "So I have several friends myself on the job. Perhaps some day we could compare notes."

He gave her a look that covered head to toe, either to capture a good memory of the outfit, or to size her up for later disposal.

"I'd enjoy that," he said. "Is this a good number?" he asked, holding up her card.

"The best," she said, and led me out of the trailer into the early fall day, crisp with harbingers brought down from Canada on the north-northwesterlies, the wind I most enjoyed sailing under, something I fervently wished I was doing right at that moment.

"It's your turn to do some explaining," I said to Jackie, when we were safely outside the cyclone fence and heading west.

"You don't have an Uncle Francisco."

"That's too bad."

"And I don't know how old Tasenka is. But I wanted to watch his reaction to her name, and André's, and his murder. Nothing showed, like my smarter clients. They should be on Mount Rushmore. Faces never budge."

"But you had foreknowledge."

"You never heard of Google? Before I drove out I did a little research on Orfio. Learned he was a big shot with the Order Sons of Italy. They're very serious about Italian Americans, the good guy, vast-majority version. On the way here, I worked out a little story. Then I spit it out before I had time to stop myself. And before you start giving me a hard time, admit it worked."

"Worked? How?"

"Our interest in André Acquillo has been delivered. Directly. He knows the rest is pure baloney."

She opened the window of her Volvo station wagon to add a little white noise to the conversation.

"To what end?" I asked.

"Who knows? I learned this technique from you, remember. You evoked Dashiell Hammett's Continental Op. When everything looks frozen in place, do something big. Shake the can."

"You shook the mob."

"I brought the Glock, like you asked. Not just the outfit."

"We're on watch. We'll have to take shifts."

"In a new hotel. I've already booked the room."

A strange sort of paternal impulse stirred inside me. A type of pride, something I usually avoided, or denied. She'd admitted learning from me over the lengthening arc of our partnership, so part of me took pleasure, while the other part wished, for her sake, we'd never met.

JACKIE'S HOTEL was a significant upgrade. People in uniforms swarming the lobby, attractive women with exotic accents holding down the registration counter, guests in designer clothing tugging luggage festooned with international baggage claims. An address on the East Side of Manhattan.

Indirect lighting and a chrome and glass bar within eyeshot.

My mood, instantly restored.

Our room was actually a suite, with two bedrooms and a little seating area, kitchenette, and a giant-screen TV in between. I asked her who was footing the bill.

"Burton Lewis. Probably owns the place."

Burton was her boss, the guy who set up the free legal practice she worked for, a kind and decent man who was also an old friend of mine. And a billionaire, though you wouldn't know it if you met casually, so polite and deferential his deportment. I was simultaneously grateful and appalled by the largesse. Jackie had anticipated that with a fierce look at the registration desk, so I had meekly submitted to being checked in as Mr. and Mrs. Sam Acquillo of Southampton, New York.

"Amanda would love that," I said.

"We're not telling her."

The suite itself achieved the aesthetic standards of the lobby, including a well-stocked minibar. I poured us our regulars and took a seat facing the door.

"You're forgetting that Orfio Pagliero severed all connections with his father's criminal enterprise," said Jackie after a hearty gulp. "Harming us would violate his legitimacy."

I acknowledged that.

"Doesn't mean he'll be any help," I said.

"Trevor Cleary must have thought differently."

I acknowledged that as well. I had him on my list of people to revisit, a list topped by Madelyn Wollencroft. So I gave her a call.

"We identified your shooter," she said, when I told her who was calling.

"Really."

"A local rat-fuck named Larry Ringer. Junkie. Would shoot his grandmother for fifty bucks."

"Did you arrest him?"

"He appears to have made a hasty departure from his last known address. Could be anywhere by now. Including the bottom of Long Island Sound, having so thoroughly botched the assignment."

"Not thorough enough. What about the old DNA from Bonnie's bar?"

"They got clear readings from the blood traces and cocktail glasses, but no matches in the national database. That's not so surprising. We rarely get hits on those old samples. It's more useful for IDing an actual suspect."

Then she asked me what I'd been up to. So I told her, leaving nothing out. She had mixed feelings about our paying a call on Orfio Pagliero. Annoyed that I had hidden the tip from Trevor, impressed that we got an audience. I gave Jackie all the credit, well deserved.

"You know he made a big show of leaving the family," she said.

"Do you believe it?"

"I do. Because Vaughn believed it, and he's in a position to know."

"Okay. Then why did Cleary think I should talk to him?"

"I don't know," she said. "I'd like to. And I'd track down your sister. She could know everything."

I sighed, though I doubt she heard it over the phone.

CHAPTER FOURTEEN

Jackie wore a pair of flannel pajamas covered in drawings by a famous *New Yorker* cartoonist of snarling, leaping house cats. I'd volunteered to take the first shift and she joined me for a nightcap. I had the Glock in my lap and a cup of coffee from the room's little coffeemaker in my hand.

"I can hear those cats from over here. How do you sleep?" I asked.

"What? The pajamas? Harry gave them to me."

"Doesn't mean you have to wear them."

"Do you remember how to shoot that thing?"

"I do. Point and click."

"You know who's hard to find on Google?"

"An honest man?"

"John Smith. Too common a name. But what about Tasenka Mikutavičienė?"

"Easier?"

"I found her. Street address, but no phone number or e-mail. Unless there's another Tasenka Mikutavičienė in the Greater New York metropolitan area."

"The Bronx?" I asked.

"West Seventy-Sixth Street. Manhattan."

"Get out of here."

"We could walk there in about a half hour."

"But we won't."

"No. We're polishing off the contents of that minibar and then sleeping the sleep of the dead."

"Pre-dead, if it's all right with you."

"What's it like discovering you have a sister?" she asked.

"Aw, Christ."

"You hate it, don't you."

Where to begin.

My sister and I never questioned the logic of my father moving us out to North Sea, the woody area above Southampton, while he kept his business and apartment in the Bronx. It was a rougher borough in those days, and the cottage, though hardly palatial, was a much more pleasant environment than the apartment, and the small-town life of Southampton, nine months out of the year, a much more agreeable place to live.

We never knew what our mother thought about it. She never said. We assumed, given the venomous storms that blew through the cottage when my father was there, that she was as grateful as we were for the weekday reprieves.

The obvious never occurred to me. Never once, not even in my wildest, booze-soaked, blackout ridden, suicidal days, did I think my father had a second life going on at his apartment. Another family, an entirely separate existence.

And now that I knew he did, my mother made sense. A gentle, dignified woman, with European manners to match her thick Québécois accent, it always seemed part of her was absent, that she also existed somewhere else, where she shouldered a burden unseen by us.

But did she know? Did she even suspect? How valid could my memories be, warped and contorted by time and the overlay of the intervening years?

"Yes," I said to Jackie. "I hate it."

She pinched a piece of the pajamas up off her chest and studied the ferocious cats.

"I rediscovered a brother I thought had died in prison," she said. "I know it's different."

"No it's not. Everyone's pain is uniquely their own. It's not a competition."

"We don't have to talk about this," she said.

"Good. Let's not."

"But we should still go see her. We've got a case on our hands."

"No. You're going to find Richie Scamporino, my father's connection to the garbage business." I turned the Glock on the minibar. "Then we kill what's in there and get in a few good hours of insomnia."

I WAS stunned by my father's announcement that we were going to spend the day at Jones Beach. It was one of my first weekends visiting his apartment in the Bronx without my mother and sister, who stayed in Southampton for reasons never broached much less explained to me.

I'm guessing I was about fifteen, since the promise of witnessing a flock of girls in bikinis, fulfilled upon, is more than a lingering memory. And though I'd been driving cars since I could look over the dashboard, mostly around the sand roads lining the Little Peconic Bay, I didn't have a driver's license.

We rode in my father's day-to-day pickup, a midfifties Ford in which I had to dig out a place to sit among truck parts, tools, repair manuals, crumpled receipts, spare eyeglasses, and similar detritus that washed back and forth as the truck turned right and left.

We'd never done anything like this before. Vacations on the water, even day trips to Jones Beach or Coney Island, were things my friends talked about, but were as alien to my sister and me as flights to the moon. Since we lived year-round a few hundred yards from the pebble beach on the Little Peconic Bay, it was one of my father's few understandable idiosyncrasies, and I was too young to know that normally functioning families went on vacations just to go somewhere else.

So I'd never seen the giant water tower and stone bathhouses, the colossal monuments to Robert Moses's ambition that rose skyward as you approached the shoreline. I recall my father saying that such things were built in a day when money was worth something and great people did great deeds, an impulse lost on today's degenerate masses, swarming like insects over the causeway and fanning out across the beach.

We parked as far away from the crowd as possible, and hiked out to a fringe area, though still a mob scene compared to the sparsely populated Little Peconic Bay. I carried a canvas tarp from the truck that my father used for roadside repairs, assuring the aroma of refined petroleum would follow us into the sea air. We both wore T-shirts and long pants, not owning bathing suits, but we made a concession to the surroundings by taking off our shoes and rolling our pants up above the ankles.

He also brought a small cooler and a short stack of car magazines. I had a dog-eared copy of *Moby Dick* stolen from the Southampton library. We picked a relatively open patch of sand and plopped down on the canvas to read, since idle conversation was never an option. I also did my best to scan the neighborhood for bikinis, with some success.

Thus distracted, I didn't notice the woman with a toddler approach until I heard her ask my father if the open spot next door was available. He said it was, without looking up from his magazine. And it wasn't until the little girl staggered over with a plastic bucket and shovel that I really registered they were there.

The child handed my father the bucket and babbled something in the language of the prearticulate. He took the bucket and asked the kid in French what she wanted him to do with it. She answered by taking it back out of his hands and squatting down so she could fill it with sand. He watched her fill it halfway, and then with some effort, dump the sand back out again. She looked at him for approval, which he gave, thanking her for returning her treasure.

"Merci de mettre le sable de retour à sa place legitime."

This became a game, which also involved my father using the shovel to help fill the pail, and occasionally assisting in pouring out the sand. The girl's mother watched the little girl with gentle adoration between peeks at her own book, a paperback with an indecipherable title.

At one point, the little girl went back over to her mother— her bulky, soggy diapers further challenging her drunken gait—and pointed back at my father. The woman brushed off the girl's butt and said something, in a language I didn't understand, though she sounded amused.

My perspective on the mother was naturally blunted by my age, though as I took a better look, I realized she filled her own bikini far more capably than the competition around the beach. She was a platinum blonde, with skinny legs, but plenty of soft curves and pale skin made slightly rosy by the sun.

My father told her the child was getting a good early start on the craft of building sand castles. In French. To which she responded:

"Elle est très bonne avec ses mains."

She's very good with her hands.

They went back to the game, and I went back to Melville, occasionally taking a break to pretend to look around the beach, hoping my sunglasses would disguise glances at the mother, who made the task more difficult by standing up and adjusting her bathing suit. She asked my father if he could look after her daughter while she cooled herself off with a quick dip, and he said sure.

I watched her over the top of my book, and listened to my father give the little girl instructions on the proper construction of a sand castle, which would someday involve moistened sand and sturdier implements.

Preoccupied though I was with my sly surveillance, I remember being struck by the gentleness in my father's voice, a tone I'd never heard him use with my sister, with whom I'd never seen him even in a moment of play.

The mother came back from the water and toweled off as she stood before us. Then she said something in the strange language to the little girl, who looked at her uncomprehendingly, but was acquiescent when her mother picked her up and prepared to leave.

"*Au revoir*," she said to my father, after gathering up her beach bag, folding chair, and tiny daughter. "*Dis bye-bye*," she said, waving the girl's little hand for her. Neither of them looked at me before turning and heading back up toward the parking lot.

My father went back to his magazines, but I'd lost interest in the White Whale, too unsettled by the surreal sequence of the day's events to reengage with the evocative, ornamented nineteenth-century prose.

CHAPTER FIFTEEN

When Jackie spelled me at four in the morning, she broke the news that there was a veritable army of Richard Scamporinos living in and around the five boroughs of New York City. After sorting for age and proximity to the Bronx, she got the list down to ten.

I referred her to the Vaughn book, in which she was able to find a Johnny "Bongo" Scamporino, who had three kids, including one of the Richards, at least based on age.

After I got in my requisite five hours of sleep, I called Donny Duxbury, who told me where Richie went to vo-tech with Donny Junior. Jackie tapped around on her computer for a few minutes, then said, "*Voilà.*"

There were only two points of corroboration, but good enough to pay a call.

If it was the right Richie, the grown-up version had ascended the socioeconomic ladder to the position of sales manager at a Toyota dealer in Remsenburg, Suffolk County, Long Island. Just inside the western border of the Town of Southampton. Our home turf.

"I can find anybody," Jackie sang, and I really believed she could.

Jackie drove us in her Volvo station wagon, which was more like a rolling storage container, but I did my part by securing coffee at two different rest stops and keeping us safe with helpful driving tips.

"I think I've got a muzzle somewhere in the back," she said.

"I'm sure there's nothing you don't have back there."

"Any thoughts on how to approach Richie?" she asked.

"No idea."

"Great."

"Planning's for amateurs. Spoils the spontaneity."

It was an unalloyed pleasure to be heading down the Sunrise Highway toward the East End. We decided to drive on after meeting with Richie so we could sleep in our own beds and reacquaint ourselves with our loved ones. We held on to the room in Manhattan, despite the expense, which Jackie reminded me represented a nanosecond's rise or fall of Burton's stock portfolio and real estate holdings.

I alerted Amanda.

"An unexpected pleasure," she said. "Eddie will be thrilled."

"Don't count on it. He'll think we're moving him back to the cheap seats."

"How's your side?"

"I'm aware it's there. We're only planning on one night. Jackie feels this ridiculous need to get back to her paying job, so I have to keep her head in this thing."

"Anything you can tell me?" she asked.

What she meant was, anything I'd be willing to talk about. So I brought her up to date, more or less, leaving out any mention of Tasenka Mikutavičienė, ignoring Jackie mouthing the words, "Tell her about your sister."

"So that's about it," I said.

"No, it's not," Jackie mumbled.

It was Jackie's turn to call her boyfriend, Harry Goodlander, the bald-headed redwood tree who ran his logistics business out of an apartment in a converted gas station. I got along fine with Harry, and not only because he was big enough to carry me around like a Chihuahua. He had the forbearance of Job and took good care of Jackie, which were complementary virtues. I suggested he meet us at Oak Point so we could spend a little social time and Jackie could get an earlier start on a bottle of red wine.

"Bring the good stuff," she told him. "Amanda's picky."

Toyota of Remsenburg was actually in the Speonk section of town. In every other way, it was like any car dealer in the United States, complete with a showroom full of Toyotas, brochures and desks, with Richie's somewhere in the back so the salesmen had somewhere to go and pretend to negotiate.

Jackie opted to skip the middleman.

"We want to see Richie," she told the first guy to approach. "We're told he's the one with the juice."

The salesman looked unperturbed.

"I can show you around, then you can talk to Richie. If he's available."

"We already know what we want," she said. "I'll tell him if you don't get the commission, he doesn't get the deal."

The salesman looked at me for help, but I just shrugged, helpless to intervene.

"I'll see if he's back there. Can I have your name?"

"Mr. and Mrs. Sam Acquillo," she said.

At least Richie Scamporino looked like he actually belonged in organized crime. Under six feet, but appearing larger with a gut of impressive proportions. His tie followed the giant globe and dangled like a pennant above his belt buckle, which struggled to contain a V-shaped view of pink flesh. His slick hair was unnaturally black, and long enough to drape over his shirt collar. The ring on his finger large enough to cause injury from a handshake it took all my strength to resist.

His aftershave triggered repressed memories of the bookmakers who used to crowd the locker rooms before a fight, kept at arm's length when possible by our superannuated, paternal trainers ("Come on, boys, give da kid a little air.").

He looked Jackie up and down while trying to crush my hand.

"Juice, huh," he said to her. "Is that what you heard?"

"Yeah. They said you got it to spare."

"They're right about that. So what're you driving outta here?"

"That depends on you," said Jackie.

He enjoyed that, finally glancing at me with a look that said, "Where'd you get this girl?"

"I'm thinking something practical. Roomy. But the missus wants a convertible," I said.

He let go of my hand as if fearing infection.

"Well, brother, that's a pretty big gap."

"Can we talk?" said Jackie, looking toward the back of the showroom. "My feet are hurting just standing here."

Richie was magnanimous.

"Absolutely," he said, turning around his bulk like a freighter backing out of the harbor and leading the way to his office.

Richie wasn't much for decoration, his office featuring a single pad of paper and two Le Mans posters that might have been stuck on the wall when the dealership first opened. He pulled out a chair for Jackie, even though she had plenty of room to sit unaided, and I took the other customer's chair. He found a way to squeeze behind the desk.

"So, the convertible," he said. "Like the wind in your hair?"

"This hair? You know how long it takes to brush it out?"

She illustrated by failing to rake more than a few inches through the strawberry blonde Brillo pad.

"More the adventure," he said.

"Exactly. Did you drive those cars?" she asked, looking up at the Formula Ones in the posters.

Richie was surprised by the question, but looked ready to admit that he indeed had. Though something stopped him before it was too late.

"Drove a lot better than that. So what're you looking for again?" he asked me, halfheartedly.

"Anything I can lay a four-by-eight sheet of ply in without scratching the vinyl."

Richie tried to explain, as diplomatically as his social skills would allow, just how wide a discrepancy we had in the Acquillo family vis-à-vis a new car.

"Maybe you folks oughta regroup and come up with a more synchronized plan," he said.

His face, as heavy as his belly, hung off his head like a loose sack of potatoes. It made him look sadder than he probably was. He sat back in his chair, causing it to roll into the wall behind.

"Ever consider a crossover? Maybe not as sporty as a convertible, but quick on its feet and roomy enough for the weekend project."

I silently applauded both Toyota's marketing strategies and Richie's sales aplomb. Jackie looked over at me, a tad condescendingly.

"Fine for him. But what about my adventure?"

I was impressed with Jackie's assumed Long Island accent, a disappearing artifact.

"Adventure's where you find it, sweet cakes," he said, not even bothering to include me in his stare.

"I'm thinking as we're talking here," I said, "you're not Johnny Bongo's boy are you?"

Richie pulled himself off the wall and set both arms down on his desk.

"Why would you be asking that?"

I let a little silence build up in the room.

"The manners," I said.

Richie was one of those Italian guys with very white skin. I often wondered about their lineage, assuming a fair dose of Viking, or Visigoth. It made it harder to conceal upset, as a bloom of red flowed up from his inflated neckline.

"Do I know you?" he asked, as they usually do.

"No. But I know you. So let's skip the horseshit."

I looked down at my hands folded in my lap, then up again. Richie's eyes drifted toward my middle, as close as he could to my lap, where I might be holding something he wouldn't like very much.

"This is my place of business."

"So don't mess it up with any nonsense. We just want to talk," I said.

His mountainous shoulders settled a little, but he kept his hands spread on the desk, still measuring the distance between us and the likelihood of reaching my throat before I stuck a shiv into his.

"My old man's dead," said Richie. "A long time ago."

"That's what we want to talk about," I said. "The good old days."

"Talk ain't cheap," he said. "What's in it for me?"

"The ability to keep talking after we leave," I said.

Richie started to look defiant, until he noticed Jackie rummaging around her ten-gallon purse. We both watched her pull out the Glock.

"Just checking," she said, before putting it back.

"Who're you people with?" he asked.

"Does it matter?" I asked. He shook his head. "You remember Donny Duxbury? You went to tech school together."

"I don't know where he is, and that's the truth. Haven't talked to him in a million years. We called him Junior. His old man was Donny."

"Donny Senior worked on your trucks," I said. "Did you know his boss, André?"

Richie's mind, probably not a fleet thing, looked down at the pad of paper on his desk and put two and two together.

"André Acquillo. Frog bastard with a gumba name. You related?"

"He was my father."

Richie tried to get more comfortable in his chair, though he was breathing heavily.

"That was a long time ago," he said.

"But you know what happened to him."

"I heard," said Richie.

"What did you hear?" I asked.

The shock of the initial moment had begun to wear off. Richie was starting to make the calculus, running the odds on how dangerous the situation really was. People like Richie often did that once they realized they weren't immediately dead.

"Lots of stuff," he said. "I heard stuff all the time."

"We heard you did it," said Jackie.

Richie flung out his arms.

"Whoa, none of that. Never laid a hand on the guy. I wanted to. A major league asshole. But I had nothing to do with any hit."

"Tell us what you heard," said Jackie. "We already know a lot, so keep the imagination in check."

"Them guys from back then are all dead or dyin' in jail," said Richie. "The whole family got put out of business twenty years ago. What's the fucking point?"

"So you have no one to be afraid of," said Jackie. "Except for him," she added, jerking her head at me.

"Come on, Richie," I said. "Give us something and we'll let you get back to work."

"Donny told us you were a good customer," said Jackie. "Paid cash for the truck repairs."

He snorted.

"That's what he told you? Funny."

"Funny how?"

"Couple a grand for a brake job? Fuckin' right I was a good customer."

My brain was demonstrably quicker than Richie's, but it took me a few moments to process that. Jackie got there ahead of me.

"We know all about that," she said. "Just tell us what he did to earn it."

"What am I, head of HR for Leon Pagliero? I don't know what the fuck he did. What he was told."

"So you never worked with him," I said. "Outside the garage."

Richie might still have been a little nervous, but now he was getting curious.

"Why now?" he asked me. "Where were you in the day?"

An excellent question.

"I was an undergrad at MIT studying to become a mechanical engineer."

I might as well have told him I was busy performing the part of Odette in *Swan Lake*.

He pointed at me and said to Jackie, "I'm supposed to be afraid of him?"

"Well, actually, yes," she said. "But he won't hurt you unless you try to hurt him first."

"We took an oath at MIT. Reciprocal conduct only."

"What the fuck does that mean?"

"So you didn't work with André?" asked Jackie, repeating my question. "Outside the garage."

"Why should I tell you?" he asked.

Another important question, one I'd heard often in the last several years from people like Richie Scamporino, some even more like Richie than he was himself. Sometimes I had a good answer, and sometimes I didn't.

"To do a good deed?" I asked.

He studied me.

"You were a fighter," he said. "I remember now. Junior said you were fast."

"Not fast enough," I said, pointing to my busted nose.

"Fast with the mouth, that's for sure."

"Like André?" I asked.

He snorted.

"I never understood a word the bastard said. I don't speak frog."

"Who worked with him?" she asked. "Who's still around?"

"I don't remember. Coulda been any of the crew. That sort of thing wasn't my department."

"You don't know because you were a nobody," said Jackie. "Nothing important ever involved you."

That raised the slight pink on his cheeks to a solid red.

"The frog was fast with a car, is what I *know*," he snapped at her. "Could outrun anything with four wheels. I brought him the cars a week in advance. Customized them himself. The rest of them guys in his shop were totally out of the loop, including Junior. Don't tell me that wasn't important."

"Wheelman," said Jackie. "Of course."

"You don't know shit," he said, his face a solid snarl, whatever fear remained turning to anger.

Jackie didn't respond. She just sat there and looked at him, with her legs crossed, the high heel dangling from her left foot.

She kept the silence going a few more moments, then gave him one of her business cards.

"If your memory improves, call me," she said.

We stood up. He almost looked disappointed we were leaving.

"And if we learn you had anything to do with my father's murder," I said, "you might want to look up the word reciprocal."

I WAS nearly through high school, by then having spent almost two years training at a boxing gym in the Bronx. I was listed as a middleweight, though for some reason most of the guys I sparred with were bigger than me, the story of my life.

I was in a bar on East 233RD, a dingy little joint among an equally rundown string of stores serving the lower end of the local manual labor. The music made it too loud to talk, though no one cared, being mostly drunk or high, and only wanting to use up the rest of the evening in an exhausted trance before going home to crash and brace themselves for another tough day.

I had my own table, hard up near the bar, where I was nursing the first of my two-beer allotment. I probably had a cigarette going, since everyone I knew at the time would have one going as well.

Somehow, despite the loud music, I heard a guy at the bar yelling something. I gazed up and saw it was directed at the girl sitting next to him. She was shaking her head and yelling something back, though I couldn't make out any of their words.

The guy was big, with lots of long brown hair, hippie-style. He wore a suede jacket with tassels and heavy cowboy boots on his feet. He leaned into the girl with so much intensity it lifted him off his bar stool, causing her to lean back and hold up her forearm in a meek defense. Someone put a hand on the guy's shoulder and tried to say something, but the guy shook him off and said something that made the intruder move off in a hurry.

The bartender slid into the scene and said something as well, but things had moved too far down the road. The angry guy put one foot down on the floor and smacked the girl across the face. She probably cried out, but it was too noisy in the bar to hear. She put her hand to her face and shrunk down in her seat. The guy hit her again, much harder this time.

I was so close I barely had to stand to get behind the guy's barstool, grab the neck of his jacket, and pull him backward off the stool and into the table I'd just left. He took a moment to get his bearings, then leaped back on his feet to look around for the perpetrator. I made it easy for him by calling him a name and settling into the boxing stance I'd been practicing at the gym most of that day.

He was easily a foot taller than me, and a lot heavier. We both noticed the discrepancy right away, though only the guy thought it was funny. He grabbed for my shirtfront, but I dodged out of the way. He told me he was going to tear my fucking head off, and might have said something else, but I socked him in the mouth before he had a chance to do so.

A fist in the mouth really hurts, no matter how big you are, so at this point his interest in me was better focused. He took another heavy swing, but the slowest boxer on earth knows how to get under those things, and as it passed over my head I stuck another right into his kidney. He came back with a lot of profanity, but I was more concerned with reestablishing proper form—fists raised, elbows tight against my sides, legs spread, and feet up on the toes. The guy took another swing, which I easily avoided and answered with a combination to the head.

Blood sprouted from his cheeks. I used it to aim my next punch, which rocked him back on his heels. I thought that was it, but he surprised me by lurching forward and grabbing my shirt again. Suddenly the weight advantage was a factor. I tried to pull back, but he held me and rammed his head into my face. Tears filled my eyes, and I almost lost control of the situation.

But then I told myself I was okay, and hit him in the temple, which was enough to get my shirt back. Thus liberated, I was free to let fists fly, which sent the guy through another row of tables, at which point the bar's management finally ran over to end the fight.

While I stood there, bleeding from my hands and face, waiting for the guy to get back up, a man came up to me and said, "You should be doing this for money."

I recognized him as one of the trainers from the gym. I hadn't worked with him, involved as he was with the few pros who came in for bag work and consultation out of view of the competition.

"I wouldn't know anything about that," I said.

The bar's bouncers hauled the guy out of there, then told me it would be preferable if I left as well. I was fine with that, especially when they waited for me to finish my beer. The smacked-around woman watched me the whole time, mixed feelings written all over her face.

When I got out to the parking lot, the trainer caught me at my car. He handed me a card.

"I've got a middleweight who could use a sparring partner. Call me."

And I did. Which led to a boxing career that paid for my time at MIT, ultimately leading to my corporate career. That the career ended with punching the company's chief counsel during a board meeting could be seen as poetic justice. Never having studied poetry, I didn't know.

Chapter Sixteen

Harry Goodlander was already there when we showed up at Amanda's house. He was out on the patio trying to explain the virtues of soccer, which everyone else in the world calls football, something Joe Sullivan found incomprehensible.

Goodlander noted that soccer principally involves moving the ball around with your feet, whereas American footballs are only kicked occasionally, and by specialists, many of whom grew up playing soccer.

"Better we called our version bullet ball or head basher ball."

"Fine by me," Joe conceded. "I was a linebacker. Head bashing was a fundamental."

"Good preparation for your future employment," I told him.

Eddie had followed our car down the driveway and greeted me like he meant it. Sullivan told me the dog spent most of the day hanging around the cottage, even with Amanda's ready indulgences right next door. He hardly looked the worse for wear.

Amanda came out wearing a flowery dress and a black hoodie, giving in to the chilly breeze off the Little Peconic. She still managed to look like the first and last word in au courant.

When she kissed me hello, her hair tumbled across her face and delivered the scent I most associated with serenity and delight.

"Where ya been, buddy?" she asked.

"I don't know. All I remember are crowded streets and frightening Italians."

"We've pacified our Italians out here. All it takes is chilled vodka and a little prosciutte."

The conversation around the patio stayed safely desultory and nonintrusive, helped along by the bounty of Amanda's larder and liquor supply. I thought I'd dodged discussing my field trip to the Bronx, but with Jackie there, I should have known better.

"So how's the side feeling?" she asked me, out of the blue.

"Healing. And thanks for asking. Any predictions on the World Series?"

"They identified the attacker," said Jackie, "but haven't located him. Seems to have flown the coop."

"We don't deal much with the wise guys out here," said Sullivan, "but I'm bettin' any flying was done off a bridge."

"Your colleagues in the Bronx share that suspicion," she said.

"Would have preferred to chat with him first," I said.

"What do you think?" asked Sullivan. "Any theories?"

I was trapped. Sullivan was too good and loyal a friend to put off, and too experienced a cop to evade, so I gave as good an accounting as memory allowed, with Jackie filling in some of the pieces. The only thing I left out was Tasenka Mikutavičienė, and Jackie had the good grace to respect that, though I knew she wouldn't forever.

"We know about Richie," said Sullivan. "Got a heads up when he moved out here, maybe fifteen years ago. Far as I know, he's been a good boy, at least around here. Don't know what he does in the city."

"I don't think anything," I said. "The Pagliero family was effectively wiped out during the big federal prosecutions.

Richie's at the other end of the hierarchy from Orfio Pagliero, but he was caught up in similar turmoil. He couldn't know if the FBI was watching his every move, and he faced competing gangsters, both Italians and newcomers like the Russians and Albanians, gobbling up the Paglieros' business. A good time to quietly seek other opportunities. Like selling Toyotas on the East End."

Sullivan also knew Madelyn Wollencroft. He hadn't heard her history in undercover, but it didn't surprise him. Semple had brought her out to Southampton a few years before to give a week's CSI training, with an eye toward helping cold case specialists like herself.

"Really knew her shit," he said. "Ross sat in on the whole thing. Took the squad out to a fresh crime scene and she made us look like a bunch of dumb fuckups. No punches were pulled, I can tell you that. Kind of a bitch, actually."

"Didn't your ex-wife go to Wellesley?" Amanda asked me.

"Exactly."

With at least some of the curiosity around the patio sated, I was able to steer things back into the pleasantly innocuous, and eventually our guests drifted away, including Sullivan, who said it was a good opportunity to check up on the staff back at his apartment.

"See if they got the wine cellar stocked and the perennials planted in the rock garden."

Amanda cranked back the patio lighting so we could better see the moonlight cast an iridescent runway across the Little Peconic Bay. She brought out blankets, knowing we'd stay out there shivering otherwise, and we sat in near silence, holding hands between the lounge chairs.

"Turns out I have a half sister," I said, finally. She gripped my hand a little tighter as I told her what Donny Duxbury told me, and the story of that one and only excursion to Jones Beach with my father.

"You think that was her? Tasenka and her mother?"

"I do. No other explanation."

"This must be exceedingly odd for you."

"More exceedingly complicated. I don't know how to feel about it. So many years repressing history, cramming this giant pile of toxic waste into a box, only to have it leaking out all over the floor, remembering things I didn't even know were there."

"I know what you mean."

And I knew she did. She not only learned later in life who her father was, it turned out to be someone she'd known all along. Or at least knew of, a prominent, wealthy person, a distant, though powerful force in her life. Dead before she had a chance to slap him, or hug him, or demand he acknowledge all he'd denied to her mother and her young self.

It struck me then, that on a subterranean level, this parental deprivation and subsequent confusion formed one of the pillars of our relationship. Something every artist and thinker knows about others, yet can rarely see in themselves. That we emerge from childhood without entirely leaving the child behind, and as we move through time and space, people likewise encumbered succumb to a selective gravitational pull, unwittingly, irresistibly, irretrievably.

THE NEXT morning I took the bus by myself into Manhattan. Jackie was so disoriented by this she didn't know whether to be pissed or relieved.

"I thought you wanted my help," she said.

"I did. And you delivered. You should get back to upholding everyone's right to quality legal representation, no matter their social standing."

"That's not how you usually put it."

"I'm getting more sensitive. If I need you again, I'll call. Or e-mail."

"That new computer is just another way to be insufferable."

"You only have yourself to blame."

I checked out of the hotel in Manhattan and had Randall Dodge get me into a different hotel in the Bronx under an assumed name. He had me ask for a man who would handle the check-in without the encumbrance of an ID.

The quality of the hotel was a sharp comedown from the one in Manhattan, but it had a kitchenette with a sink and refrigerator, and I was on the eighth floor, ensuring that the next guy to jump out the window would have a harder time running away.

"Ah, Mr. Archer," said the man. "Your room is ready."

"Call me Miles."

After settling in, I saw that Madelyn Wollencroft had pinged my cell phone. So I called her. She told me her partner, Jake Johnson, had tied Larry Ringer to people who also had ties to the moribund Pagliero family, though way down the food chain. Ringer was also known to freelance for other families, and ethnic gangs like the Albanians.

"In other words, he worked for anyone who'd pay him," she said. "Doesn't help us."

I told her what I'd been up to, ending with our visit to Richie Scamporino's Toyota dealer. Though I left out mention of half sisters. I expected the usual grumpy cop complaint about interfering with an official police investigation, but she just said, "I've learned a few things myself. Disturbing things."

Ready to invoke the right of private citizens to talk to whomever we wanted, anytime we wanted, I was caught off guard. So I just said, "Can we meet?"

"We can. Where?"

"You tell me. It's your town."

"It could be my office, but as much as I love Jake Johnson, he doesn't work for me. Rather not have him dropping by in the middle of the conversation."

"My hotel room has a table and chairs, and a refrigerator," I said.

"Hotels are traps."

"Okay, so where?"

There was a pause.

"Stay tuned."

A few minutes later an address popped up as a text on my cell phone. I ripped off a piece of paper from the hotel's notepad, wrote down the address, and stuffed it in my pocket.

IT TURNED out to be a strip joint a block north of Boston Post Road. I rechecked the address three times, but it kept coming up the same, so I had to accept the truth.

It was midafternoon, so Elegance Gentlemen's Club was just catching the early happy hour trade. While neither a club, nor elegant, with no one present you'd consider a gentleman, the place did have the feel of a well-established, professionally run enterprise.

The ten-dollar entry fee included one free drink, and a menu card promising an all-you-can-eat buffet, for an extra charge, later that evening. I found a spot at the bar where I could get a drink in my hand before surveying the territory.

There were two low stages, each equipped with a brass pole employed with some agility by a topless woman staring vacantly into middle space. Better-looking women trolled the lounge seating and tables, picking up and dropping off drink orders. A bouncer stood next to the dressing room door, and giant TV screens—silently accompanying the heavy metal sound track from stadium-grade loudspeakers—hung above the bar and around the larger room, drawing at least as much attention as the dancers.

At the back of the room was a raised area behind a brass rail, with plush seating gathered around glass coffee tables. Once my eyes were fully acclimated, I could see Wollencroft sitting there at a table by herself, wearing sunglasses, with her hair pulled back in a ponytail.

The bone-crunching volume from the loudspeakers was remarkably muted up there, something she must have known.

"I know the owner," she said, as I sat down at the table. "He thinks my name is Chardonnay. Don't disabuse him of that."

"No abuse from me. He's got the edge on manpower."

"There's no safer place in the Bronx. At least for me. They'll tag a cop the second he comes through the door," she said, taking a pull off a cocktail glass the size of a soup tureen.

"We're concerned about the cops?"

"For this discussion, yes."

She flagged over a waitress, who seemed happy to see her. They kissed both cheeks and Wollencroft ordered another double bourbon on the rocks. When the waitress looked over at me, with my full drink, Wollencroft said, "Just a friend. We're hanging out."

The waitress took it in stride.

"Whatever you want to do, sweetie," she said, and left.

Wollencroft took off her sunglasses and put her legs up on the table, settling down into the overstuffed chair. She wore a grey skirt and heels, and a plain white blouse, giving her the look of a junior executive at a downtown bank.

"You're polite not to ask," she said.

"None of my business. I appreciate that you're still talking to me."

"Even here?"

"The drinks are overpriced, and I like my naked women less commercially inclined, but it'll do."

Once she got her bourbon, she let out the ponytail and used her rough nails to comb her hair down over the blouse.

"Do you remember checking into the property room?" she asked.

"I do."

"Back in the day, they used to have a similar procedure for accessing case files on open investigations. It was a limbo land, full of active but still unsolved cases before they were declared utterly cold and shipped to the archives, which you've seen. Today we trust our detectives to handle files without so much supervision, but in those days, not so much trust."

"I saw *Serpico*," I said.

"That's the gist of it. It's hard to imagine how much crap the feds had to clean up in the eighties and nineties to deliver to us the paradise we live in today."

It was hard to know which part of that was earnest.

"I was noodling your bartender's story of the senior cop coming into his bar and warning him off your old man's murder," she said. "Not surprised, but curious. So I went into the old sign-in books, which are still at the squad head-quarters. They go back into the thirties. We're all so used to seeing them on the shelves, it's like wallpaper, but they come in handy sometimes."

"What did you find?"

"It's what I didn't find. Fitzy knew about a prior assault charge from the arrest records, which are kept in a different place. But there should have been a complete file, which he never noted in his investigation. Because it wasn't there."

I told her vanishing police files would come as a surprise to the general public. She smiled.

"Most people hate paperwork. Cops are no different. You could probably fill Yankee Stadium with all the paper that's gone missing from official police investigations. It's not that it's gone that bothers me. It's why."

She stopped talking when her waitress friend showed up unbeckoned with another double bourbon on the rocks for her, and a vodka for me. Wollencroft thanked her and squeezed the hand that delivered the drink.

When the waitress left, I said, "And you know why."

"I strongly suspect. A week before your father was killed, the file was checked out by Captain Francis X. Kelly. It was never checked back in."

"Really. And no one complained?"

"Kelly was in charge of records. He was the one you'd complain to."

"Where's Kelly now?"

"Woodlawn Cemetery."

"I keep forgetting this all happened so long ago."

"Cold cases will do that to you."

"So what do you think it means?"

"Kelly wanted to destroy information. Hide evidence. If he wasn't already dead, I'd remove his testicles with a butter knife. My job is hard enough without my own people making it harder."

The waitress came back over with another girl, a stripper, who had some exciting news to share with Wollencroft.

"Strawberry got her new tits," said the waitress. "They're awesome."

Strawberry looked like a teenager just named captain of the cheerleading squad. Wollencroft stood up and they had a group hug. Only Wollencroft didn't prance like a show pony or wiggle her shoulders like she'd just caught a winter chill. But she did smile effusively, and gave Strawberry a maternal caress on the cheek with the back of her hand.

"I'm so happy for you."

Strawberry unsnapped the glitter-covered brassiere that barely contained the freshly enhanced breasts and asked Wollencroft if she wanted to feel the product.

"They're, like, so natural," said the waitress.

Wollencroft obliged with a hearty handful.

"You're right. You had a very good surgeon."

Strawberry looked up at the ceiling, her face clenched with pleasure. Then she hugged both the other women again, causing her to turn her head toward where I was sitting in the comfy chair.

"You want to feel?" she asked me.

"I'm all set," I said. "I can tell just by looking they're as real as Marilyn Monroe's."

Whose were undoubtedly real, since they didn't look like the pair of porcelain salad bowls sewed onto Strawberry's chest.

I suffered another few minutes of congratulations and exuberant hugs, which paid off, since the waitress said our drinks were now on the house. I toasted with my near empty glass of vodka, which the waitress grabbed with a big nod.

"Make the next one coffee," I told her.

"Comin' right up, friend of Chardonnay."

As I watched the pair of thong-outlined rear ends retreat, Wollencroft said, "You're a good sport."

"How'd they feel?"

"Like a Hefty bag stuffed with a softball."

"Never understood it."

"Me neither, but we occupy a different spatial dimension. You should visit it sometime."

"I grew up in their dimension. Didn't understand it then either."

She might have taken that as a dig at her upper class background, though it didn't show. She just sat back in her chair and slid a little farther into its welcoming embrace, taking a big pull on her bourbon on the way.

"Why would Kelly do what he did?" I asked.

Wollencroft sighed an exhausted sigh.

"Who the hell knows," she said. "It could be anything from absentmindedness to intentional obstruction of justice. It's too long ago, Sam. It's like finding a dinosaur bone on the side of a mountain. Once covered in sediment, now solid as a rock."

"But you thought it was current enough to meet me here. Undercover."

She studied the waning glass of bourbon as if there were tea leaves settling on the bottom.

"It's you," she said.

"Me?"

"Don't get coy with me. It's insulting. I know a lot more about you than you know about me. Do you think I'm the only one that's bothered to look you up? This is the information age and you're all over the public record. People know what you're trying to do, and they don't want you to do it. They want you to go back to Southampton and leave everything be. I've seen it before. My predecessor in cold cases was a real crusader, idealist college boy. He's now keeping Frank Kelly company up in Woodlawn Cemetery. You're like a man in a blindfold walking naked into a lit room full of psychopaths with swords. They'll carve you into chum before you have a chance to say 'Hey, what's up, dudes?'"

I realized then that she was slightly drunk.

"So what do you think I should do?" I asked.

"Come home with me."

The moment was interrupted by an announcement that Strawberry was about to take stage one. A spirited performance was probably in the offing, but I still wasn't interested.

"I can handle myself," I said.

She smirked.

"I'm sure you can, until you can't."

She was right about that, at least when it came to matters of sexual innuendo. Back in the days of dreary parties around my old suburban neighborhood in North Stamford, various isolated housewives would put out signals, which I was the last one to pick up on. It was usually my wife who clued me in, whose signal-reading skills were nonpareil.

My basic problem was one of chronic fidelity. Even in our darkest days, when gutting that house and hauling the contents down to a landfill in New Jersey seemed like a reasonable thing to do, I never cheated on my wife. Or Amanda, who lived in her own house and never once mentioned the word marriage.

On the other hand, maybe Wollencroft just wanted to keep me safe.

"I appreciate the offer, but a friend of mine got me a room under a fake name," I said.

"At least come see my house before you make a final decision," she said. "Might be a better venue for confidential meetings."

I looked around the strip joint.

"I don't know. This one's growing on me."

Wollencroft must have considered that an invitation to have a few more drinks, bourbon for her and coffee for me. So I did get to see her house after all, since I felt the need to follow her home after she turned down my offer to drive her.

Her house was in Riverdale. A blond stucco and fieldstone Tudor, with a slate roof and two-car garage, it was hard to imagine such a place could exist within the official confines of New York City. She pulled her SUV into the driveway, then walked out to the Jeep, which I'd parked at the curb.

"Come back tomorrow," she said, then turned and went into the house, her stride as determined as ever, if a little short on equilibrium.

THE MOST incongruous thing about my father's 1967 Pontiac Grand Prix was the four-speed stick shift. He installed it himself, with my help, though you could order the ten-ton, 428-cubic-inch monster similarly equipped direct from the factory. The appeal was a potential second or two off its already impressive zero-to-sixty performance. For my father, the point was a few extra miles per gallon.

Why he owned the car in the first place was a mystery to me. All I'd ever seen him drive were disheveled pickups, usually abandoned at his shop by people who considered the repair estimate a death sentence.

It was late at night and we were on the Southern State Parkway on the way to his apartment in the Bronx. He rarely had much to say to me when he drove, reserving most of his commentary for the other drivers, whom he addressed with invective both various and original.

Traffic was light, but there were still ample targets of opportunity, usually cautious drivers who made the mistake of cleaving to the outside lane, or others who moved to the right so hastily they neglected to signal. I was so used to this

I'd almost fallen asleep when I heard him murmur, *"Merde,"* nearly under his breath, which made it all the more ominous.

I opened my eyes to see the inside of the Grand Prix lit up like a Broadway stage from the high beams of a car following only a few feet from our rear bumper. We were in the left lane, moving about ten miles over the speed limit, boxed in by a line of cars on the right. My father edged the speed up, but the other car kept the same distance, its headlights still on high.

This went on for a few minutes, my father moving his eyes back and forth between the windshield and the rearview mirror, surprisingly quiet as he processed the situation.

Then he did the trick I would use myself many times, decades later, with a variety of consequences. He slid the gear shift up from fourth to third, then used his heel to touch the brakes, setting off the brake lights, before jamming down the accelerator, rocketing the big car ahead.

I watched the front end of the car behind us dip toward the pavement, then swerve as the driver fought to regain control. My father chuckled and called the guy a string of foul names in both English and French, a special bilingual honor.

Too soon, as a moment later the car was back on our ass. My father began to hum a little tune as he slowed down, allowing the cars in the right lane to pass us until there was a space to slide over.

The car that sped by turned out to be a Porsche, as if the driving behaviors weren't offensive enough.

As soon as the Porsche cleared our front bumper, my father stuck the Grand Prix back into fourth gear and slid into the left lane. Then he moved up until you'd have trouble slipping a dollar bill between our front end and the rear of the little sports car.

And that's where things stood until the speed of the two cars reached about 110 miles an hour, with frequent lane changes to avoid the innocent, and when necessary, using the shoulder and slivers of the parkway's grassy median.

The Porsche held the curves better, though the layout of the Southern State Parkway was kind to American cars, and this specimen of Detroit excess was also equipped with heavy-duty racing shocks and anti-sway bars that kept the big car on a reasonably even keel.

Any other deficiencies in the Grand Prix were made up for with raw horsepower and the driver's heedless intemperance.

Coming out of a wide curve, a straightaway loomed out ahead, free of other cars. Both of us were in the right lane, with the Grand Prix still inches off the rear bumper of the Porsche, but then my father jerked the wheel and our car was suddenly on the left. He floored the accelerator and the tach pushed into the red zone, but he managed to bring the Grand Prix side-by-side with the Porsche. I got a look at the driver, a guy about my father's age, with thin red hair and thick-framed glasses. But only for a moment, because my father gave the steering wheel another little jerk, this time to the right, which sent the tank-sized Pontiac thudding into the much smaller Porsche. The driver looked over at us for the briefest moment, in horror, before turning his attention to a series of 360-degree spins executed by the runaway Porsche before it crashed sideways through a tall stockade fence.

What happened to the car and driver after that, I have no idea, because we were long gone, my father dropping down to the speed limit, which felt like standing still, and with no further comment, either reflective or profane, calmly drove us to his apartment in the Bronx.

CHAPTER SEVENTEEN

"Nice house," I said the next day, when I picked her up in the Jeep. I'd told her I'd take her out for breakfast, and she didn't argue.

"It was my mother's condition for letting me join the NYPD," she said. "I let her think it was a concession, but I really just wanted the house. My condition was her signing over the deed."

"Sounds like a complicated relationship."

"You don't want to know."

"I don't," I said, sincerely.

I figured she needed a place that big to contain her wardrobe, which changed character with every encounter. Today, she wore blue jeans and sandals, and a blue scoop-neck top that offered a glimpse of cleavage. And a baggy, mustard-colored, all-weather jacket that looked fifty years old. She brought along her briefcase, of a similar vintage.

"I know a place," she said. "They have great tea."

"I won't hold it against them."

She needed the jacket, since it had turned cool overnight, and the November sky was a surly harbinger of weather to come. She told me to get on the Hutchinson Parkway and drive to the next exit. Most of the traffic was heading the other way toward Manhattan, though I took my time, the Jeep being a sturdy thing, but not perfectly suited to the curvy Hutch.

"Jackie Swaitkowski thinks my father was a wheelman," I said. She asked me why and I said Richie Scamporino more or less told us so.

"Would suit his professional credentials," she said.

"And temperament. You think they might have mentioned that in the missing file?"

"Maybe. No way to know."

I told her about my father shoving the Porsche off the Southern State Parkway at more than one hundred miles an hour.

"I guess that supports the theory," said Wollencroft.

"It was the kind of thing he did," I said. "Didn't know it had a professional application."

The restaurant shared a building with a yoga studio and a store that sold nutritional supplements. I was braced for the worst, but the place actually had scrambled eggs with bacon on the menu.

"What would a wheelman do, exactly?" I asked her.

"Anything involving a steering wheel. Boosting cars, driving family members around, fleeing various scenes of the crime. Skill sets include the ability to drive anything, sometimes very fast, but just as often very carefully in order to evade notice. A good man to have in those days. Not so much in the age of surveillance cameras and GPS tracking."

"Wouldn't they have to be part of the family?"

"Too low on the totem pole," she said. "Just an associate. Skillful and invaluable, but an associate nevertheless."

The eggs came with a sprig of parsley and an orange slice, but otherwise an acceptable product.

"Would Pagliero stay in touch with the family's working staff?" I asked her. "Keep his hand in?"

She shook her head.

"Not likely beyond doing an occasional *legal* favor for a family member or former colleague. Successfully retiring

from the mob is not easy. There's no percentage in jeopardiz-
ing that. Doesn't mean his excavation business doesn't benefit
from the halo. Wins him a lot of work and keeps his job sites
free of illicit interference. And for all intents and purposes,
the mob world of Orfio's father is dead and buried. It has
been for twenty years."

"That's what the Tyler Vaughn book seemed to insist."

"You're familiar with the eighty/twenty rule?" she asked.
"Twenty percent of the people in any given organization do
eighty percent of the meaningful work?"

"I think it's more like ninety/ten, but yeah, I know," I said.

"It was the underlying principle the senior Vaughn and
the feds employed to essentially gut the Italian Mafia. The
brains of these operations were all at the top, as a result of the
hierarchical structure they'd imported from Sicily. When you
don't nurture up-and-comers in the lower ranks, providing
legitimate career paths, you can effectively kill off the creature
by severing the head. It's a lesson any corporation should take
to heart."

"The people I worked with stayed safe by hiding their
heads up their ass," I said.

She liked that.

"I think you've proved my point. Another factor was the
requirement that you kill someone before ascending to the
upper ranks. This meant a management structure overly represented by violent sociopaths."

"So you think my father might have been murdered just
to establish the killers' bona fides?"

"Wouldn't be the first time."

"If that's the case, then Orfio would surely know who
they were."

"As sure as the sun rising. And just as surely, he'll never
reveal their names."

Few things irritated me more than being told I could
never achieve something that was, in theory, achievable. I
didn't blame Wollencroft, who was doubtless sincere in her

opinion. No less sincere than the made men at my old company when they handed back one of my proposals with the words, "Can't be done."

That was probably at the heart of my troubles there. It didn't matter that I did enough of the undoable to end up running the company's R&D division. Each new effort to push into fresh territory was met with the same resistance, the same stubborn terror of the unknown. It made me feel more like a merchant of fear than a design engineer.

Or maybe it was just me. A person you were just naturally afraid of. And then, I guess, I proved their point.

WOLLENCROFT ASKED me to come in when we got back to her house in Riverdale. This time I said yes.

I'd been in rich people's houses before, and Wollencroft's was up to the highest standards. It was a full-scale house, at least 3,000 square feet, vintage, but entirely modernized. I had one more cup of coffee in the kitchen at a center island under a wrought iron rack filled with huge copper pots I hoped were well secured.

"You didn't like it when I told you Orfio's a dead end," she said. "I could see it in on your face."

"He's not a dead end. He just won't tell us what he knows. He wouldn't tell you his name if it wasn't already public knowledge. As a source, he's completely bolted down."

"So what do you do?"

"Find a way to loosen the bolts."

After I downed the coffee, Wollencroft offered to show me around the rest of her house, but I demurred, telling her I still had plenty of unproductive work to do that day. She told me to keep her informed about what I did, unproductive or not, and I took off.

I STAYED off the highways and just meandered through the unfamiliar streets between Riverdale and Edenwald, where my father had his apartment. It wasn't until I drove into the big public housing development, which people like my father just referred to as "the fucking projects," that I knew where I was.

I wondered if any of the people who conceived of these towering concentrations of human misery, hope, and aspiration still remembered the utopian dream. It wasn't for me to say, only to pray the future would sort in favor of the aspirants.

When I got to my father's old apartment, there were two guys in front of the house working on a ten-year-old BMW. I asked if they needed any help. One of the guys looked wary, but his buddy seemed happy with the distraction.

"Just changing out a valve-cover gasket," he said, wiping his hands with a blue mechanics rag. "I think we need to drop the engine."

"Don't have to drop no engine," said the other guy. "Just got to get to the damned thing."

"I told him not to buy any of this German shit. Too complicated."

"You like driving this German shit, so don't start on complicated."

"You're right about that. Goes like a motherfucker."

I looked into the engine compartment and had to agree with both of them. I said in the old days I'd switch out a valve-cover gasket in about ten minutes. We all shared a moment of quiet reminiscence.

"I think you can lift the valve cover without taking that hose all the way off," I said, pointing to where the car's owner was struggling with a recalcitrant clamp. "Keep it connected here and just pull it out of the way."

The owner brightened, but looked unconvinced.

"And how do you propose getting all this other shit out of the way?"

"Can I show you?" I asked.

He stood back and I took off one end of the big intake ducts and stuck my hand into the tangle of overengineered components, feeling my way around the ignition system that stood in the way of progress.

"If you remove this, this, and this," I said, pointing, "by disconnecting here, here, and here, you're good to go. Make sure you note how those wires come off, because they have to go back exactly the same way."

I watched as the two guys leaned into the engine compartment and felt their own way around. I followed their hands and told them they had it right.

"Nothing complicated about that," said the car's owner.

"Building a rocket to the moon is easy once you know how to build it," said his friend. He offered his hand and I gave it a shake.

"You know the people who live in there?" I asked him, nodding toward the three-story house.

He said he knew at least one.

"Cause that'd be me. I'm on the top floor. Got a view of the world up there."

"I used to live on the second floor," I said. "Long time ago."

"Old Jewish lady in there now. You related?"

"No. Like I said, it was a long time ago."

"She been there long as I know. Nice lady. I carry shit up the stairs for her."

"I wonder if she's home," I said.

"Almost for certain. Don't go out much. I can take you on up there if you want."

"I'd appreciate it."

"Don't want to be scaring the old girl."

We left his friend with the repair and climbed the metal stairs. On the way he thanked me again for the mechanical advice, telling me his friend was actually a decent mechanic himself, but more used to Japanese and American cars, and thus somewhat thrown by his newly acquired BMW. I told him my father worked on cars in the day, but wouldn't know one end of a modern engine from the other.

"I hear you," he said.

It took awhile, but eventually the door was answered by an elderly woman in a pink sweat suit and running shoes. She smiled.

"Who's your friend?" she asked the guy.

"He's a visitor, Mrs. Nadelman, used to live in your place." I introduced myself. Her smile faded into puzzlement.

"Not the Frenchy. He's dead."

"I'm his son. I used to stay with him off and on."

"*Oy gevalt.* The kid. What's with my memory?"

"Don't let her fool you," said the guy. "Nothing wrong with her memory."

She asked us to come in, but he told her he had to get back to helping his friend.

"More like moral support than any actual help," he said.

"We all need it," I told him.

Like the rest of the neighborhood, the apartment had shrunk into an approximation of the place I remembered. The layout was the same, of course, though the rest completely unrecognizable. The petroleum aroma was replaced by something far more floral and the austere walls were now covered in prints, ancient photos, and narrow shelves cluttered with tchotchkes. Mrs. Nadelman walked with her arched back canted to one side, though briskly, as if unable to give up the habit of a lifetime in motion. We sat in the living room.

"Your father's name again?" she asked.

"André. My mother was Jeannine, but she wasn't here much."

"I thought it was something like Rosie. Snazzy-looking blonde."

"You mean Rozele. That wasn't my mother."

"Oh."

And there it was, in less than a minute, the central issue.

"Well," she said, "I didn't know him very well. We owned the house across the street. With my husband gone, I couldn't keep it up. So me, Mrs. Brilliant, decide to move into a walk-up. I don't mind. Keeps me limber."

I struggled to recall her and her husband, but it wouldn't come. The street was full of people back then, and despite the startling diversity, to a part-time kid, all generically adult.

"What about Rozele," I said. "What do you remember?"

"What I told you, snazzy," she said, almost on the defensive. "Wore dresses every day. I wish people still did. Though look at me. All comfort, no style. Oh, well. Nobody wants to see me in a dress. I think she cleaned houses. Carried a couple big bags with spray bottles in and out of that apartment. Had an accent. No idea what kind. Not German, which is the only kind I can identify. Not sure if she really spoke English, though so what. We're used to that around here."

I felt a familiar sag in my mood, the type brought on by confronting the dark hole of the past. Here this woman sat across from me, in the same physical space I'd occupied with my father, where the mysteries of his life played out in detail, yet now removed to somewhere entirely inaccessible. Another spatial dimension.

She must have read it on my face.

"I'm sorry I can't tell you anything more," she said. "It's been a long time."

"So they keep saying."

She suddenly jerked her head, as if hearing an unexpected sound.

"Wait a minute. I'm so stupid."

She pulled herself back onto her unsteady feet and left the room. I sat and looked at the birds pecking around a flat bird feeder hung outside the window. The hum of the city barely intruded, as if the accumulated experiences of the apartment's dwellers had constructed an additional layer of soundproofing.

I heard Mrs. Nadelman patter back into the living room. She went over to where I sat and handed me a slim book. I recognized it immediately. It was faded green, with the word "Ledger" embossed on the cover and framed by ornate art nouveau designs. The corners were protected by brown leather, and on the dark spine were the dates January 1, 1969, to January 1, 1979, written in white ink.

"The movers found it stuck behind a dresser that was left by the former tenants," she said. "I just remembered the words were in French."

The pages were divided by tabs listing entry category, protected by Scotch Tape. Each page showed two columns, assets in black, liabilities in red. Credits and debits.

I knew pencil erasures were under many of the inked figures, where my father reconciled projected amounts with actuals, balancing the books. If you looked closely, you could see the faint remains, made by a type of pencil preferred by my father, a bundle of which I'd once stolen and tossed in the Little Peconic Bay.

"My husband kept books just like that when he first started the business," said Mrs. Nadelman. "They're all gone now. I didn't have the heart to throw that one away, even though I have no idea what any of it means."

"Double-entry accounting. My father recorded every penny he ever made and every penny spent. Personal and business, all in one book. It'll tell you what he spent on socks and hydraulic wrenches."

"That sounds like my husband."

"For your sake, I hope that's where the resemblance ends."

She looked inordinately pleased.

My favorite professor at MIT was a physicist who taught a course on Zen Buddhism. It wasn't a crowded class, the relevance lost on the scientifically inclined student body, though nearly everything he said stuck with me long after the engineering equations faded away. He advised that the moment you truly ceased striving for something, it would appear before you. That great gifts were available to those who had abandoned all hope and desire, who sought only the vast emptiness of nonseeking.

"Take it," said Mrs. Nadelman, the Bodhisattva of the Bronx. "One less thing for my children to throw out after they haul me down those damned stairs."

Chapter Eighteen

I lay no claim to being hyperobservant. I might think a lot about the things I see, but a lot gets past me. The inhibiting factor is my preoccupation with all the clatter going on inside my head, which I often attend to with more devotion than the readily apparent, the stuff right before my eyes.

So it was astonishing that I not only noticed the white truck driving behind me along East 223RD, I realized I'd seen it before on the way over to my father's apartment. The distinguishing feature was a brand new bumper winch mounted on the front of a battered pickup. Only slightly incongruous, it still somehow stuck in my mind.

At the next light, I took a left into another residential neighborhood, this one more heavily stocked with multistory brick apartments. The truck followed. I kept a slow, but steady speed, and worked my way south until I reached Boston Road. Although several cars had now come between us, the truck continued to follow.

On Boston Road, heading east, I stayed in the right lane and slowed to just under the prevailing speed, encouraging the cars between us to pass until the white truck was directly behind, though keeping its distance. This took me past where José had his garage, but away from my hotel. Traffic thinned a little, so I picked up speed, though still well under legal limits.

I pulled into a gas station and up to the pumps. The truck continued on, but I could see it pull off into a small shopping strip, backing into a space so it faced the exit of the parking lot. No one got out.

I put in a half tank of gas, and went into the convenience store as if to pick up a few things. When I came back, the truck was still there. I left the gas station and it fell in behind.

I made another stop at a hardware store. I bought a cordless drill, a set of bits, a heavy claw hammer, and a box of four-penny common nails. At the cash register I asked the clerk if they had any half-inch ply.

"This is a hardware store. We don't sell lumber."

"I can't believe there's no plywood in the back. All I need is an eighteen-by-eighteen-inch piece of half inch, though three quarters would work."

"We don't sell it."

"I'll give you fifty bucks for an eighteen-by-eighteen-inch sheet."

He went into the back and I heard power tools. He came back five minutes later with a piece of half-inch birch ply.

"I trimmed it to eighteen-by-eighteen," he said, handing it to me. I rubbed my hands along the edges.

"And sanded."

"For fifty bucks I'll stain it and put on a coat of varnish."

After I paid I asked if he had a restroom.

"That'll be another fifty bucks," he said. "Kidding."

I locked the restroom door, then drilled a constellation of holes separated by no more than four inches. I drove a nail through each of the holes, using the sink as a workbench.

The clerk was waiting for me outside the door.

"Looks interesting," he said.

"You got a bag big enough to fit this?" I asked, holding up the nail-festooned plywood.

"This is a hardware store. We got everything."

When I got back on Boston Road, I didn't see the white truck, figuring I took too long in the hardware store. But then as if through a magic trick, it was back behind me. It was close enough that I could see the driver, who was bald, with a full beard and wraparound sunglasses. The other guy was just oversized—head like an artillery shell sitting neckless on round shoulders.

We caravanned into New Rochelle. The roadway was still pretty congested, but the scenery improved. Other vehicles slipped in behind me as I drove, but the white truck never let more than three of them get between us.

I entered a riotous retail area with shopping plazas on either side of the road. A third lane was introduced to allow people to exit into the parking lots. I slowed down as I approached the turnoff lane on my left and put on my turn signal, causing the car immediately behind me to pass on the right. The truck was now only one car behind as I turned into the parking lot and made for the far end.

When I reached the edge of the lot, I turned down an access road that led to the rear of the enclosed mall, watching the white pickup follow at what he likely thought was a safe distance. Behind the mall I saw the usual loading docks, dumpsters, and employee parking. To my great relief, no people.

I drove into an area full of trucks and maneuvered the Jeep until I was perpendicular with a tractor trailer that was backed up to a loading dock. Moments later the white pickup rolled by at about twenty miles an hour. I left my hidden spot behind the semi and pulled up alongside the pickup. The guy in the passenger seat noticed the Jeep in time to see me start to pass, then watched as I opened the door with one hand, and while steering with my knee, used the other hand to toss the plywood bristling with framing nails under the pickup's right front tire.

Almost simultaneously, I heard a loud popping sound. I nearly lost control of the Jeep getting myself back inside and both hands gripping the steering wheel, but still managed to get ahead of the truck, which swerved to the right before coming to a stop.

I stuck the Jeep into low gear and spun the wheel hard, forcing it into a sliding 180-degree turn that pointed me back toward the pickup. The bald guy was just stepping out of the truck when I arrived, with one foot on the ground, using the door as a shield and stabilizing his stance to make it easier to get off a shot with the semiautomatic cannon stuck through the open window.

I aimed the Jeep as well as I could, holding the steering wheel steady as I slid down below the windshield. He got off two rounds before I slammed on the brakes and yanked the Jeep's left front fender into the bald guy's door, which really didn't amount to much in the way of protection.

His screams got louder after I scrambled over the center console and tumbled out the passenger-side door. When I hit the pavement, I saw the automatic, equipped with a suppressor, lying about ten feet in front of the Jeep. I stood up and pondered the next move. I'd brought the hammer with me, so I had a convenient way to club the head of the fat guy who came at me, arms spread, and bellowing, looking and sounding like a psychotic sumo wrestler. I used the flat side of the hammerhead, hoping to knock him out without performing a frontal lobotomy.

I had to jump out of the way when he fell, his eyes still open, but with the light switch turned off. I walked around the rear of the Jeep and saw the bald guy squirming in his seat. He'd lost his sunglasses. By the time I opened the passenger side door, he'd stopped screaming and was pulling at his leg and thudding his thick shoulders into the door, as if that would push the Jeep back out of the way.

"Who're you working for?" I asked.

"Fuck you, you fucking piece of fucking shit."

I swung the hammer into his dashboard. He turned toward me and looked at the tool, appreciating the situation.

"Who're you working for?" I repeated.

He, in turn, repeated his opening statement. I hit him on top of his shoulder with the hammer. Then on the backswing, drove the claw into the radio, which until that moment was still playing selections from the adult contemporary playlist.

He grabbed at the hammer, and I swung at his hand. He made another try, and so did I. We both missed, initiating a contest that lasted until I smashed the hammer claw into the meaty part of his palm. He didn't start screaming again, though his eyes were clenched in a more expressive display of pain and frustration.

"Give me your wallet," I said.

He didn't answer, but his eyes blinked open for an instant, casting a traitorous glance up at the visor. I stepped up on the running board and grabbed a wad of McDonald's napkins off the dashboard to cover my fingertips. A quick pull of the visor and the wallet fell into my hand. He watched as I used the same napkins to pick out the cash and throw it on the seat. Then I shoved the wallet into my pocket.

"You're so fucking dead," he said.

"Tell them all I want is an answer. Won't go beyond that."

"You can tell them in hell," he said, a curious twist of logic, but understandable under the circumstances.

I got in the Jeep, backed it up, and headed out the access road. I saw a woman in a green jumpsuit tentatively approach the pickup, and just before I turned the corner, the bearded bald guy falling out on the ground.

I left the radio off as I drove back to my hotel room, letting the pain in my side accelerate into the nearly unbearable while I listened to the adrenaline crackle and buzz in my ears, and the hectoring voice of alarm, usually ignored, fill my mind.

CHAPTER NINETEEN

The next morning, Madelyn Wollencroft brought her some-time partner Jake Johnson along for a meeting at a diner close to my hotel. She wore wedge sandals, a short pleated skirt, and a nylon jacket with NYPD stitched on the front. Johnson wore his regular grey suit.

I had Dante Marino's driver's license, credit cards, lottery tickets, and a membership card at the Eastchester Gun Club. I'd called Wollencroft the night before, so she had time in the morning to run a check on him, along with the license plate on the white pickup.

"New Rochelle police are looking for an early model Jeep Cherokee in connection with a hit-and-run behind the Cloverdale Mall," said Johnson. "It looks like one of the victims also lost his wallet."

"I'll get it back to him," I said.

"Send it courtesy of Montefiore Medical Center," said Wollencroft. "According to New Rochelle, Mr. Marino failed to provide a clear description of the vehicle or the man who hit his truck. Another witness said it was an old Jeep Cherokee."

"Lots of those things still on the road," I said. "Can't kill 'em."

"Mr. Marino has a rather long résumé," said Johnson. "Assault and battery, attempted homicide, extortion, grand larceny, possession of drugs with intent to distribute, et cetera, et cetera."

"Although since getting out of Ossining, he's been on his best behavior," said Wollencroft. "Even holds down a good job."

"Who's the lucky boss?" I asked.

"Superior Earth Moving," said Johnson. "It was their pickup."

"Orfio does strive to support his fellow Italian Americans," I said.

"We're not sure what Marino actually does for Superior," said Wollencroft, "but I'm guessing something to do with labor relations. He has experience in that from his younger days with Orfio's dad, Leon."

"Unfortunately for Mr. Marino, his clean streak is probably broken," said Johnson. "They found an unregistered, long-barreled semiautomatic with a suppressor and laser sight near the damaged vehicle. Mr. Marino claims to have no knowledge of the weapon or how it happened to be there."

"Or its intended purpose," said Wollencroft.

"Though we can guess," said Johnson.

"Where's your Jeep, by the way?" Wollencroft asked.

"Over at José's garage. Needs a little work. They gave me a loaner."

Johnson left to scare up a waitress and make a call on his cell phone. I got the feeling it was rehearsed, since there were plenty of waitresses within earshot.

"You could have found an easier way to ID Marino," she said.

"One of my old trainers advised me to stay out of street fights, but if I couldn't avoid it, hit first."

"Apparently taken to heart."

"What's your theory?" I asked.

"Orfio's taking a big risk. Has to be a very good reason."

"Such as?"

"There's no statute of limitations on homicide," she said. "Why your dad was killed probably doesn't matter as much as who did it."

"Every witness had it as two big guys. Orfio's maybe 150 pounds soaking wet."

"Leon kept his kin away from anything that conspicuous. But there could be a trail. Orfio's smart enough to know about DNA. He'll know we're checking, he won't know it's turning up blank."

"Doesn't it make you wonder? They were young, but presumably had long careers ahead of them. Pretty lucky to stay out of the data base."

"I do wonder," she said, sitting back in the booth and tapping her fingers on the table. "There's a lot to wonder about with this case. Are you all right?"

I admitted I wasn't. The tussle with Dante Marino and his fat friend had played havoc with the wound on my side. Adrenaline and other salubrious hormones had masked the damage as it happened, but they'd worn off overnight, leaving a residue of sickening pain.

"You should get it checked out," she said.

"They'll just tell me to rest up and give me a bunch of pills I won't take."

"You look pale. Barely Italian at all."

"I am barely Italian. That must be the problem."

I distracted her from my state of health by telling her about my father's ledger book delivered by Mrs. Nadelman.

"Really. Have you looked through it?"

"Started to. I'll need a French dictionary."

"You need to give it to me. It's evidence," she said. "You wanted an active investigation. That's the deal."

"Then I can hardly look through it."

"I'll have it scanned into PDFs. If the handwriting is blocky enough, it'll work with OCR and we'll have searchable files," she said. "We can each have a set."

"I have no idea what you just said."

So she explained it to me.

"What a world," I said, handing over the ledger just before Jake Johnson rejoined us with a waitress in tow. They each ordered a hearty breakfast, which did little to improve my condition. I stuck with coffee, though with little joy.

By the time she came back with their meals, I was hunched over in my seat, fighting the urge to let my head drop to the table, or vomit, or both.

"Did somebody just take all the oxygen out of the air?" I asked.

"Sam," Wollencroft said, reaching across the table to put her hand on my shoulder. I don't know what she said after that, because by then I was out cold.

YOU'D THINK with my deep-seated aversion to hospitals I'd do a better job staying out of them. I knew I was back in Montefiore, awake, but groggy from all the painkillers they pumped into me when I was helplessly unconscious.

I found a button meant to retrieve a nurse, which only took about an hour to achieve. She was actually a doctor, so I guess worth the wait.

"Welcome to the living," she said.

"Thanks for answering my first question."

She looked at my chart and studied it, then asked me if I wanted to know what happened.

"Sure, why the hell not."

"You were in circulatory shock resulting from intra-abdominal bleeding." She looked back down at the chart. "It looks like you had a rupture in the tissue below one of your fractured ribs. They didn't tell you not to exercise until the ribs were fully healed?"

"They did, but failed to inform the guy who was trying to shoot me."

She looked at the chart again.

"My suggestion is to avoid further gunplay until all existing wounds are securely sealed."

"Noted. Do you know if Dante Marino is anywhere nearby?" She asked why. "He's the one who wanted to shoot me. He might want to finish the job."

"That explains the police officer sitting outside your door."

"Really? Excellent. I've always wanted one of those."

She handed me a little device at the end of a thin white tube. "You can push the button when you want another dose of pain medication."

"Hell no. Rather have the pain."

"You won't be saying that in about an hour."

"Try me."

She shrugged and left the room. As predicted, an hour later that button started to look pretty alluring. But I didn't push it. I just let the pain fill up my mind, until it became a type of abstraction, almost detachable, a strange but observable thing. I thought of nothing else until I passed out again, waking up a few hours later to slightly graver torment. And that's how I spent the next two days, until I could form sentences coherent enough to call Wollencroft and ask her to get me the hell out of there.

I told her to drop me off at my hotel, but she ignored that and drove me to her house. When I said I wanted my computer, she asked for the key to my hotel room, telling me she'd retrieve it.

I made it up the stairs without her help, but when I reached the bed, I was happy to lie there on top of the duvet like a corpse in a coffin. She left and came back a few hours later with my suitcase, computer, and a bowlful of chicken and rice soup. When I eyed the laptop she said, "Eat first," and sat cross-legged in a nearby Windsor chair after helping me sit up in bed.

"It took a month to feel even close to normal after they put my throat back together," she said.

"I don't have a month."

"Yeah, you do."

"My daughter will be back from France before then. I worry about her safety."

"I'll make you a deal. Stay put for a week. Give your side a chance to heal. It'll save you time in the long run, to say nothing of your life. And if you don't agree, I have handcuffs."

I agreed and went back to sleep, which I mostly did for the next week, so there's nothing left to tell, except that her plan worked. At the end of the week, I was making regular trips down the stairs to take long walks on a treadmill she had in the basement.

We ate together the last night at her house. We were in the living room, an arts and crafts masterpiece incongruously encased within the Tudor house, though with undeniable success. She'd brought bags of fried chicken and catfish gumbo from a place she claimed was run by real live Creoles, and by the taste, I wasn't in a position to argue.

After polishing off the food, she disappeared for a while, then came back in a change of clothes—a floor-length dress and a pair of battered leather sandals.

"You're welcome to stay, you know," she said. "You can see I have plenty of room."

"That's good of you, but I'm used to having my own place."

"I did make a deal."

"You did. And I deeply appreciate you looking after me. I'm not so good at doing it myself."

"Me neither. What is it with that?"

"Probably biological."

"Do you also try hardest to obtain that which is the most unobtainable?" she asked.

I shook my head.

"Quite the contrary. Having once obtained more than I wanted, only to lose it all, I'm eternally grateful for everything I have now and want for nothing."

"But you fear losing it all again."

A variation on *"Out of the mouths of babes."*

"I do. That's the catch."

WOLLENCROFT HELD up her end of the bargain, driving me
back to the diner to retrieve José's loaner, an ancient Honda
Accord that looked like the wrinkled suit of a valiant salesman, which I drove to my hotel. I'd kept Amanda more or
less informed, but once actually in my hotel room, where I'd
claimed to be the preceding week, I put in a long call and
brought her up to date. More or less.

"When are you going to see your sister?" she asked.

"Probably never."

"And why?"

"She doesn't need to know me and I don't need to know
her. Once we meet, that's no longer an option. This way, the
can of worms stays sealed and on the shelf."

"Very well," she said, the first time I ever heard a breath
of crystalline ice in her voice, a harbinger of disruption more
feared than anything Dante Marino, or Larry Ringer, or any
army of brainless thugs could ever engender.

Dead air accumulated on the phone line for a few moments,
then I said, "I'm sorry. You're right."

Chapter Twenty

The next afternoon, I took a cab to the 149ᵀᴴ Street-Grand Concourse subway station where I grabbed the #5 train into Manhattan. You wouldn't call the experience urban utopia, but like most things in the city these days, much less of an experiment in survival than it was in the midseventies, when I frequently made the trip into Greenwich Village, attracted by the music, flexible morality, and other anarchical impulses.

That day, I had a different destination, so I switched to the #2 train over to Manhattan and the Upper West Side in time for happy hour at a place I once haunted after clenched and dreary meetings at corporate HQ in Midtown. I fortified myself at the bar, chatting with the bartender who remembered my drink, if not my name, or what I did, or where I lived. He just set down the drink and welcomed me back. I had the drink, overtipped, and left.

I didn't have much of a plan, except to estimate a likely time for Tasenka to be home, and to show up at her apartment. There were many ways to approach these things, though I usually preferred direct. I didn't like the phone, and e-mail was either too distant, or too fraught with misinterpretation. And I had the coercive forces of my friends to consider. No one could accuse me of avoiding the deed if I just walked up and rang her apartment.

It was in a nineteenth-century, eight-story building with a stone facade, and a grand entrance you reached by way of a sweeping stone stairway. At the top of the stairs there were modern glass double doors behind which you could see a counter commanded by a doorman in a dark blue suit. He buzzed me in.

I told him I was there to see Tasenka Mikutavičienė, who wasn't expecting me. I said I wasn't sure she was the right Tasenka, whom I'd never met, seen, or spoken to.

After correcting my pronunciation, he said, in a thick, Slavic accent, "And what is this in reference to?"

"It's a family matter. I can sit right over there." I pointed at a visitors' lounge. "If she doesn't mind coming down. Tell her my name is Sam Acquillo."

He took out his smartphone and told me to stand still as he took my photo. He used his thumb on the device as he lifted the receiver of the desk phone.

"Ms. Mikutavičienė, you have a visitor name of Sam Acquillo. I'm sending you a picture. He's here in the lobby." He listened for a moment, then handed me the phone. "She want to talk to you."

"Hello, Tasenka."

It was so quiet on the line I thought she'd hung up, but then she said, "Are you related to André Acquillo?"

"I'm his son. My mother was Jeannine." I gave her the address in Edenwald. "I have a note from your mother to my father. Written in French."

"Qu'est-ce qu'il a dit?" she asked. What did it say?

"Une liste d'épicerie." A shopping list.

"What kind of car did he drive?" she asked, in English.

"A 1967 Pontiac Grand Prix. Cream colored with tan leather seats. And a four-speed stick shift on the floor. I still have it. I have a photo on my phone. You can come down and see it, or I can send it to you."

There was another long pause.

"Please give the phone to the concierge."

He listened for a moment, then said okay and hung up.

"There are cameras at every angle in this lobby," he said to me. "And I am armed security. Ten years with the Ground Forces of the Russian Federation."

"Understood," I said, and went to sit on a straight-backed wooden chair.

While I waited, I dug the photo out of the files on my phone. It was of me in a T-shirt leaning against the Grand Prix, its hood open, wiping my hands with a paper towel. Amanda thought the moment captured well my ongoing relationship with the car.

Tasenka was a tall brunette with a nice face, marred only by dark pools under her blue eyes. She wore a sweater and blue jeans, and held her arms folded across her middle in a defensive posture. She looked over at the concierge as she moved across the lobby and they nodded to each other. I stood up.

"I don't favor surprise appearances," she said.

"Few people do."

I handed her the phone with the photo on the little screen. She looked at it carefully.

"Why now?"

"That's a long story. No sense starting it if you don't want to talk to me."

"Give me the top line."

"The bartender who was there the night André was killed got in touch with me. He thought I should look into the murder. I didn't want to do it, but some friends twisted my arm. I didn't know about you or your mother until a few weeks ago. The same friends thought I should pay a visit."

"To what end?"

Her voice was deep, calm, and reserved, but not what you'd call hostile, or even guarded. More businesslike.

"Reasons both simple and complicated beyond my powers of comprehension. So let's stick with simple. To say hello."

I stuck out my hand. She took it, with a dry, confident grip.

"I was very young," she said.

"I know. I'm not here to talk about any of that. Just to say hello."

She studied my face like it was a strange artifact. Which I guess it was.

"I never saw you," she said. "Only pictures. Along with a few of André, it's all I have."

"I think you saw me on Jones Beach, but you were too young to remember anything."

She let her hands drop and stuck them in the pockets of her jeans.

"I have a son. He actually looks like you when you were his age. Funny thing, genetics."

"My daughter takes after her mother, thank God."

"My mother died ten years ago. Cancer."

"I'm sorry."

"Don't be. She was a strong woman. Wouldn't abide weakness."

That was enough of a visit for me. I told her that, and stuck out my hand again. She took it, but said, "We can talk a little more. Unless you have to leave."

"I have nowhere to go."

"Is it okay if we just sit here?" she asked, looking toward the sofa and chairs.

"Okay with me."

She sat with her hands in her lap. I tried to match her face with the foggy memory of the day at Jones Beach, but there was no way. The only morphological clue was her slimness. None of my family on either side knew how to grow fat. And I might have seen a bit of me in her eyes, puffy though they were. Her nose was at the other end of the spectrum from mine, though I did remember the woman on Jones Beach had small, fine features, something you didn't see much in the neighborhoods I hung around in.

"My mother wouldn't talk about André's death," she said. "I didn't ask, or rather demand, until I was a bratty teenager, which I guess is redundant. She would only say he was a good man, that we were lucky to have him for the time we had him, and that he made sure we would never want for anything. I don't know about that last part. We wanted for plenty."

"But you knew what happened to him," I said.

"Only after I was old enough to look it up in the newspaper archives at the library. I think I cried for a week. Teenagers are dramatic."

"That's rough. I'm sorry."

She sat quietly, her lips pursed.

"It doesn't make me special," she said. "Everyone's pain is the same."

"I say that all the time. Must be genetic."

Her face softened.

"I haven't let you say a thing about yourself," she said.

I looked down at the floor and shrugged.

"Nothing that interesting," I said. "I have a grown daughter who lives just a few blocks from here. One ex-wife. A girlfriend and a dog. I think most guys could say the same thing."

"You went to Harvard or some such."

"MIT. Had a career as a mechanical engineer, but I messed it up. Now I'm a cabinetmaker. The training came in handy."

"I went to Carnegie Mellon," she said. "Mathematical science. I do quantitative analysis for an investment bank. Not as much fun as cabinetmaking."

I knew it had to be something like that, given her apartment building.

"You probably never tried making curved raised-panel doors or cutting a compound miter with a coping saw. Makes quantitative analysis feel like a trip to Hawaii."

She sat back in her chair and finally took her hands out of her pockets. It almost made her look like a different person.

"I thought you'd come here to condemn me," she said. "I had a whole speech ready, but I didn't get to use it."

"Why would I do that?"

She looked down.

"My mother was your father's mistress. His wife was your mother."

I made a dopey sound, a sort of dismissive laugh. Made me realize how nervous I actually was.

"Who cares about all that? Not me. It was almost forty years ago. I have no right nor reason to judge anybody, much less a little kid. My old man did what he did, for his own reasons. Same with your mother. None of that matters anymore."

Tasenka closed her eyes and took in a deep breath through her nose and let it out through her mouth. Then she looked at me.

"She never got over it," said Tasenka. "Her grief consumed our lives. I think it's what killed her. The cancer was merely the proximate cause."

"Not so great for you."

"She was good to me. Made sure I had a childhood. I just grew up thinking mothers were people who were very kind, but sad."

I didn't tell her my mother was very kind, but pissed.

"I cleaned out his apartment after he died," I said. "Walked away from the lease. If I'd known I would have let you and your mom stay there."

"You would? I'm not so sure. Easier to say now."

"Maybe you're right. I was more confused in those days."

She pulled out a smartphone and looked at the screen.

"I'm taking too much of your time," I said.

"It's not that," she said. "I'm concerned about my son. He's up there making dinner. Give me a moment."

She called him and said she'd be back later than planned. I could tell by her expression that he took it well. She signed off and said to me, "He doesn't know anything about André. I can't bring myself to tell him. It must be cowardice."

"My daughter was about thirty when I told her."

"We think we're protecting them. I'm not so sure."

"So what did you do?" I asked. "After he died?"

She put her hands together, prayerfully, on her lap, which turned out to be a harbinger.

"The priest gave us a room in the rectory. On the top floor. It had its own bathroom, but smelled of mothballs. I still associate the odor with equal parts humiliation and deliverance."

The concierge strolled over to where we sat and asked Tasenka if everything was okay. She said it was, and asked him if he was on for the night. He said, for her, of course. He tapped me twice on the shoulder before going back to the front desk.

"The Father had helped Momma come into the country. Cleaning the rectory was the only way she could pay him back," she said. "She did the laundry, and sorted out the kitchen drawers, and swept the salt and grit out of the garage. She cleaned and pressed his robes and went to the pharmacy to pick up his imported cigars. Putting us up for a whole year was a good deed, though you could argue self-interest played a part."

"But you liked him," I said, guessing.

"I did. I thought he was a good man then and I still do."

"Is he still around?"

"Of course. Father Cleary at The Mother of Divine Providence Catholic Church. Our guardian angel."

"Is that how she got in the housecleaning business?"

"Momma was a very smart woman, but she struggled with English."

"Though she spoke French."

This surprised her.

"How did you know?"

"I heard her on the beach."

"She lived in Paris before coming to the states. I don't know any more than that. Protecting our children from history must run in the family."

She stole another look at her phone, so I stood up and said I should probably get out of her hair.

"You probably should," she said. "But I'd like to talk more. When some of the jolt wears off."

"Sure." I wrote my e-mail, cell phone number, and address on a piece of paper ripped from the little notebook I kept in my back pocket. "Anytime."

"What do you think would have happened?" she asked.

"Sorry?"

"If he'd lived. How do you think it would have worked out?"

I wanted to say I don't answer the unanswerable, but she was my sister, and though our experience together could be measured in minutes, she deserved family-grade consideration.

"Your mother would have had less sadness."

"Thank you."

I don't know if I lied to her, because it might have been true that my father reserved his wrathful animus for his first family, and after exhausting it, was left with a residue of cherished benevolence, unknown by us, and reserved solely for Tasenka and Rozele.

At least at that moment, I was content to let history remain unknowable, and the questions unanswerable.

Chapter Twenty-One

I killed the morning lying on the bed, trying to rest my body. My brain made up for the indulgence by nattering at me like a deranged monkey. I was familiar with this situation and had a partial remedy.

I pulled out a yellow legal pad and a pen, and propped myself up on the bed with a pair of pillows. Then I wrote down what I'd learned since visiting Marcelo Bonaventure.

My father had a police file prior to his murder. At least one arrest, for assault, though no convictions. Which would have shown up in separate court records. More important, someone had removed the file, presumably the records manager himself, a ranking officer.

Another officer essentially warned Bonnie off the case, fairly clear evidence that at least some in police leadership had an active interest in sandbagging the investigation. No evidence Gerald Fitzsimmons or his partner were in on that.

Richie Scamporino had funneled money to my father by overpaying for occasional garbage truck repairs. Compensation for his services as a professional driver for the Pagliero family, an open brief that would include anything you could do with an automobile.

My father had a second family who lived with him whenever members of his first family weren't at the apartment,
which was most of the time.

Orfio Pagliero had ostensibly severed all ties with organized crime, yet so far two killers with whom he was associated, one closely, had already tried to kill me. Orfio may
or may not have been directly involved, but the fact of these
attempts was a crucial data point. A murder nearly forty years
ago was still of fresh importance in someone's mind.

I made boxes around these statements and tried to connect them with arrows, usually a comforting exercise, but
since none of the connections made any sense, it was mostly
frustrating. So I gave it up.

Just in time to get a call from Madelyn Wollencroft.

"Dante Marino's apparently checked out of the rehab
facility," she said.

"Really. Fast healer."

"The cops on watch are now on report. Got to hand it to
Marino. Smarter than we thought."

"What about his fat friend?"

"We don't know. Seems to have disappeared as well."

"Maybe they ran away with Larry Ringer," I said.

"The next guy to come after you is going to be highly
motivated."

"No more than me."

"You won't know where it's coming from."

Not even noon and I was already in a debate. Weakened
by my failed attempt to diagram the situation, I capitulated.

"You're right. Why don't you just come over here and
shoot me dead and we'll get that part over with."

"I'm busy settling cold cases, otherwise I would."

"Do you know where Orfio Pagliero lives?"

"I do, but I wouldn't tell you."

"I can understand that," I said.

"Ross was wrong. You can be reasonable," she said, and
hung up.

A few moments later an address in Manhattan showed up as a text on my cell phone. I was beginning to get how communication worked in the twenty-first century. Nobody tells anybody anything, but there are no secrets in the digital world.

THE HONDA was an ideal car to park on the city streets. Nondescript to the point of invisibility. I was about a half block down from Orfio's townhouse off University Place. The streets were filled with kids from NYU and those who catered to them. I sat at a metal table a coffee shop had out on the sidewalk and nursed a creamy confection that only had a passing relationship with a cup of coffee, trying to look like a preoccupied professor, noodling on my yellow pad and gazing about in an existential fog.

Patience is among the long list of laudable human qualities I utterly lack. I can happily concentrate on a specific task for hours, but I'm incapable of just sitting there doing nothing. Though at that point, I didn't know what else to do, and thought maybe the forced tedium would unlock a more effective strategy.

Instead, I nearly overdosed on heirloom, free-range, sustainable coffee beans before the effort bore fruit.

It was seven in the evening, and the autumn light had long faded away. Luckily a streetlight reflected off Orfio's yellow windbreaker as he descended the brownstone stoop from his townhouse. He carried a soft briefcase and moved away from me down the block. I followed him to the corner of Sixth Avenue.

I was no better at managing an effective tail than holding down a stakeout, but felt the crowded sidewalks and general city bustle would provide adequate cover. It didn't help that Orfio walked with a brisk stride, making speedy headway despite his small stature. I would have lost him immediately if it weren't for the pedestrian lights, which Orfio strictly obeyed, allowing me to catch up every few blocks at a saunterer's pace.

He made a westward turn toward Seventh, but before the next corner, entered a building affiliated with the Episcopal Church next door. Before I had a chance to dwell on what I was doing, I followed, running straight into a wide hallway filled with people chatting quietly with each other and drinking coffee freely dispensed from two large chrome urns.

Fearing another belt of coffee would trigger hallucinations, I used a water cooler to fill a tiny paper cup. The people in the hallway looked like they'd been gathered there by a casting director seeking maximum diversity. All ages, races, and genders, biological and otherwise, seemed to be represented. They also seemed to know each other, forming into various conversational clusters. I hovered near the water cooler and stayed as far away as possible from Orfio. A middle-aged man in a grey suit without a tie approached me.

"Welcome," he said, reaching out his hand. "Have I seen you here before?"

"Don't think so. Just dropped by."

"It's a good meeting," he said. "I think you'll like it. Though that's for you to decide."

"You must be a regular," I said.

"Twenty-five years. Give or take a few years spent abroad with the company. Are you familiar with the drill?" he asked.

I admitted I wasn't.

"First time, huh. Nothin' to be afraid of. You can tell us who you are, or not. First names only, plus 'and I'm an alcoholic.' Or not. Say something about yourself, or not. See how easy that is?"

"Yeah. I think I'll opt for 'Or not.' At least for now."

My fear of being identified by Orfio was eclipsed by a sense of utter violation of these people's privacy. I would have felt less out of place at a powwow or Wiccan sabbat. It must have been written all over me.

"Do you know how many of the people here felt exactly the way you're feeling when they came to their first meeting?" he asked.

"Everyone?"

"Exactly."

"How long is the meeting?"

"About an hour. Little more, depending on announcements and how chatty everybody's feeling."

"Do people hang around afterward?" I asked.

"Some do."

I thought about Ray Osmund and the receptionist at the retirement home. It made the insult of my presence there even more personal. While I'd managed to crawl back from the program of self-annihilation via alcohol I'd undertaken after losing my job at Consolidated Global, I wasn't what you'd call a paragon of moderation, much less abstinence. It seemed shameful to pretend to this gentle man that I was seeking anything of the kind.

"You're not staying, are you," he said.

"I can't."

"Won't do you any good if you aren't ready," he said. "No pressure."

I thanked him and left, and took off for the nearest bar. It was a few blocks away, leaving enough time for some basic fortification before heading back to the church. There were a few people grouped on the sidewalk, and others were chatting as they walked away. I went through the door and nearly ran into a young couple, an old Asian man, and Orfio Pagliero, clumped together in conversation.

Orfio looked at me blankly, as if trying to believe his own eyes.

"Do I know you?" he asked, cutting off the young woman.

"Not well," I said. "We've only met once."

"The phony Italian with the lawyer." He took my arm with a tight grip and pulled me aside. "You've got some kind of nerve."

"Not as much as you'd think."

"Were you in the meeting?"

"No. I waited till it was over. And I'm not exactly a phony Italian. My grandfather came from Viareggio."

He pushed his glasses up onto his forehead, as if to increase the intensity of his malignant stare. I backed up against the wall.

"You must not know me very well," he said. "Otherwise you wouldn't be standing here."

"I intend to keep on standing. And sitting and walking around, no matter how many of your goons come at me."

"If I'm not mistaken, I think I just heard an accusation."

"Call it a hypothesis."

He moved closer to me and lowered his voice.

"You're out of line, and way over your head."

"I can't be both."

He grabbed my arm again but I shook it off.

"Touch me again and I'll put my fist down your throat."

He looked over his shoulder at the remaining meeting-goers, none of whom seemed aware of our confrontation.

"This is not the place to have this conversation," he said.

"I don't need a conversation. I just need you to tell me what you know about my father's murder."

"Why the hell would I know anything about that? And if I did, why the hell would I tell you?"

"To clear your conscience?"

I got the feeling Orfio was so used to automatic intimi-dation he'd forgotten what to do with a frontal assault. So he did the only thing he could do, spinning on his heel and walking away, with his briefcase tucked under his arm, as if fearing I'd snatch it away.

The guy who'd greeted me before the meeting was out on the sidewalk. He lurched in front of me and offered his hand.

"Same time next week?" he said. "We'll all be here."

I told him if I was still alive by then, I might give it a try.

CHAPTER TWENTY-TWO

The next day was Sunday, so I went to church.

Having been out of the devotional loop for most of my adult life, with the exception of unavoidable christenings, weddings, and funerals, I didn't know you could show up without a jacket and tie. So feeling overdressed only heightened my sense of profound displacement and alienation as I walked through the towering front doors of The Mother of Divine Providence.

A few white-hairs were clustered in the front pews, but most of the parishioners were spread around the church. I sat with the serious misanthropes and introverts near the back. Father Cleary was sitting up on the altar in silence, stealing occasional glances at the congregation, counting the house.

At precisely ten A.M., I was startled by a thunderous chord from the organist, who until then had been playing a sort of aimless, ambient baroque. Father Cleary stood up and was joined by another priest who came in from the sacristy. This pulled everyone to their feet and it went from there.

I went through the motions, literally—standing, sitting, and kneeling—though I didn't follow along with the back and forth bits, or sing any hymns or clasp my hands in prayer. I only perked up at some of the Latin Cleary and his sidekick tossed in, though usually not fast enough to pick up the whole meaning. Sitting alone at the back of the church, I didn't think my lack of involvement would offend anyone, and I wouldn't play the hypocrite even if it did.

So I had a chance to look over Cleary's flock, most of whom were Latinos—Puerto Rican and Dominican—mostly older than I, some with fidgety grandchildren under constant whispered threats. There were at least a half-dozen African Americans, beautifully groomed, and a hodgepodge of white people representing a range of demographics. Among the dispersed loners were some very old ladies, at least one in gym clothes not unlike Mrs. Nadelman's. Though some were fully decked out. One young guy, in a leather jumpsuit, held a motorcycle helmet.

I stayed in my seat during communion and browsed through the hymnal, recalling a few from when my mother dragged me along so I could sit there and listen to her scoff and snigger at half the things the priest said. It wasn't the religious inculcation she probably had in mind, or maybe it was.

I admit to great relief when things finally wrapped up. I followed the procession out of the church, helping along one of the old ladies who grabbed ahold of me like the survivor of a sinking ship. She thanked me between pleas for God to damn old age and everything that came along with it.

Outside the sunny day had turned grey, though it didn't seem to darken the general mood. Father Cleary was shaking hands and kissing cheeks. I had to wait awhile for him to finally retreat from a small crowd of hangers-around. I caught him at the door.

"Mr. Acquillo," he said, somewhat taken aback. "Nice to see you here."

"Father, I'd like to talk a little bit, though you're probably busy now."

"Not for the next hour I'm not," he said, looking at his watch. "People tend to leave me alone after Mass. They must think I need a cooling down."

He motioned for me to follow and we walked the length of the church and back into the sacristy where we'd first met. He used both hands to remove a large crucifix from around his neck before peeling off the white alb.

"I'd offer you a drink but all I have is burnt coffee and sacramental wine," he said.

"I'm all set. I've learned a lot since I was here before. I hope you don't mind if I ask a few more questions."

"I hear you've met with Trevor. I'm sure he knew a thing or two. How about some water?"

Women tell me black is slimming, but seeing Cleary in his head-to-toe priestly under-outfit made him look like a giant bear. He poured us each a glass of tap water and we sat at the table.

"Your brother wasn't actually much of a help. Not his fault. Nobody seems to know much of anything, and if they do, they aren't talking."

"It was a long time ago."

"With all due respect, I'm a little sick of hearing that. I don't think memory's the problem."

I told him about Larry Ringer and Dante Marino, and Dante's missing associate. As a man who'd heard it all in the confession booth, he had a good grip on his composure, though the consternation peaked through.

"Oh, Lord God," he said. *"Dimitte nobis debita nostra."*

"I'm sure He will, but in the meantime, what does this tell you?"

"Latine loqueris?"

"Sort of. I'm a little rusty. The only guy I get to practice on is the chief of Southampton Town police."

"Interesting cop."

"You have no idea. So what do you think?"

He shook his head and looked down at the table.

"You're in terrible danger."

"And you're holding out on me. With all due respect."

He held on to his poker face.

"I've shared with you what I'm permitted to share."

"You took Rozele and Tasenka Mikutavičienė into the rectory after my father was killed."

He cocked his head like a startled Jack Russell Terrier.

"I don't understand."

"They were living with him. At least when I wasn't around. Tasenka's his daughter."

He stood up from the table and moved away from me. Gaining a safe distance, or perspective, I couldn't tell. He sat down again, shoulders slumped.

"Rozele worked for me from the time we sponsored a group of Lithuanian immigrants," he said. "I knew nothing of her personal life. She never mastered English. When they came to me, Tasenka had to translate. She told me they'd been evicted from their apartment. The landlord was a violent man. She was clearly distressed. That's all I needed to know. Our church has given refuge to hundreds of people, probably a thousand, over the years. All this space and so few parishioners," he added, veering into a deeper lament.

He put his head in his hands and took a deep breath.

"Sorry for the harsh tone," I said. "My nerves are a little on edge."

"I forgive you," he said, with a weak smile. "We do that a lot around here."

I told him how I'd learned about Rozele and Tasenka, even the story about the day at Jones Beach. I must have been in a confessional mood. He told me how as a young priest he'd lobbied to be assigned to the once-busy church, now barely in operation as a house of worship. He said he favored the pastoral aspects of the job over the liturgical, but hadn't foreseen the nearly overwhelming social service needs of his constantly evolving congregation.

"The so-called safety net is more like a wet tissue," he said. "We're the last stop before utter dissolution and despair."

"It must be expensive for the diocese," I said.

"If it weren't for a few private givers, we'd have folded years ago."

"How do you close down a giant church?"

"With a phone call. Don't get me started."

His pale Irish face had reddened a lot, which I felt bad about. It didn't stop me from asking if he knew any of the Pagliero family.

"We minister to all who come before us. I never had the privilege of knowing any of them personally, though for a few years they significantly boosted our funeral business. Sorry, poor joke."

"It's a pretty sure thing they're the ones who killed my father. I still don't know why. Or why they still care so much about keeping a lid on it."

"I didn't think you cared so much about lifting the lid."

He had me there.

"I guess I'm bad at walking away from these things," I said. "It's a character flaw."

He checked his watch, telling me we'd used up his spare hour, but before I left I asked him one more time if there was any light he could shed on my father's murder, now that he knew the connection with Rozele and Tasenka.

"There was a type of wariness, a heightened vigilance, among the immigrants we took in from the old Communist countries," he said, after collecting his thoughts. "It made them secretive, reticent, even cunning. You can understand that. They'd lived in fear of the authorities, but also their neighbors, even friends and family. This made trust very hard to establish. I never pressed Rozele for any information beyond what she was willing to provide. That's just the way it was. But in my business, you learn to read the unsaid. After she came to stay that one year, she was not the same woman who'd cheerfully cared for me and the rectory. She'd changed."

"Fearful?" I asked.

He tilted his head, considering that.

"No, not really."

"Then what?"

"Angry. She was very, very angry."

WOLLENCROFT CALLED on my way back from Father Cleary's. She had the scans of my father's ledger book, exact images of each page along with a searchable OCR document of dubious quality.

"Those things are getting better all the time, but still not perfect," she said.

"How imperfect?"

"About 50 percent. The thing's trying to read human handwriting, for Christ's sake. Give it a break."

"How do I get this stuff?" I asked.

"You ask politely and I give it to you at my house. I'm not chasing you around the Bronx just to complete a favor."

"Fair enough. When will you be home?"

"Tonight," she said, and hung up.

I ONLY met one of my grandparents, and he was dead. It was a funeral parlor in New Britain, Connecticut, and he was lying in an open coffin. My mother had announced that morning that her father had been living up there in public housing for the last five years, and I had to drive her to see him off. He'd shared a studio apartment with his cousin, who died the year before. She didn't volunteer how he ended up there, or why we'd never gone to see him. She said the projects were full of people his age who spoke Polish, which was the only explanation I got out of her before boarding the ferry at Orient Point.

We took the old Chrysler New Yorker my father had left at the cottage ostensibly for my mother's daily use, though since she didn't know how to drive, it was up to me from the time I was able to see the road to provide chauffeur service.

At the funeral parlor, there were about a dozen people standing around where they had him laid out. When I saw the priest in a black suit and clerical collar I reminded my mother that her father was Jewish. She said they didn't know that, and anyway, what was the difference. He was dead.

I'd seen a few pictures of him and my grandmother, but nothing that would help me recognize the withered, wax mummy in the open coffin. Except maybe his nose, which made me wonder if my father's genes really were responsible for my own nose, which had yet to be refashioned in the boxing ring.

We sat in folding chairs that were arrayed theater style for the service. No one approached us, and she didn't bother telling the staff or the priest that we were the only relatives in the room. The service was nicely done by the young priest, who threw in a lot of Polish that my mother said she mostly understood, though she claimed not to speak it. Her mother was Parisienne, though thoroughly egalitarian on which language was used in their home in Montreal. They'd immigrated there in the thirties, wisely prescient about Hitler's ambitions and predilections.

Two ancient Poles stood and gave witness to my grandfather's good nature and love of fine Polish *wódka*, which might prove the power of genetic predisposition. A young man, barely in his twenties, thanked my grandfather for teaching him how to play chess, apologizing for their last game, which the kid won in just a few moves. I could see it pained him. My grandfather's hospice nurse also spoke, though her defense of his poor behavior at the end of his life seemed more like damning with faint praise.

My mother was silent throughout all this, and when I whispered in her ear that she should at least say something to these people, she elbowed me in the ribs.

For my grandfather, the last step in the process was a trip to Sacred Heart Cemetery a few miles away, where there was to be another brief invocation. My mother leaned over to me and said, "Let's get the heck out of here."

At the door, one of the funeral parlor staff was handing out an obituary they planned to send in to the *New Britain Herald*. My mother asked the name of the obit editor. The guy asked her why.

"So I can write a rebuttal."

On the way down to the ferry dock in New London, I asked my mother again why we never went to see her father. She took a tighter grip on her handbag, clenched the whole time on her lap, and said, "Your father and him didn't get along."

"But we could have just gone up there ourselves. I've had a license for a year."

"That would not be good. There would be fights with your father."

I told her that was horribly unfair, and cruel, and too tragic to comprehend.

"None of that," she said. "Your grandfather was a bastard. When I knelt by his coffin I wished him a nice trip to hell. That was the most positive thing I could think to say."

I let it go at that, getting the sub-rosa vibe from my mother that further conversation on the subject would not be welcomed.

When we got back to the cottage, my father was waiting for us in the driveway. My mother was clearly stunned, since it was the middle of the week when he was supposed to be at his apartment in the Bronx. I pulled our car under the floodlight that lit the parking area next to the work shed. My father opened my door.

"What is this shit? What are you doing out this late?" he yelled in French. "Is this what you do when I'm not here? Go joyriding?"

My mother, sitting stoically in her car seat, said, "André, we just went for a little meal. At the place where we go in the Village with hamburgers and milk shakes. It costs very little."

"Get out," he yelled at her.

I kicked open the car door, pushing him out of the way, and ran around to the passenger side. I could hear him recover and come after me, so I whipped open the door to get my mother out, forgetting the solid window frame on the old Chrysler, which took out a large slice of flesh covering my collar bone, and apparently in the process severing a packet of nerves that provided sensation to my upper arm.

I scooped up my mother and carried her into the house, faster than my father could pursue, despite the extra weight. I got her into the bathroom where she had the door locked before he plowed me into the frame, cracking open my cheek and blackening my left eye. I slid to the floor and covered my head with my hands, though only ferocious French diatribe followed, the overuse of which had destroyed its destructive power.

To this day, my right shoulder is utterly without feeling. It works fine, but when I touch it, I might as well be touching someone else's arm. I do this whenever I need reminding that there's no cost to devotion, when devotion is deserved.

CHAPTER TWENTY-THREE

Wollencroft met me at the door wearing a sweat suit and giant fuzzy slippers. She was eating out of a large bowl of fruit cocktail, which she offered to share, but I politely refused. We went back to her Greene and Greene living room where she had her work spread out on the coffee table. Four of the stacks were copies of my father's ledger, PDFs and the searchable OCR versions, a set for each of us.

"Have you looked at the ledger?" I asked when I was back in the living room.

"I did."

"Anything interesting?"

She leaned over and picked up her PDF version. She went to where a paper clip secured a selection of the pages and handed it to me.

"It's a subaccount, detailing expenditures drawn off his personal bank account," she said. "Note the title."

"RM. Rozele Mikutavičienė?"

"Apparently. It records what and when he paid her for cleaning, laundry, shopping, and so on. It was fair and reasonable based on the value of the dollar in those years." She took out a thicker section bound by a bigger clip and handed it to me.

"Accounts receivable," I said.

"I haven't done a deep dive, but there's no evidence of out-sized payments made by Pagliero Waste Management, just a few hundred dollars here and there that they paid for routine maintenance and repair."

"Even an accounting freak like my father wouldn't log cash bonuses."

"I agree. But look at the chart of accounts."

"RM is there too."

"He managed her billing. There's an aging report showing thirty, sixty, ninety days. The clients have codes."

I studied the columns.

"Hardly anything got past thirty days, and nothing past ninety," I said. "Is there a code key?"

"Not that I could find. Why hide their identities? Why is that funny?" she asked, seeing me smile.

"He did it for efficiency, not secrecy. The box is too small to fit full names, and their status as weekly, biweekly, and monthly customers, simple cleaning or more elaborate service. And he liked symmetry, so no more or less than five letters per box."

"Rather anal."

"He was an asshole, I won't argue that."

I let my mind get comfortable with the rhythm of the entries, which allowed me to focus on a few standouts.

"Two of the weekly full-service clients had the initials TC/RC. If TC is Trevor Cleary, who's RC?"

"Robert Cleary. The city councilman. In those days he was a junior master of the universe at the DA's."

"You know him?"

"He presented my commendation for being stupid enough to get shot in the throat. We sort of became friends until he got too friendly."

"Not interested?"

"Less than his wife."

"That must happen to you a lot."

"When I said I only want the ones I can't have, I didn't mean married."

"Can you introduce me?"

"I'm starting to feel like an escort. With a license to carry."

"You're not the first."

"I'll make the call."

IT TURNED out we got two Clearys for the price of one. When we pulled into the parking lot that served Robert's office building, his brother Trevor was waiting for us.

"Bobby called to check you out after hearing from Madelyn," he said to me. "I invited myself along."

"Still think we have a story?" I asked.

"TBD," he said. "But that's why I'm here."

Robert was taller than the other two Clearys, with a little less girth, but the brothers all looked stamped out of the same mold. Same basic shape and features, and now in their sixties, with uniform grey to white hair. Robert also dressed better and kept a spare and finely furnished office, a man with a long familiarity with power and social standing.

He shook our hands and gave Wollencroft a little peck on the cheek, which she endured with just the slightest flinch.

"Trev has filled me in a little about your quest," he said to me, after we gathered around a mahogany conference table with a coat of gloss varnish you could use to shave with, "but let me hear it from you."

So I went through it again, pitched to the audience. Meaning I left out my father's missing police file, my run-in with Dante Marino, and subsequent stalking of his boss, Orfio Pagliero, but emphasized my visit with Tasenka and what I knew about her mother.

"Which is why we wanted to talk to you," said Wollencroft. "We know Rozele worked for your brother Nelson, and we think she might have worked for you too."

"Absolutely," he said. "Trev and I shared the apartment. It was before either of us were in relationships, when we had the domestic skills of Kodiak bears. Not that my wife took over those duties. She's a liberated woman."

"What do you remember about Rozele?" she asked.

"Lovely woman," he said. "And I'm not just talking about her looks—easy on the eyes—but how she was as a person. Very diligent and responsible. No complaints there at all."

"Did you ever meet André Acquillo?" I asked. "She lived with him."

He made a gesture that most resembled tossing an imaginary ball. He must have acquired the habit punctuating key points of a political speech.

"As a matter of fact, I hired him, too. To fix my car. An old Mercedes. Sort of a rattle trap, but all I could afford in those days. But it had to be a Mercedes. Your father really knew his foreign cars."

"Rozele must have referred you," I said.

"She did."

"How did he act?" I asked.

Cleary seemed unsure how to answer that.

"He had a pretty thick accent. Found him hard to understand. Of course, she could barely speak English, though they talked to each other in French, which I know a little of. It all worked out. This is New York City. If you don't enjoy hearing all kinds of accents you don't belong here."

"We think he moonlighted for the mob. Wheelman," said Wollencroft.

He sat back in his chair, both hands raised as if to catch the imaginary ball.

"Whoa, whoa, I didn't know anything about that."

"We're not saying you did. We just learned this ourselves and thought you should know."

"I appreciate that," he said. "Jesus, let's forget he fixed my car. Wouldn't want the press to get ahold of that," he added, looking at his brother.

"You're safe with me," said Trevor.

Robert's concern seemed to deepen.

"You think this is why he was killed?" he said to Wollen-croft. "Mob hit?"

"Certainly looks that way," she said.

"So let's also keep my connection with Rozele out of this," he said. "I want to help, but confidentially, if you don't mind."

"Not an issue for me," I said.

"Me neither," said Trevor. "Which you know. Though, if I write anything, connecting Nelson would be unavoidable."

Robert made another of his flamboyant hand movements. I figured he'd cleared his share of wine glasses off the table.

"Of course. That's not a biggie. Just remind him not to mention my name in this context. He's got a tin ear for politics."

"Anything else you can tell us about André?" Wollencroft asked. "It'll stay in this room."

"Now that you mention it, he was a good driver. Not what you're thinking," he added with a laugh, pointing at Wollen-croft. "He used to drive me to the airport so he could work on the Mercedes while I was out of town. The damn thing needed a lot of work. Cool car, though. A two-seater with a stick shift. Chick magnet. He would drive and we would discuss all the maintenance issues. I still know a lot of auto parts by their French name. Will come in handy if I ever break down on the Côte d'Azur."

"Must have been expensive to have a go-to French mechanic," said Wollencroft.

He grinned at her, though more as a nod to his youthful self.

"At every stage of life, you spend money on what matters. I still drive a Mercedes, only now I own the dealership."

Chapter Twenty-Four

Tasenka called to ask if I wanted to hear her sing.

"If you're not doing anything else tonight," she said. "I'm a cabaret singer, which sounds a lot more glamorous than it is."

"Let me be the judge of that."

She said her singing offered a soothing haven from advanced mathematics, and had basically paid for college and graduate school. I told her I had no musical inclinations beyond a steadfast commitment to long dead musicians and composers.

"Then you might like my set list."

She gave me the address of a club called the Majestic Lounge on the Upper East Side. I'd been to the place more than once, though not since my days at the company. Pretty swanky venue, I told her.

"I'm a decent cabaret singer," she said. "Still doesn't make it all that glamorous. I thought we could talk a little before I go on, and between sets. For some reason I feel more like myself in that world. Maybe it's the preparatory martini."

I told her they used to require a tie.

"Just a jacket, tie optional. No sneakers, though if they're expensive enough, they'll let you through. I gave your name at the door in case there's a line. Just go up to the huge man and tell him who you are. Do the same thing with the hostess and she'll give you a good table," she added.

I truly loved that place, and thanked her as earnestly as I could without sounding phony. She returned the favor by admitting to a lifelong yearning for a more coherent personal history.

"These childhood things," she said, "they have a pull."

I didn't burden her with Newton's thoughts on the reciprocal dynamics of attraction and repulsion.

It's NOT as hard to buy a blue blazer in the Bronx as you might think, if you think the Bronx is somehow a less regular place than anywhere else in the country. I found a shop near the hotel run by an East Indian guy dressed up like it was his last chance to impress the world.

"I just need a blue blazer," I told him.

"How many buttons?"

"I don't know. How many do I need?"

"Double- or single-breasted?"

"Two breasts are standard, though in this case one will do."

"So, single-breasted, two buttons. Very American. Sleeves?"

"Two."

"Over or above the cuffs?"

"Let's split the difference."

He whipped out a cloth tape measure and captured my specs.

"Your torso is too short for your arms, which are long, and your chest, which is too wide," he said.

"Nobody's perfect."

He looked over his shoulder at a long rack of blue blazers as if seeking their advice.

"I think custom is the only alternative," he said.

"How long?"

"A day."

"I need it now."

"One hour. We have magazines," he said, pointing to a dismal waiting area.

It actually took two hours, but the jacket fit like a glove. The tailor seemed pleased with his accomplishment.

"It sits on your body like it's normal," he said.

"The jacket or the body?"

"What about those trousers?"

I was making my escape in the Honda when Wollencroft called me.

"Do you know what makes for a successful cold case detective?" she asked.

"A decent sweater?"

"Attention to detail."

I recognized that tone of voice. I'd heard it often from Jackie Swaitkowski. Triumphalism mixed with a certain insecurity, the subtle kind, tentative, yet poised for defiance.

"You found something," I said.

"No, I discovered something. Big difference. I was looking at your father's ledger and went through the subaccount covering auto maintenance and repair. A sizable category, as you might guess."

"The shop?"

"No, the personal account. His own cars and trucks."

I'd flipped over that part, holding it for a later look, but she was right. It was thick with entries.

"So you know how many miles the '55 pickup got on a quart of oil," I said.

"More important, the '67 Grand Prix."

I thought about it.

"Less than a thousand, though a lot of it drips on the ground."

"Not a problem for André. It was all part of the deal," she said.

I pulled over to the side of the road so I could concentrate on what she was saying.

"Okay," I said. "I'm listening."

"The Blue Book on a fully loaded 1967 Pontiac Grand Prix in 1975, the year your father took possession, was about $1,500. How much do you think he paid for it?"

"I'm done with the twenty questions."

"Five hundred. Included in the purchase price was a monthly maintenance check. All new points, plugs, oil change, filters, flushed radiator, full inspection of belts, brakes, tires, transmission fluid, and timing adjustment. No seller does that, and no buyer writes it all down."

"You didn't know my father."

"And you didn't know mine. Sorry, why did I say that?"

One of my problems with relationships is a tendency to overlook things going on with people in my immediate proximity. It's not so much a lack of empathy, it's an assumption that what they say is actually what they think, and how they act is actually how they mean to act, when all the while, it's something else entirely.

"What happened to your father?" I asked.

"He killed himself. On my eighteenth birthday."

I knew then I was caught in a conspiracy, conceived by a cabal of dead fathers, each having left children behind to be tormented by their mysteries, their sins against innocence and adoration.

"I'm sorry."

"Don't be. I wasn't."

"Okay."

"So Richie Scamporino didn't technically give your father the required performance car," she said, pulling the conversation back on track, "he just arranged for its easy purchase and regular maintenance."

"He didn't maintain it himself?"

"According to the ledger, it went back to the dealer once a month for service. I told you, it's all written down. You can see for yourself."

I pulled back onto the road, now eager to get back to the hotel room and the stack of PDFs.

"Who was the dealer?" I asked.

"Didn't say. So I got Albany to pull the registration. They had to dig to find the original title, which you can imagine caused great gnashing of teeth, but they found it."

"And?"

"Cleary Pontiac Oldsmobile of Mount Vernon," she said. "The crown jewel of William J. Cleary's General Motors Auto Group."

AS TASENKA suspected, there was a line outside the Majestic Lounge, though as promised, the bouncer at the door had my name on his list. The VIP treatment was also extended by the hostess, who not only got me a nice table, but brought a waiter along to get a nice start on the drink ordering.

The place was all black, white, and chrome art deco, the only color provided by a wall of bottles behind the bar. The crowd was a mix of people like me there for the music and a younger coterie who liked the mood and what the lighting did for their complexions. On a small stage about a foot off the ground an Asian woman wearing opera gloves with the fingers cut out played "They Can't Take That Away from Me" on a grand piano.

On the wall behind the stage, between open floor-to-ceiling curtains, was a painting of a flapper bent over impossibly by a swell in a tux with a cigarette holder between his teeth. I knew the stage could fit a small trap set, bass viol, and one other musician if they didn't mind cozy, but tonight there was just a single mic stand.

Tasenka came out from behind the curtain on the right, walked off the stage, and over to my table.

You're not supposed to notice that your sister is an actual female, much less an impressive beauty, but Tasenka's transformation from exhausted financial drone into glittering entertainer was too decisive to avoid.

Her brown hair had somehow deepened and threw off blonde highlights at the same time, and her blue eyes matched the sapphire necklace that draped down over ample cleavage.

I thought of my other sister, her face knitted into a permanent frown, jaw set for battle, a being so tightly wound it kinked her hair.

Tasenka slid into her seat in time for a martini to appear along with my Absolut on the rocks. She held it like she'd trained one hundred years of women in the art of holding a martini glass.

"I'm glad you could make it," she said.

"Glad you invited me," I said. "I like this joint."

"You know the Majestic?"

"Sure. Our corporate headquarters was in Midtown. They'd drag me down there every once in a while, and I took the opportunity to spend the night and crawl around places like this."

"By yourself?" she asked.

"Yeah, sometimes my wife would come along, but it was hard to pry her out of the suburbs. I think the city scared her."

Tasenka looked over her shoulder at the piano player when she slid into "The Way You Look Tonight." They smiled at each other, message sent and delivered.

"My ex-husband never left the city," she said. "Claimed all that fresh air gave him panic attacks."

"Funny guy."

"Literally. A stand-up comic. Met him at a club downtown. Melvin Minklestein. His real name is Jerry St. John, but Melvin worked better with the act."

"I think I've heard of him."

"He's a very nice man, and a good father. No acrimony, it just wasn't meant to be. How about you?"

"Plenty of acrimony, but that's all in the rearview."

I gave her the basic outlines of the story, focusing mostly on my daughter, how we'd managed to configure a semblance of good will out of the wreckage of the past. I told her my life had been less a trajectory than the path of a pinball, but I wasn't complaining, as long as I still had the faculties necessary to contemplate it all.

"Is that in doubt?" she asked.

"Technically, I'm over the limit for concussions," I said. "For all I know, I'm already crazy and these last few weeks have been one big delusion. I could make a case for that."

She smiled, letting a little of the gentle sadness I'd seen before creep into her face.

"I like being part of someone else's crazy dream," she said. "Explains a lot."

"You look like you're doing okay," I said.

She brightened.

"I am now. And I have you to thank for that. It's why I wanted to see you."

"What did I do?"

"I've been a little nervous about seeing you my entire life," she said. "How many times do you think I heard my mother say, 'We have to go to the church house, Sam is coming.' I was a child. For me, the name Sam equaled disruption, if not dread."

"You always went to stay with Father Cleary?"

"It's what I remember. Anyway, I've been carrying around this foolish burden, not even realizing it was there most of the time, and you just show up at my door one night and take it away. So thank you."

She wriggled her wrist to get a watch, loosely secured by a silver chain, around to where she could see it.

"When do you go on?" I asked.

"I still have some time."

"Speaking of crazy dreams, I got a crazy thing to ask," I said. "If you don't mind."

"Sure."

"You remembered André's Grand Prix. You couldn't have been more than eight years old when he died. Why do you think it stuck in your mind?"

She made a quiet laugh and looked down at her necklace, as if just realizing she'd wrapped the string of blue stones around her finger.

"I thought I told you. Photographs are all I have for memories. My mother must have taken it because she's not in the picture, but I'm there with André and some other people. We're all dressed up for a summer party. That car was so huge, everyone looks like midgets standing next to it. Especially me."

"Maybe I could take a look at it sometime," I said.

"You can look at it now," she said, rising up from her chair and going back behind the curtain. A few moments later she was back holding her smartphone. "I scanned them all to save to cloud storage. You never know, there could be a fire."

She handed me the phone, telling me to hold it horizontally. The old snapshot rotated and filled the little screen. Tasenka was squinting, her long, skinny legs sticking out of a white linen dress. My father also wore white—baggy trousers—over a tan rayon jacket I remembered almost keeping for myself before throwing it out with the rest of his stuff. It was from the forties, with lots of gussets and pleats. The other two men in the photo looked more like they belonged in that time, with shaggy hair and sideburns. One was younger than my father, the other closer to his age. They looked like they were having a much better time, grinning, with their arms over each other's shoulders.

"Can you zoom in?" I asked Tasenka.

She took the phone and flicked around on the screen, then gave it back to me.

"Just use the tip of your finger to move it around," she said.

I filled the screen with close-ups of the two other guys. It wasn't the sharpest image, but good enough to make out features, easily recognizable despite the extra hair.

I asked Tasenka if she knew them as well, but she shook her head.

"Just a couple of guys."

"No," I said. "Not just."

CHAPTER TWENTY-FIVE

José called the next day to say the Jeep was ready. I put the repairs on my credit card and asked if I could add two more items.

"I'd like you to run it out to Southampton and let me rent this Honda," I said. He was agreeable and I gave him Hodges's boat address at Hawk Point Marina. "I'll explain the fresh paint job when I get the chance. Don't let him try to worm it out of you."

"I'm sending two of my best *compadres*, but unless your friend speaks Spanish, there'll be no worming."

"Excellent."

Then I drove the Honda over to see Donny Duxbury.

This time calling ahead really didn't matter, since the odds of a blind old guy addicted to audiobooks being away from home were slim. The larger danger would be Esteban visiting, but only Donny was there when he answered the door.

I announced who I was and followed his shuffling feet back into the sitting area. I saw the orange blur of its hind-quarters just as the cat fled the room. I apologized to Donny for barging in on him, but he said he wished people would barge in more often.

"It's not for the company exactly. I just have so much information rattling around in my head, I feel the need to let some of it out."

"How's the war going?"

"We're finally out of the Ardennes. Patton was one lunatic bastard, but we're lucky we had him."

"Every age needs them," I said.

He stopped and turned toward me a few feet away from his easy chair.

"You just hit on my theory of history," he said. "Serious events call forth the right lunatic bastard for the job."

"Like André Acquillo," I said.

He laughed.

"Yeah, a lunatic and a bastard, though I'm not sure if the times had the right place for him."

I waited until he was safely in his chair.

"Can I get you anything?" I asked.

"What time is it?"

"Eleven A.M."

"Too early for a beer."

"Not where I come from, though I'll stick with coffee."

"Go look in the fridge."

I didn't recognize the brand, and you needed a bottle opener to get the cap off. I put one in his waiting hand.

"My daughter would not approve," he said. "Do me a favor and stash these things if she knocks on the door."

The cat reappeared, sitting in the doorway to the kitchen, watching me, its tail sweeping randomly through the air.

"It's a deal," I said. "I tracked down your old friend Richie Scamporino. I thought you'd like to know."

"No friend of mine. What's he doing? Guarding a junkyard?"

"Car salesman. Toyotas, not far from me in Speonk."

"Rice burners? That's rich. Fucking Richie Scamporino. All attitude, no brains."

He took a long pull on the beer to punctuate his point. I saw in the gesture the younger man, a slender Anglo-Saxon surrounded by beefy Italians and ruddy-faced, hotheaded Irish. A man with secret intellectual aspirations resigned to the oily purgatory of the auto repair business, struggling with his fading eyesight, an even more lethal secret.

"Did the Paglieros hire my father to drive for the family?" I asked.

He returned his attention to the beer.

"I'm an old man, but I still want to die in my own bed, not with my throat slit, thank you very much."

He was startled when the cat jumped in his lap, and almost lost control of the beer. A little wad of foam fell on the cat's fur, but I decided it could stay there.

"Christ Almighty, you little fucker," said Donny. "You're lucky I don't toss you across the room." Though his hand gently followed the contour of the cat's arched back.

"Surely those days are long gone," I said.

He continued to pet the cat, which encouraged the process.

"Nah," he said. "Them days just moved to another address. Same bullshit, different zip code. And unlike most people in this country, guys like the Paglieros appreciate history. Everything that's ever happened to them is like yesterday. My suggestion for you is to go back to where you came from and forget about the whole thing. Being a stubborn shit is just gonna get you killed."

"Like my old man."

He picked the cat off his lap and held its limp body up to his face, breathing the animal aroma deeply into his lungs. He closed his eyes as the cat slid like liquid feline back into his lap.

"Like your old man," he said. "Only you didn't hear it from me."

"You can tell me more than that."

He shook his head.

"I can tell you what I know. A few weeks before André got killed he took a call in the shop. Spoke French into the phone, so I have no idea what he was saying, only that something bad was going down. The other clue was him ripping the phone off the wall and heaving it across the bay into the wall. He ran out of there, and we didn't see him again for a day or two. Pretty surly when he came back, not that he was usually Mister Congeniality."

"You don't know why."

"No."

"So why connect it to his murder, and why the Paglieros?"

"No other explanation. I meant it when I said I stayed clear of all that stuff. Once you start playing around with the mob, it's a Faustian situation. You think it's all nice and fine until they want something from you, and then you come home to Mephistopheles sitting in your living room. Not a good situation for a headstrong guy like André."

He asked me again if I wanted a beer. I turned him down, but got one for him.

"Did he introduce you to Orfio Pagliero, or was it the other way around?" I asked, as I handed him the beer.

He settled it down between his legs and sighed. His sightless eyes fixed on something at the far end of the room.

"Wisenheimer," he said, in a soft voice.

"Sorry?"

"That's what your father called you. Herr Wisenheimer."

"I never heard him say that."

"It sort of means wise ass, though I think he also meant you were a smart kid. Too smart for your own good."

"I don't think it's possible to be too smart for your own good."

"So you're still a Wisenheimer."

"I have a photograph taken a few years before André was killed. He's there with Tasenka, and the Grand Prix, and you and Orfio, yuckin' it up like a pair of best buddies."

He sat quietly, staring blindly into middle space, his face impassive.

"You could be lying," he said, finally. "How would I know?"

"Easy enough to prove I'm not," I said.

He nodded.

"Okay, so I knew the Paglieros. Leon ran my neighborhood. All I did was introduce them to André. So they owed me, not that I'd ever collect."

"If you stayed out of their business, what's to worry about?" I asked.

"You can know too much for your own good, how's that?"

"Funny coming from a knowledge freak like you," I said.

He squinted and pinched his lips, as if the strain of holding back his words was beginning to show on his face.

"I can't talk about it," he said.

"You did ask for something," I said. "You made a deal with Mephistopheles."

He shook his head and we sat in silence. For some reason, it felt easier to do that with a blind man. Which might be why the answer came to me.

"Donny Junior," I said.

His face went from clenched to defiant.

"Who told you that?"

"Nobody. It was just a guess."

He turned away from me and spat into the air. I didn't look to see where it landed.

"Fuckin' kid. Him and that meatball Scamporino. I could see where it was going. So yeah, I asked if they could drop him from the outfit before he got in too deep. Unfortunately, part of the deal was Junior had to get out of town. As far out of town as possible. I don't know what they said to him, because he never spoke to me again. Him or his old lady. There's gratitude for you."

I tried to get a little more out of him, but he'd confessed enough for the day, so I got up to go. He looked at me without making eye contact, the way blind people do.

"Too bad you never knew Rozele," he said.

"You liked her."

"I did."

"How did he treat her?" I asked.

"André? Pretty good, far as I could tell. She seemed happy with him, at least until the end there."

"What do you mean?"

"I mean, she acted different after André got that phone call. Stopped working. Sat around the apartment. I don't blame her for it, but I think I know what happened."

"What?"

"I think she got him killed. That's what I think happened."

Chapter Twenty-Six

I'd probably just turned sixteen. It was Friday afternoon and I arrived at my father's apartment after a long walk from the subway station. He wasn't home, though he'd left a note telling me he had to go to Canada for a few days. He didn't explicitly say that I could stay, though he wrote that he'd left TV dinners in the freezer, two quarts of Hawaiian Punch, and milk.

I took my things into my bedroom and sat on the bed, deliberating. To help that along, I turned on the jazz station, something my father never allowed. This set the mood for more improvisation, beginning with a trip to the liquor cabinet. I'd long been aware of a large, open, but unused bottle of vodka, my father's preferences running to wine and a daily Canadian whiskey, the other liquors presumably kept on hand for social occasions.

I put on a pair of leather gloves and poured about a quart of booze into an empty milk bottle. (If someone asked if my father had either the inclination or ability to lift fingerprints, I would have said yes, and yes.) I replaced the pilfered vodka with an exact quantity of water.

I don't remember what that first sip on the rocks was like, but a few sips later I thought the next obvious thing to do was take a quick spin in the Grand Prix.

By this time it was dark outside, but I knew where to find the spare key on top of the jamb just inside the access door to the garage. Once inside, I pulled open the big door, casting the die.

I used a piece of electrical tape to mark the position of the car seat before adjusting it for my shorter legs. Backing the Pontiac out of the garage required some precision, since there were only a few inches to spare on either side. I rolled down the sloped driveway to the street, and pulled away as quietly as the souped-up V8 would allow.

I continued to drive with care, getting a feel for the manual gearbox, an improbable feature in such a gigantic car. I followed my nose through the tangled streets over to the Hutchinson Parkway, where I put the accelerator to the floor and gloried in feeling all those G-forces pressing me into the leather seats.

I backed off at about eighty-five mph, and settled into a steady cruise. I bailed off the Hutchinson before reaching the Throgs Neck Bridge, and dove into the city streets, somewhere in the southern reaches of Brooklyn.

I took my time getting back up to the Bronx, motoring along with the window down, burning down cigarettes in the breeze. At a stop sign at the end of a one-way street, a girl about my age came up to the car door and asked if I had a match.

She had long, shiny black hair combed straight down so I couldn't exactly tell what she looked like, though I knew she was a native by the sturdy Brooklyn accent. I took the cigarette from her and lit it with the car's lighter. She asked me if my car was a Cadillac, and I had to disappoint her. She said it was the biggest fucking car she'd ever seen that wasn't a Cadillac. I told her she was an astute observer of cars, a rarity among the girls I knew. She said she got it from her brother, a die-hard greaser who drove a '65 GTO. When I told her the Grand Prix was the GTO's big brother, she leaned into the window to get a better look. She smelled like a mix of calamity and endless horizons. I told her I'd drive her somewhere if she wanted a lift.

She directed me to a liquor store. She went inside and came out with a bag of ice, plastic cups, a quart of Coca-Cola, and a bottle of rum. Her parents had been in the Bahamas the year before, and she'd developed a taste for it after raiding their imported supply. I told her I'd pinched some of my old man's vodka, and this cemented the bond between us.

She said she was twenty-one and I told her I was eighteen, so the average inflation was probably around two and a half years. She directed me to a parking lot behind a bowling alley, which she said the cops never patrolled. She called it the BDZ, the Brooklyn Demilitarized Zone. We sat there and drank and lied about our current status and future prospects.

She eventually asked me why we were sitting in the front bucket seats when the rear seat was bigger than a suite at the Waldorf Astoria. I'm not crystal clear on everything that happened after that, though I know it was something that had never happened before.

Through the good offices of the hearth gods that attend to young idiots, I got the girl back to her parents' house and the Grand Prix back into the garage without a hint of a scrape. The next morning, I wiped the car down, checked the trunk to make sure the jack and a bundle of tools were in their proper places, cleaned the faint ashes off the otherwise virgin cigarette lighter, and wrote down the miles on the odometer. Then I used the special pencil to reconcile the mileage logged in the general ledger with the reality on the dial.

I didn't see my father until a few weekends later, and judging from his general demeanor, the caper was a success. Reinforcing a lifelong belief that attention to detail is key to both larceny and love.

JACKIE SWAITKOWSKI e-mailed me to say that Orfio Pagliero wanted to meet.

> *Really. About anything in particular?*
>
> He didn't specify. Not Orfio, his lawyer. He's the one who called. And he wants me there.
>
> *Get out of here.*
>
> Christian Arnell. That's the lawyer's name. He insists on a face-to-face, but said I could pick the spot.
>
> *I say no Italian restaurants.*
>
> I have a better idea, but you'll have to wait till I get there.
>
> *When?*
>
> In about two and a half hours. Text me your address.

She called me when she reached the hotel lobby and I came down to meet her. She carried a briefcase and wore jeans, cowboy boots, and a shapeless jacket that did a decent job hiding the Glock. We found a quiet corner so I could bring her up to speed.

It took awhile to tell her about Dante Marino, my week off courtesy of internal bleeding, securing André's general ledger from Mrs. Nadelman, my chat with Orfio Pagliero at the Episcopal Church, visiting Robert and Trevor Cleary, and Father Cleary, and all the ensuing data and ramifications.

"We've been busy," she said.

"Yeah. Busy spinning in place."

"You seem to have attracted Orfio's attention. That must be worth something."

"I guess we'll find out."

"No theories?" she asked, a question we often asked each other in the absence of tangible information, pretending raw speculation was just as good.

"I think I know a lot more than I think I know."

"Don't tell me we're going into Zen mode." She gave me a gentle kick with her cowboy boot. "That stuff gives me a headache."

"I'm sitting here thinking I have a lot of information, but zero knowledge. But others disagree. Otherwise they wouldn't want to kill me. This is empirically sound logic, no Zen required."

"So maybe we should bag the meeting with Orfio."

"That's the last thing we should do. This is a gift. I have no idea why it's been bestowed, but accepting is essential."

Jackie told me her plan. Her deal with Arnell was to pick a place you could reach in an hour from anywhere in the Bronx, assuming normal traffic. So she drove us in her Volvo over to an old estate turned public park called Wave Hill in Riverdale set above the Hudson River with a nice view of the Palisades. There was a relatively open lawn with folding chairs and a pergola the original owners had designed for just this purpose. Conveniently there were four unoccupied chairs, which we snagged and settled into before she called Arnell. Judging from her side of the conversation, the choice was agreeable, since he and Orfio were already nearby.

The day was sunny, with a stiff breeze blowing up from the river shuffling the first fallen leaves of the season around the lawn. Few tourists had taken advantage of these seasonal wonders, so we had the place mostly to ourselves.

Arnell was a head taller than Orfio, which wasn't hard, and dressed in a similar polo shirt and sport jacket ensemble. He held a slim accordion folder under his arm. They walked with purpose across the lawn and made no effort to shake hands when they reached us, and neither did we. They sat in the chairs, which was a relief, since I didn't relish looking up at them the whole time.

Arnell thanked Jackie for agreeing to meet with them. She admitted she was curious about the meeting's purpose.

"I feel it's important for you to be fully aware of Mr. Pagliero's position before we embark on any discussion relating to your client," said Arnell.

"He means me," I told her.

"Let's hear it," said Jackie.

Orfio looked relaxed in the folding chair, legs crossed and hands folded in his lap. He kept his eyes on me, not staring so much as observing, slightly bored.

"Mr. Pagliero is a respected, successful businessman, with a long commitment to charitable work and selfless service to the community," he began, in a tone hollowed out by the infinite repetition of those words. "Any suggestion otherwise, any utterance or allusion to prior accusations, would be considered libelous, and subject to civil action, rigorously pursued to the fullest extent of the law."

"Jesus Christ," said Jackie. "We're not going to have one of those conversations, are we?"

"I beg your pardon?"

"You know as well as I do that's a bunch of happy horseshit, devoid of meaning and completely unactionable. We stipulate that Mr. Pagliero is a prominent businessman engaged in active public service. He's also a former member of organized crime, as concluded by the district attorney and US Attorney's Office in the 1995 plea bargain that kept Mr. Pagliero's former mobster's ass out of jail. As a matter of public record, expressing opinions on that subject is no more libelous than commenting on the Yankees' pennant prospects, however poorly they're playing."

"Well," said Arnell, reaching around inside his accordion folder. "Perhaps we should move to the matter of Mr. Acquillo's harassment of my client."

He went on to paint the picture of a vindictive crusader (me) suffering under the delusion that his client (Orfio, aforementioned prominent businessman) held some responsibility for his father's death, a preposterous allegation in every way, one categorically denied. He gave a fairly accurate description of our visit with Orfio at his excavation business, including an insinuation that we had misrepresented the purpose of the meeting (true enough) and had made veiled threats against Mr. Pagliero (not exactly).

His description of our encounter at the AA meeting in Manhattan was technically sound, if slightly embellished, exaggerating the delivery of the threat, if not the spirit. An outside observer would find it easy to sympathize with Orfio's position and accept the legitimacy of his attorney's complaint.

"I hope you see this meeting as a professional courtesy," Arnell said to Jackie, "an attempt to avoid the aggravation of legal action, including, but not exclusive to a restraining order against your client, which we will obtain immediately should there be any further effort to contact, encounter, speak to, or communicate in any way with Mr. Pagliero going forward."

"Does this mean I'm not allowed to break the legs of the next thug he sends to kill me?" I asked, sort of spoiling the official mood.

Arnell pointed at me.

"That is precisely the type of irresponsible and slanderous allegation that must cease from this moment forward," he said, "or you will suffer the appropriate consequences."

"Look who's allegating now," I said.

"We hear you," said Jackie. "And I appreciate the heads-up. Though it would be reassuring to hear Mr. Pagliero disavow the recent attacks on Mr. Acquillo, both of which were life-threatening and the cause of serious bodily harm."

"Mr. Pagliero has given his statement to the police," said Arnell, sticking the accordion folder back under his arm.

"I'll make it easy for you," I said to Orfio. "I don't have to talk to you anymore. You've already given me everything I need to know. If you think I care about what happened to my old man, you're wrong. I should be thanking whoever did it. The only reason I'm still hanging around is people keep telling me to go away. That it happened a long time ago. That if I don't let up, it'll get me killed. What's up with all that? What do you think, Arnell?"

The lawyer just looked at me, impassive. Not opening your mouth at the wrong time is something they must teach in law school. It's a useful practice, though Jackie might have missed that course.

"If thinking is something you do," she said.

Arnell's face went a little pink, but his trap stayed shut.

I stood up and Jackie followed, giving us a chance to look down on them for a moment. Neither showed much affect, though it's hard to muster adequate defiance from a folding lawn chair. We walked away, in close unison, as if we'd rehearsed the move.

It wasn't until we were nearly at the parking lot that Jackie said, "Asshole."

I didn't know exactly who she meant by that, but thought better of asking her.

Chapter Twenty-Seven

I called Amanda after Jackie let me off at my hotel. She was in her pickup loading up on incidentals for one of her restoration projects. I asked her how things were progressing and she said fine, which meant no better nor worse than any other. She put the same question to me.

"Fine," I said, and I went on to give her a fairly complete update, allowing her to decide if things were better or worse than usual.

"You must be frustrated," she said.

I deflected that by asking after Eddie, Joe Sullivan, and anyone else we knew in common. She played along and gave a thorough and lively report.

"Hodges wonders why you had his Jeep repainted," she said. "I told him I knew nothing, since I don't."

"I sort of cracked it up," I said. "Anyway, it's my Jeep now. As soon as I pay him."

"Any idea when you might come home?" she asked, as lightly as the question would allow.

"How about tomorrow? So you remember what I look like."

"That would be lovely. How will I recognize you?"

"I'll be the one with the frustrated look."

"But still determined," she said.

"More than ever."

"How did that happen?"

"Can't explain it."

"I feel responsible. I goaded you."

"Goading is too strong. You encouraged."

"I'll be here."

RIGHT AFTER I hung up the phone it made a little sound. It was a text from Madelyn Wollencroft.

Take a ride with me to Breezy Point.

I called her.

"Sure," I said, when she answered. "What's the occasion?"

She said we'd talk in the car and hurried me off the phone. It was still a nice day, so I didn't mind sitting on a bench outside the hotel waiting for Wollencroft to pick me up. I occupied myself guessing what she'd be wearing, though beyond Alpine chalet wear or a ballroom gown, the possibilities were manifold.

Instead she looked like a regular, professional police detective, in a plain blue suit and sensible flats. She had, however, changed her hairdo, somehow finding enough length in the front to have it sweep across her forehead and add in some wave over her shoulders. I took a chance and told her it looked good on her.

"I get bored with the same thing," she said, accepting the compliment.

"Apparently."

On the way to Breezy Point, she filled me in.

"I got an anonymous tip," she said. "It was written on a slip of plain white paper sealed in an envelope left on the windshield of my SUV when it was parked at the house."

"Pretty traditional approach."

"No. Slick as it gets. Completely untraceable. Written with the left hand by a righty. No prints, no DNA. Whoever did it knew there were no security cameras in my driveway."

"And?"

"It said, 'About the mechanic. Look at the cops.'"

"Really."

She glanced over at me.

"Funny thing is, that's what I've been doing."

"Looking at the cops?"

"That missing file is stuck in my gut. Okay, maybe I'm overreacting, but nothing pisses me off more than fucking with evidence. You have no idea how hard it is to re-create these cases that are buried under mountains of time and stupid, lazy process. Every little piece of data becomes like a precious jewel. To think that some fat-headed, bought-off shit of a cop, a captain no less, had intentionally destroyed an entire file makes me absolutely fucking crazy."

I got the feeling she meant it.

"So?"

"So I've been searching through everything I can find connected to your father and I keep running into this big hole. We know he was arrested and charged with assault about two weeks before he was murdered. I'm clear on that. I have the officer's report. I don't know the preceding circumstances, since all the officer had to do was report the time, date, and nature of the arrest, which was not resisted, by the way."

"Must have been an off day."

"It doesn't add up," she said, smacking the steering wheel.

"Which is why we're going to chat with Fitzy."

"We are."

Along the way I told her about our meeting with Orfio and his lawyer. It didn't seem to faze her that much.

"The legal card is just one of his available options. No reason not to play it."

"Can he do that? Get a restraining order?" I asked.

"He can try. I know the judges he'd have to convince. Be an uphill battle. And not good for maintaining a low profile with the DA. I think you were right to tell him to stuff it."

"All the credit goes to Jackie Swaitkowski."

"She showed up a lot when I Googled you. Attractive, if you like that type. Your girlfriend?"

I barked out a little laugh, shorthand for a big, long story. She left it at that.

Wollencroft flashed her ID at the guy manning the little security hut at the entrance to Breezy Point. There was no argument or hesitation. She told me the co-op's security detail were mostly ex-cops, as if I needed an explanation. I directed her to where we could park the SUV within easy walking distance of Fitzy's place.

"Hi, Fitzy," she said, when he opened the door.

"Madelyn," he said, clearly startled, darting his eyes from her to me. "Long time no see. Hey, Sam."

"You gonna let us in, or do we have to talk out here?" she asked.

He burst into overt friendliness and ushered us into his house. The smell of cooking fish and stale beer competed for dominance. The backside of his Crocs were all busted down, his calves bloated and filled with varicose veins, but it didn't seem to slow his progress.

"You look great," he said to Wollencroft. "Stayin' in shape?"

"If you think I'm in shape, then I guess I am," she said.

"Yeah. Sure."

He offered the outside space, which we eagerly accepted.

"So," said Fitzy, dropping into a swayback lounge chair, "what brings you to these parts?"

Wollencroft took random steps around the patio, gazing at the darkening sky above the low roofs of the neighboring houses, huddled together like stubborn sheep.

"You know what I do now, right Fitzy?" she asked.

"Sure. Cold cases. Tough stuff if you ask me."

"Not as tough as lying around stinking squats making small talk with crack whores."

"You did that too. I know that Madelyn."

He looked over at me, probably wondering if he should have said that.

Wollencroft pulled a chair up to Fitzy's lounge and sat down, her knees nearly touching his legs. She leaned into him.

"I was a history major at Wellesley," she said. "Does that surprise you?"

"Not a bit."

"Do you know what animates historians? Not a love of the past. But rather the thrill of feeling the past as a living thing, a force gripping our present lives. The nowness of everything that's ever happened."

He sunk into his lounge.

"That sort of stuff is over my pay grade, Madelyn. I'm just a retired cop."

He grinned over at me, assuming a comradery of working stiffs.

"It was different in the day, wasn't it," she said.

He shrugged.

"Yeah. More complicated. But we still got the job done. You know that. Without us the whole city would've gone down the drain."

"I know that, too, Fitzy. I admire you. I always have. You were one of the good ones."

"What're you gettin' at, Madelyn? You didn't come all the way out here to pin a medal on me."

She shoved her chair even closer in.

"I found a stack of index cards," she said, "in an old file box on the bottom of a bunch of other boxes in the archives. Do you remember when they used to record things like court appearances and trips to the DA's to comply with union rules on overtime and extraordinary duty?"

He thought about it.

"Yeah, I do, but I wouldn't 've remembered if you hadn't reminded me."

"They were organized by individual officers, which was all the union cared about. You'll probably love it that I found yours. The whole stack."

He did look pleased. As a guy who kept duplicates of all his reports, that didn't surprise me.

"That's pretty cool, Madelyn. Can I get copies?"

"Absolutely, Fitzy. Fact is, I've already scanned them all in, so you can have PDFs."

"That's good of you, Madelyn, but you didn't have to go to that kind of trouble."

"I did. Makes searching a lot easier."

That confused him.

"Searching? For what?"

"A name. And I found it."

"Still don't get what you're drivin' at. What name?"

"André Acquillo." He looked at me again, though less genially. Wollencroft leaned into the look to recapture his attention. "You came in on your day off to do an interview. You spent two hours with André after he'd been arrested for assault. Two hours after that, he was released on his own recognizance. All charges dropped. What did you two talk about, detective?"

You'd want to play poker with Fitzy, since he wasn't very good at hiding his feelings, which at that point had moved from confused to apprehensive.

"How the hell would I remember that?" he said. "It's ancient history. It'd be in the file."

"It would be, if the file was still around, but apparently it's skipped town."

"I don't remember any of this, honestly," he said to both of us. "I'm almost seventy years old. I'm lucky I remember my own name."

"You remember Frank Kelly," said Wollencroft. "He ran records."

"Sure. What's he say about it?"

"Not much at this point. He's been dead about five years."

He held up his hands as if showing us no missing files were in his possession.

"Did you look at the logs?" Fitzy asked.

"First thing I did. Kelly checked out the file and never checked it back in."

"Get out of here. No way."

"That's what it looks like."

Fitzy got up from the lounge chair with some difficulty and walked over to the spot on the patio from where you could see a patch of Jamaica Bay. His back was to us. He had his hands on his hips and shook his head in little bursts, as if considering, then rejecting, a series of thoughts.

"Did anyone tell you to lay off the investigation of Acquillo's murder?" Wollencroft asked.

He turned around and pointed at her.

"No. Nobody told us that, and even if they did, I wouldn't go along with it. We worked that case as hard as we worked anything, and that's in the records. If it isn't, I got copies in the house."

"It's there," she said. "Except the things that aren't."

"I'm a little insulted, Madelyn."

She stood up and got up in his face.

"I'll apologize after you tell me about the interview with André Acquillo."

So there it was. An actual stand-off. I kept my seat.

"Nothing to tell," said Fitzy.

"*Vous mentez*," I said.

He turned toward me and took a step, then caught himself.

"What the fuck does that mean?"

"*Ça veut dire que vous êtes grosse, laide, et stupide.*"

His eyes narrowed and his lips drew into a straight line. But he held his ground.

"I think the two of you better get the fuck out of here."

I stood up to join Wollencroft in her leisurely walk through the house and out to the street. Fitzy followed us. Before we left, she said, "If your memory improves, you know where to find me."

He didn't respond, though it looked like his flare-up had cooled a little, a touch of doubt softening the set of his jaw. He had his eyes on me when he shut the door.

"MY FRENCH is a little rusty. Did you call him fat and ugly?" Wollencroft asked when we were back in her SUV.

"And stupid. And a liar. I think I'm only right about three out of four."

"Smart enough to speak French? How did you know?"

"Dumb luck. Even better than being smart."

"If it's in his personnel file, I have a good reason to pay another call," she said.

"He'll just say he used to speak it, but can't anymore. That happens. The only thing my sister remembers is *je ne sais pas.* Though that might be willful amnesia."

"It's why they brought him in to do the interview on his day off," she said.

"But why lie? You said he was one of the good ones."

"Good is relative in the context of the times."

"What next?" I asked.

"Research. I'm an historian. It's what we do."

BEFORE DRIVING out to Southampton, I figured it was time to go see Bonnie again. The tiny woman guarding the residents of Saint Anthony's was at her post, and this time she let me in without all the rigmarole. We made a little small talk, then she called Flora down from upstairs. She still had trouble pronouncing Acquillo, but I didn't care. Nice enough to see her pleasant face.

She said Bonnie was in his favorite chair in the reading room, which reinforced the feeling that nothing in the place had changed in the weeks since my last visit, that the logic of time had a different meaning within the tall brick walls.

Bonnie gave me the same firm handshake. I sat across from him as Flora made her silent retreat.

"I thought I'd seen the last of you," he said.

"No such luck. I've been in the Bronx pretty much since we last visited."

"Got it all figured out?"

"No, but I know a lot more than I did."

"Me, too," he said, holding up his book. "Only now there's not so much I can do with it."

"I know a blind guy about your age who's in the same boat, though he sees the learning as an end in itself. His name is Donny Duxbury. Know him?"

He shook his head.

"The name rings a bell, but a very distant one. Might be imagining it."

"He worked for my father. Might've come into your place sometimes."

"Nope. Your old man always ate alone. That I remember."

"No female guests?"

He shook his head again.

"Always alone. But he'd be in and out early, which made me think there might've been a woman at home. That was usually the case with the early bird beer and shot boys."

"You talked about wise guys. Apparently the Paglieros were the main family in the Bronx. You must remember them."

That he did.

"Oh, yeah. Leon had his fingers in a lot of pots in those days. Most of them I never knew about, I'm sure. He'd come in once in a while with a woman clearly not his wife. Never gave me any trouble, though. Always polite, paid his check, left a tip. No arguments from me."

"The two punks that night, you think they were with Pagliero?"

"Most likely. The families tended to stick with their own neighborhoods. It wasn't like the gangs today that whack each other for stepping over a border. But they were happier going where their asses got kissed and people knew to keep their mouths shut."

He reached inside his sweater and took out a piece of tissue, which he used to save his place before shutting the book.

"I'm disturbing your reading," I said.

"Okay with me. I got plenty of time for that."

"But they left you alone."

"They did. Like I told you, my uncles were old friends of Leon's, and frankly, that little bar wasn't worth enough to mess around with. Tell me what you heard and maybe I can fill in some blanks."

So I did, leaving nothing out, so it took awhile. Bonnie paid close attention, and only asked me to repeat something when his poor hearing missed the words. He didn't have much to fill in. Nothing, actually, though he'd heard of Father Cleary and was flattered that the father had heard of him.

"Never went to church, though," he said. "Couldn't warm up to it. I guess I'll find out pretty soon if that was a mistake."

He also knew that the elder Cleary had been the city councilman back then, but not that his son had followed him in the same role.

"I never paid attention to that stuff," he said. "My job as a bartender was to keep politics and religion off the agenda."

When I brought up Detective Fitzsimmons, he remembered him, probably because of his Chinese partner. He liked both of them and felt they were serious about the case. Even after he got the visit from the captain.

"So it was a captain, you remember that?" I asked.

"Yeah, didn't I say that?"

"Francis Kelly? Captain Francis Kelly?"

He tried hard to loosen the memory, but it wouldn't come.

"I saw it on a little brass name tag, but all I remember was him telling me he was Captain something. For some reason that stuck. There were still a lot of Irish cops around back then, but I gotta admit, none of them names stick with me."

"I can understand that."

"This guy was actually a real Irishman, though. Like from Ireland Irish."

"Had an accent?"

"Oh yeah. Big Irish cop with a brogue. Right out of the movies."

ON THE way to Southampton I called Wollencroft to see if she could pull Frank Kelly's personnel file and check on his place of birth. She said she'd have to call me back. I was about to turn onto Oak Point when the cell phone trilled at me.

"Killenaule, County Tipperary, the Republic of Ireland," she said. "And I pulled Fitzy's ancestry off the Internet. Mother's maiden name was Charbonneau, born in Lyon. How do you say bingo in French?"

CHAPTER TWENTY-EIGHT

I synchronized my arrival at Oak Point with the sunset. The clouds over the Little Peconic Bay were in a cooperative mood, spreading themselves out along the horizon in a way designed to gather up the sun's lavender and magenta extravagances.

Eddie trotted across the lawn toward the driveway I shared with Amanda, his tail waving an unconditional welcome. Anyone could have been driving that old silver Accord, proving his worth as a watchdog. When he saw it was me he tried to climb up into the car, as he always did, which no admonishments would ever deter. I let him walk over my lap to the passenger side so he could stick his head out the window during the 150-foot journey to Amanda's pretty house.

Joe Sullivan stepped out the front door when I was about fifty feet away. He put up his hand for me to stop, which I did, getting out of the car so he could see it was me. He waved me forward.

"What were you doing?" I asked. "Staring at the driveway?"

"Motion sensors. Covers the whole perimeter. Alerts are geo-specific." He held up his smartphone. "It's an app."

"How does Eddie get through?"

"Sensors are set three feet off the ground. If a bad guy comes at us in a fast crawl, we're screwed."

The air was unusually humid for that time of year, and had the effect of releasing the perfume of damp grass and midautumn decay from the oaks overhead and Amanda's waning flower garden. I probably wouldn't have noticed if I hadn't been in olfactory exile in the Bronx.

Amanda walked out the front door. Maybe floated was a better word, since she wore a floor-length, billowy thing that obscured the movement of her legs. She held a jelly jar glass at about shoulder level. It was filled with ice and a clear liquid.

It probably took less than thirty seconds for her to reach me where I stood in the driveway, but that was plenty of time for me to do a full review of my life, the highlights reel anyway, recalling the flow of mood states, the rise and fall of expectations, a flickering catalog of miseries and bliss, global swashbuckling in giant petrochemical plants and fetid, urine-soaked alleys, concluding with the recognition that Oak Point was the place I wanted to be for all eternity, or whatever time was left to me.

"Hello there," said Amanda, handing me the drink.

Sullivan left us so I had Amanda and Eddie to myself for the rest of the evening. Amanda reviewed the state of her construction business, leavening complaint with satire aimed mostly at herself, and I caught her up on my project in the Bronx. Eddie focused on formations of Canada geese flying overhead.

"You were right about Tasenka," I said. "Meeting me absolved her of some unnecessary apprehension."

"If we knew the outcome of every encounter in advance, what would we do with all that extra anxiety?"

I waited until the next morning to tell her I was going back for another go, which she expected, and was prepared for. She didn't ask for a possible end date, and I didn't offer one. I just called Sullivan and asked if he could secure the house again before she got home from the job site.

She did say, "I'd prefer it if you stayed safe yourself, and return with most of your vital parts intact."

I didn't ask her which parts she considered vital before climbing in the old Honda and heading back into town.

WOLLENCROFT CALLED me just as I was entering the busy streets of the Bronx.

"I got a text from Orfio Pagliero," she said. "He wants to meet with the two of us. Just us, and just him."

"No other headline?"

"Nope. Just a time and place. One of his excavation sites. He said I'd understand his desire for discretion."

"Do you?" I asked.

"Understanding and giving a shit are two different things."

"So much for slapping me with a stalker injunction."

"Something must have changed," she said.

"What do you want to do?"

"Meet with him."

We agreed to catch up at her favorite diner at seven, right after sunset. After consuming overflowing plates of diner food we could decide if we really wanted to go through with it.

Wollencroft was punctual as always, wearing a baseball cap, baggy jeans, running shoes and a bulky jacket presumably to hide her usual panoply of lethal ordnance. Her face was tight, distracted, though energetic. Like a boxer before a match. Keyed up, but eager for the bell to ring.

"What do you make of this Pagliero?" I asked her. "I feel like I'm missing something."

She weighed the question.

"I'm not sure, which is one of the reasons this interests me. I would have thought his deal with the prosecutors put him out of harm's way, but he's engaged, like he has a stake in the situation. Maybe it's just you stirring the pot. I can't tell. But he's got my attention. And he knows that. Otherwise, I wouldn't be on the invitation list."

"It's like a dance."

"Yeah, but not a waltz. No Strauss involved."

Despite our appreciation of the diner's vast menu, she ended up with a fruit cup and coffee and I had a ham sandwich on wheat toast. The waitress looked disappointed.

"Let's get this over with," said Wollencroft, and I paid the bill.

THE JOB site was up in Westchester County, in an industrial park not far from my old office in White Plains. Wollencroft drove us in her Suburban, playing songs by folksy women singers through a smartphone plugged into the truck's stereo. I gritted my teeth and pretended not to care.

As we closed in on the destination she asked if I knew how to use a gun. I told her the truth.

"Don't like the things, though I've shot people. Not that hard to use. Just point and pull the trigger."

She dug a slim automatic out of her jacket and handed it to me.

"Untraceable," she said. "You might need it. Use your discretion."

It was an old piece, but I located the safety and flicked it off, then back on again. It felt light in my hand, though well-balanced.

"How many rounds?"

"Only six. Make 'em count."

The project was a big expansion of an existing building, a brick and glass box where they did something effectively camouflaged by their unpronounceable name. The lights were on and a few cars were in the parking lot, which we passed through on the way to the construction entrance. The cyclone fence was open, with emphatic signs to either side admonishing subcontractors to report in to the office trailer. When we got there, the lights were out and no one appeared home. We got out of the Suburban and Wollencroft banged on the door.

"Are we in the right place?" I asked.

She looked down at her smartphone and nodded.

We were about to get back in the Suburban when a bright flashlight lit us up. It came from an otherwise murky area deep in the construction site. The beam swept side to side, as if beckoning. Wollencroft leaned back against the hood of the Suburban. I leaned next to her.

"We'll wait here," she called.

The beam stopped moving for a moment, then advanced toward us. Wollencroft had her arms folded and hands tucked inside the open flaps of her jacket. I followed her lead, reluctantly, gripping the little automatic as I thumbed off the safety. The ground was muddy, muffling the approaching footfalls.

The flashlight was now trained on our faces, effectively blinding us to our surroundings, though I could make out the rough shape of a man behind the beam moving toward us.

"This is bullshit," Wollencroft muttered. "Far enough," she called to the man. "Show your face."

The man stopped, but the light stayed on us.

"Move away from me," she whispered.

"Nah, stay put," said a voice directly behind us. "I like you where you are."

Wollencroft had her police-issue Glock out from under her jacket and pointed at the flashlight wielder in the time it took to inhale a breath. I looked over my shoulder at a guy wearing a Venetian Long Nose mask and using both hands to point a very big revolver at my face.

"Go ahead," said the guy to Wollencroft. "The first one in the head of the dude, the next for you."

She didn't move her gun, and neither did he. Everyone held their position, though I seriously considered adjusting mine. It must have showed, because the guy said, "Ah-ah-ahh."

Then he said, "Don't make me count to three. I might not get past one."

Wollencroft lowered the Glock, but kept it in her hand. Venetian mask came around the front of the Suburban and motioned for her to give it up while he kept the heavy revolver trained on the center of my face. The other man finished his walk while Venetian mask felt around Wollencroft's jacket, pulling out another automatic and a can of pepper spray. He handed them to one of the other guys, who wore a ski mask, less inventive, though equally impenetrable. He didn't speak.

Venetian mask gave his gun to ski mask and told him to keep it aimed at my head. Then he gave Wollencroft a more thorough body search, yielding her wallet, badge, car keys, smartphone, handcuffs, pen flashlight, and a short stiletto extracted from her bra.

"Cute," he said, pocketing the knife. "Nice tits, by the way."

I got the same treatment, losing fewer items, none but my twenty-year-old Swiss Army Knife irreplaceable.

"You're not gonna compliment my balls?" I asked him.

He looked at me down the long nose.

"Sorry. Nice balls. Let's take a walk."

"You might know the NYPD frowns on kidnapping their investigators," said Wollencroft, as he pulled her in front of him and we started to walk in the direction ski mask had come from.

"Well, that's good news, since you're not being kidnapped," said Venetian mask. "Not in the traditional sense."

"My people know where I am," she said.

"That must be very reassuring to you."

"Where's Pagliero?" I asked. "One of you?"

"The name rings a bell," said Venetian mask. "You're not talking Paganini are you? Love that guy."

Venetian mask formed a line: Wollencroft led the way, then me, then the two masked men. He guided us by telling Wollencroft to ease to the right or left, pointing the way with a flashlight.

It's a pleasant fantasy that two unarmed people arranged as we were would have any chance of turning the tables on two armed goons, in the dark, in an unfamiliar place. Not that I didn't think about it furiously, playing split-second film clips in my head, running the scenarios and odds of success.

All Venetian mask had to do was pull a trigger at the slightest unauthorized movement, so nothing could come of it, but I needed something to control my growing fear and desperation.

"Where are we going?" Wollencroft asked. "What's the plan here?"

No one answered her, but she kept up the questions, and threw in a few threats and propositions. I focused on the probability of spinning around, grabbing the gun, surviving the subsequent bullet long enough to get a fist down the guy's throat, and the gun out of his hand, which I'd toss to Wollencroft, who might manage to take it from there.

Thus occupied, we completed the trip to one of Orfio Pagliero's specialties: a hole in the ground.

Venetian mask pointed the flashlight into the hole, lighting up the roof of a freshly installed, concrete holding tank, a big one, designed for a commercial-grade septic system. The hatch cover, with a chain wrapped around the hook, was off to the side, leaving another hole into the empty tank. He lined us up at the edge of the chasm and stood back.

"Here's where you make a decision," he said. "You run at me and we shoot you both in the belly and toss you into the tank, where you bleed to death in the next few minutes. Or, you just climb in there on your own so you can use the next few hours to take stock of your choices in life."

Wollencroft tried to tell his silent partner they wouldn't get away with it, that the NYPD would never relent in their pursuit, and would likely make sure the inconvenience of a trial would be avoided. Both seemed unmoved.

I'd already made up my mind to go for option A and was about to make the leap when she grabbed the sleeve of my jacket.

"Okay," she said, "let's go," and pulled me over the edge where we hopped onto the roof of the tank. Guided by a light shot down through the hatch, we dropped down six feet or so to the concrete floor. Just enough room to stand. Looking up at the glare, I watched Wollencroft's penlight fall through the hatch and heard it hit the floor.

"Fuck you people," she said, more declaration than insult.

CHAPTER TWENTY-NINE

We heard the sound of a backhoe as it lifted the hatch cover and dropped it into the opening. The light went down to zero until Wollencroft snapped on the penlight, which did a decent job of fighting back the utter darkness. We stood in silence, looking around the concrete walls and roof, listening to the dulled sounds of the backhoe dumping earth around the tank, filling in the big hole.

About ten minutes after the sounds ceased, she asked, "How're you with claustrophobia?"

"Not great, but better than with slow suffocation."

She sat down, leaning against the wall.

"We need to conserve air." She flicked off the light. "And battery power."

I joined her against the wall.

"Sure, Wollencroft, but to what end? Nobody knows we're here."

"Not true. Johnson's about ten minutes away, waiting for my first check-in text. If he doesn't get it, this place will be swarming with NYPD before you can spit."

I let myself enjoy the thought of that before the obvious sunk in.

"We're buried underground. In a concrete box."

She didn't respond to that right away, which bothered me a little, especially since I couldn't read her face in the dark.

"There's also a beacon marking our location," she said. "I hope."

I took another excursion from denial to hope and back again, this one of shorter duration.

"Why don't you give me the whole picture," I said. "Burn a little air."

"I was able to drop a rescue beacon as we approached the hole."

"Really. After that search?"

"Wasn't that thorough."

"Looked thorough to me."

"I really don't want to discuss the details. I had a beacon and was able to deploy it. I don't know if they saw it on the ground, or if it got buried, or malfunctioned. I just hope it's out there somewhere."

She didn't offer more than that, but I pressed her.

"Wollencroft, we're sitting here in the dark, buried alive, probably on the way to a lousy death. What difference does it make at this point?"

After a little more silence, she said, "It dropped down my pants leg."

I thought about that, using my deductive, analytical skills until I realized what she meant.

"You didn't do what I think you did," I said.

"I did, and it may have saved your life."

"No, I'm impressed. That takes control."

"I hold the Bronx record for time undercover by a female detective. You learn a few things."

"Like control."

"Don't push it."

"What's the range? Can't be that big a beacon."

"Enough to reach Johnson's position."

"Is Johnson smart enough to figure out what happened? Presuming the beacon is working."

More quiet deliberation.

"I sure as shit hope so."

AFTER AN hour sitting in silence, in total darkness, on cold, hard concrete, with my only company near hallucinations caused by a confused visual cortex, and thoughts of mortality that went well beyond mere intimations, I said to Wollencroft, "I'd rather talk."

"It wastes oxygen. We need every molecule."

"What if we're already dead? Do you really want to spend your last hours deaf and dumb?"

She sighed.

"These aren't our last hours, unless you screw it up with a lot of talk."

"You're a hard drink, Wollencroft."

"Don't get sentimental on me. I'll be disappointed."

So I left her alone for a while, before asking, "Why did you become a cop? Waspy rich girl like you."

"Oh, Christ," she said, annoyed enough to shut me up. For a few minutes.

"I know why I became an engineer," I said. "I like to fix things. Asserting human intellect over the forces of entropy. Finding and realigning anomalies and malfunction. Ordering chaos."

"I'm not doing this."

"You do the same thing in your own work. We're in the same business."

She didn't respond, resulting in the definition of dead air. I closed my eyes, which caused a subtle change in the texture of the blackness. I listened for her breathing, but the sound of my own, restrained as it was, drowned it out.

"There's no sympathy for people who don't have to work," she said, surprising me. "And there shouldn't be. Though being free to choose what you do without considering financial consequences is harder than it sounds. The standard model is to squander your inheritance. But that's too easy. And hollow. And leads to early, miserable dissolution."

"Like your father," I said.

"Jesus, Acquillo. Maybe I should eat up all the air just to get you to shut up."

"I came within a hair's breadth of killing myself, with booze, the most cowardly way possible. Anesthetized. Though once you decide to die, it's not that frightening anymore. You can embrace the relief. Though I'm glad I didn't go through with it."

"Next time give me a call. I'll shoot you and put us both out of your misery."

I let the silence fall back into place after that, for maybe another hour. I used the time to wonder foolishly if there was any way to push the hatch cover up though the dirt, something my rational mind succeeded in telling my panicking survival instinct was impossible.

Then Wollencroft surprised me again by moving closer and gently pushing her shoulder into mine.

"I've had a dry streak," she said.

"Meaning?"

"Physical. I can't date other cops, but the only people I know are cops, and I work too many hours to meet people who aren't cops, and even when I do, they're scared off by my job."

"Oh."

She pressed a little harder and put her hand on my thigh.

"You want to communicate, how about a little nonverbal? We're probably going to die anyway. Isn't this everyone's fantasy?"

"Talk about oxygen consumption."

She moved her hand to the north till I stopped her.

"It's not a betrayal if it's a kindness," she said in a near whisper. "You might actually like it."

I felt her climb up on top of me and as she worked on buttons and other fasteners, took in the fragrance of her long straight hair when it fell across my face, felt the cool shock of flesh on flesh, and before I could get all the components of my fractured mind and terrified soul under control, it happened. And that was that.

WITH NO way to keep track of the hours, we didn't know if ten or twenty had gone by, but the strange heaviness of the air told us that the conversion of the O_2 in the tank to CO_2 was reaching completion.

With all the nonverbal communication out of the way, we saw little value in mere words, and thus sat very still with her head on my shoulder as I stroked her hair. After a while, the lack of movement began to give me a backache, which I found useful, giving me something to focus on, keeping my mind from slipping passively into the void.

They report that as the brain loses oxygen, it loses higher function, which somehow brings about a sort of tranquility. I can't say that's exactly what happened to me, though maybe the hard edge of panic was mercifully dulled.

It was too slow a process to say my life flashed before me, but I did think about Amanda, and my daughter, and my dog, not necessarily in that order. What I decided to believe was that they would likely grieve my passing, but had each other, and deeper bonds would grow without me hanging around disturbing the peace.

What I didn't dwell on were regrets, maybe for the first time in my life. They seemed trivial in the face of the good fortune I hadn't deserved, and the second chances the universe had unwittingly bestowed upon me.

As the miasma inside my mind thickened, a thought grew—that once we'd lost consciousness, it would extend our lives well into the future, so when revived, we'd be well-rested and ready to burst into the light with vigor and divine purpose.

I tried to share this theory with Wollencroft, but discovered I couldn't speak, and when I squeezed her, she didn't respond. I managed to lick my finger and stick it under her nose. I felt the faintest of breaths, which pleased me, since she'd already assumed that blessed state of suspended animation, preserved like Snow White awaiting rebirth from a kiss.

THAT'S JUST how fucking crazy I'd become before slipping into a dreamless abyss, rudely interrupted by yet another flashlight stuck in my eyes and someone putting a thing on my face that streamed cool vapor into my lungs.

"Sam! Sam! Look at me, buddy. Stay with me!"

I tried to yell, but it was only a hoarse whisper. I grabbed at the thing, but strong hands held it in place. I saw an IV taped to the crook of my right arm and used my left hand to rip it out. Blood sprayed my face and other strong arms joined in. I kicked something firm and heard someone yell a profanity. The original voice kept talking to me, reassuring me in a steady insistent tone.

"We're trying to help you, Sam. Come on, calm down. We're on your side."

My right arm was locked in place and I felt the sting of another IV going into the vein. I let it happen, staring up into a space filled with hard light and milling people in paramedic uniforms wearing stethoscopes and holding electronic gadgets.

"Wollencroft," I finally managed to yell. Or thought it was a yell.

A young woman with a broad face and short hair put her ear next to the mouth.

"Say it again."

"Wollencroft," I repeated.

"She's okay," said the woman. "They're working on her."

If she's okay, why are they working on her? I thought. I tried to say that out loud, but the words were too hard to form.

"We need to get you out of here," said the woman. "Will you please cooperate?"

I nodded. She studied me for a moment, then waved at someone out of my eyeshot.

Seconds later I was lifted onto a stretcher and pulled out of the tank head first. I'm not sure how they did it, but it felt like I was in the hands of people who'd trained their whole lives to extract people from septic tanks. The cold night hit me and I tried again to get the oxygen tubes off my face, longing to breathe fresh air, a substance I'd recently regarded as the most wondrous of indulgences.

A gentle hand restrained me and I let it. The world was now filled with earthmoving equipment, patrol cars, ambulances, and people in reflective outerwear. Yellow tape cordoned off sections of the job site inside of which men and women in blue jump suits were scanning the ground with strange devices lit by klieg lights, and kneeling over forensic chores.

I felt no elation over being alive, since I never once doubted my survival, despite the overwhelming odds. I didn't know what that meant at the time, and still don't. Probably hubris. I wasn't ready yet, and assumed the universe would simply have to fall in line.

I wasn't ready because the people I loved weren't ready, and I still had some work to do, a job to complete. The oxygen starvation might have played a role, clearing my brain of distractions and allowing me to see the story in stark relief. There were details to fill in, but I finally knew what was going on.

And why.

CHAPTER THIRTY

The young ER doc at Montefiore looked disappointed to see me back there again. I shared her feelings.

I told her about a fighter I knew whose strategy was to let his opponent beat on him for the first few rounds, fighting back just enough to lure the other guy into unrestrained exertion, exhausting him, at which time he would reveal his hidden reserves by knocking out the drained boxer with just a few vicious blows.

"What kind of strategy would you call that?" she asked.

"Incredibly stupid."

A nurse who'd looked after me the last time came into the room. The doc said she'd leave us alone so we could catch up on our latest news. She actually spent the time determining my current vital signs and checking me out on the bed controls and med regimen.

"No drugs," I said.

"We're not going through that again, are we?"

"We are. There's nothing wrong with me that a little atmosphere can't cure. I don't know why I'm here."

"For observation. If everything's still okay by the morning, we'll spring you. How's your mood?"

"Irritable. Why?"

She looked at her paperwork.

"Asphyxia can result in cognitive impairment, often indicated by uncharacteristic and inappropriate emotional responses."

"We're good there. I'm always irritable."

"We'll get you out of here as soon as we can."

"Can I walk around?"

"We encourage it. You'll have to take the IV with you."

"Do you know where they have Madelyn Wollencroft?"

"Just follow the cops."

Wollencroft was sitting up in bed looking about as happy with her circumstances as I was. I told her irritability could land her a psych evaluation. She patted her bed and I sat down.

"So I guess Johnson found the beacon," I said.

"He did. Went right to it, but didn't figure out right away what it meant. Not until he was interviewing the construction manager and learned the septic system had been freshly backfilled."

"By Pagliero."

"Not according to his crew. They said they had nothing to do with it. Supported by solid alibis."

"The doc told me we were down there a little over twenty-four hours."

"Felt shorter," she said.

"Time flies."

She told me what forensics had found so far, which was very little. No cigarette butts or soda cans. Just a few partial footprints in the thoroughly trampled mud.

"Johnson spent some quality time with Orfio himself, but surprisingly, the man didn't confess."

"What about the phone text?" I asked.

"From a disposable. I didn't expect him to use his own phone."

That didn't surprise me either, though not for the same reason. I lowered my voice so the cop outside her door couldn't hear, and shared my recent thinking, born in my cognitively impaired brain as they were pulling me out of the tank.

"I have a new hypothesis," I said, "but no evidence to support it. I think I can work that out, but now wouldn't be a great time for you to be involved."

That made her very unhappy.

"I could be offended by that."

"If you chose to," I said. "Or, you could trust me."

"I don't trust anyone."

"I could be your first. I'd be honored."

"You'll do what you want no matter what I say."

I agreed that was true.

"But I'd rather you stayed on my side. I think a lot of you, Wollencroft. When I think a lot of people they get me for life. I'm like a Labrador. Loyal and devoted till the end of time. You don't know that about me yet, but you will."

She sat still as a sphinx for a few moments, then pinched a piece of her hospital johnny and pulled it away from her chest.

"Do you know how ridiculous I look in this thing?" she asked.

"I'll have them put 'daily change of wardrobe' on your chart."

She let go of her johnny and gave me a little shove.

"Stay in touch," she said, and I got up to leave. She stopped me before I could get out the door.

"Sam?"

"Yeah?"

"We're going to forget about what happened, right?"

"Something happened?"

"Get the hell out of here."

I HAD to wait a few extra hours the next morning for the forensics lab to return my shoes, which they'd borrowed to make elimination casts. I was ready to walk out of there barefoot when a patrolman showed up with the shoes and an offer to drive me to the diner where I'd left my car.

José arrived with a replacement key. He checked the Honda's fluid levels and waited till the car started. I thanked him and drove directly to the hotel so I could call Amanda. I told her my wallet and cell phone had been stolen, leaving out some of the nettlesome details as to how that happened. We transferred my hotel charges to her credit card and talked the hotel manager into giving me a cash advance.

I took some of the money to buy a new phone, which I used to order a new credit card for myself. A new license would have to wait until Amanda could FedEx a stack of documents that proved I was me.

I cleaned myself up, scrubbing the patches of adhesive off my arm where they'd stuck the IV, got into fresh clothes, and headed back out. I was hungry, but didn't want to burn time at a restaurant, so I bought an overstuffed wrap and bottle of fruit juice at a deli near the hotel and headed for The Mother of Divine Providence Catholic Church.

The giant pile of European architecture rose up from the weary neighborhood like a forgotten fortress. I knew where to park the car by then, and how to find Father Cleary's rectory. I rang the bell at the front door and looked up at the surveillance camera so he could get a good view of my face. Ten minutes later, the door opened.

A big woman stood at the door, polite, but ready to do combat if I tried to push by. I gave her my name and asked if the father could give me a few minutes. I was also polite, verging on obsequious, which seemed to win her over. She shut the door, then came back shortly to let me in.

I followed her through the poorly lit old house to a back room that was part library, part office. The father was there to greet me, wearing a dark blue sweat suit and smoking a cigar.

"You've caught me in a moment of transgression," he said, shaking my hand.

"A cigar? You gotta work on your transgressions. I can help with that."

"Do they include brandy?"

"Sometimes. Not now."

He poured himself a hearty drink and ushered me into a sitting area furnished with once-elegant, now ratty old sofas. An air of broken-down comfort permeated the room.

"I thought I'd see you again," he said.

"Really. Divine insight?"

"Google. You acted like a guy just curious about his father's death. You're more than that."

"Don't believe everything you read."

"I don't," he said. "So to what do I owe the pleasure?"

"Just a single question. Shouldn't be that hard."

He swirled his brandy around the glass, took a sniff, then a gentle sip.

"Didn't I tell you all questions are hard? If you're a priest."

I took a moment to shape my words, more a hypothesis than a question, assuming I'd only get one chance.

"You knew what happened to Rozele Mikutavičienė. It's why you took her under your protection after my father was killed."

He continued to swirl his brandy, keeping his eyes trained on me.

"You know I can't respond to that," he said.

"You just did. Now I want to know why."

"Protecting the helpless is what I do."

I noticed there were at least three old clocks in the room, ticking away in their anachronistic glory. I looked around and located an ancient tree of a grandfather's clock. It was due to chime in twenty minutes. More than enough time for me.

"And the powerful?"

He hardened up a little at that.

"Everyone deserves the love of the church."

"When does preserving confidences become obstruction of justice?"

"People have been trying to draw that line for a long time. I think it's up to the conscience of the priest."

"How's yours?"

He didn't seem ready to answer that, but he did.

"Agonized."

"You could have saved me a lot of trouble. Including a few fun stays in the hospital. Might have eased that conscience a little."

"Some dilemmas are unsolvable. I've had to learn that on the job. All you can do is the best possible under the circumstances."

I suddenly felt a great need to get out of there. Before I did something that wouldn't do my own battered conscience any good. I stood up.

"I don't buy it, Father. Clear moral choices are the stuff of cartoons. The best you can do is the right thing, no matter what. And to hell with the circumstances," I said, and I left him, finding my own way out, hoping someone would try to stop me.

Chapter Thirty-One

It was late afternoon before I got back to my hotel, where I put in a call to Leon Pagliero. He wasn't crazy about hearing from me.

"You are the most fucking obstinate, aggravating, self-destructive fuck I have ever met in my entire life," he said. "As soon as I hang up on you I'm calling Arnell."

"Before you do that, I have a proposition. Just hear me out for two minutes, then hang up on me and call anyone you want."

I got more than two minutes. In fact, it was nearly an hour before we ended the conversation.

THE ENGINEER in me liked to go into difficult situations as prepared as possible. I learned that dealing with complex systems with multiple moving parts and critical dependencies. But I also learned that anticipating every contingency was impossible. That's not how the designs of nature or man worked. The functioning of the world depended on chaos and unpredictability.

And then there was the element of time. Conditions rearrange themselves every second, or less, and I knew I had very little time to act before the forces of disorder snatched away the opportunity.

So I called Wollencroft.

"What are the chances you could get your hands on a medical report from about forty years ago?"

"Not terrible, if the report still exists and the paper trail is still intact. Just takes time."

"I don't have any time," I said. "I need it now."

"They ordered me to rest at home."

"How's that working out?" I asked.

"Not so great. I'd rather be back at work."

I told her what I wanted.

"To repeat," she said, "that takes time."

"I know. I appreciate everything you do."

"You know I hate nice."

"So get me that fucking report."

I DROVE into Manhattan as the commuters were fighting their way back out, so it was relatively easy to get in and find a spot on the street where I could legally park the car.

Then I walked about five blocks to Orfio Pagliero's townhouse and rang the bell.

Seeing me was undoubtedly a mixed experience for Orfio, but he shook my hand and brought me into a study right off the vestibule and offered me a drink. I could have any kind of booze I wanted, but I'd understand if he just had a seltzer and cranberry juice. I told him one of the same on the rocks would suit me fine.

The study was spare and modern, more a vision of an interior decorator than a place serious students would want to work, but pleasant nevertheless. When Orfio had us settled, he said he'd asked his wife to go visit her friend Uptown for the evening. Nothing personal, he just wanted to spare her from hearing any of our conversation.

"Reasonable," I said.

He said his father had purchased the townhouse in the sixties as an investment, and a place to store his family when things were looking a little dodgy in the Bronx. When Orfio inherited the place, his wife did a full renovation, the result of which surrounded us. I told him she did a great job, and his pride in that sneaked through an otherwise neutral manner.

Finding common conversational ground, I talked about my ex-wife's decorating skills, equally impressive, though not generally to my taste. I skipped the part where I gutted our home after we split up and buried the entire contents in a landfill in New Jersey. Or when I removed all the lally columns from her lover's ski house in Vermont, allowing their love nest to settle irredeemably into the basement. Being more or less in the construction trades, he might have appreciated my demolition skills, but it wouldn't have set the right tone for the rest of the evening.

Luckily, the doorbell rang before we had to find another nonthreatening topic. Orfio got up and let Robert Cleary into the house. I could hear them greeting each other in the gentle mocking way old friends will do. But all that came to an abrupt halt when Cleary saw me standing in the middle of the study. Bewilderment and alarm competed for a hold on his face.

"Orfio, I'm confused," he said.

"We need to talk to you," said Orfio.

"We? You and this man? Unacceptable."

He spun around as if to leave, but Pagliero stepped in his path.

"No, Bobby. You got to sit down."

He was probably two-thirds Cleary's size, but the tone of his voice alone was enough to push the other man back into the room.

Cleary looked over at me, venom creeping into his eyes.

"I frankly do not understand what is going on here," he said, his voice rising to the stentorian.

"Like Orfio said, have a seat. He'll pour you a drink."

"Single malt, with two cubes, if I remember right," said Pagliero, as he walked over to the dry bar.

Cleary drifted into an upright chair as if drawn there by invisible forces. He continued to stare at me. Orfio handed him his drink, which he grasped without looking. He took a long sip.

"Where's Lieutenant Wollencroft?" he asked.

"Recovering from severe asphyxia," I said. "She'll be fine, I'm certain you'll want to know."

He looked back at Pagliero.

"Really, Orfio, I have no idea what this is about."

"It's about Rozele Mikutavičienė," I said.

"The cleaning lady? Surely you're joking."

I let that sit for a moment so I could keep my temper on the tight leash I'd promised myself.

"You pulled off a brilliant diversion, Cleary," I said. "You had me totally convinced that your friend Orfio was responsible for my father's death. Convinced me and Wollencroft and everyone I talked to. And why not? He was the perfect foil. My father even had a history with his family. Pitting me against him would not only send me down a false path, but would likely end with me on the bottom of the East River, because that's what gangsters do, right?"

"Orfio is not a gangster," said Cleary.

"Spare me," I said. "The world knows he was. Only he didn't follow the script. The worst he ever did to me was threaten an antistalking injunction, which frankly, I sort of deserved."

"Thank you," said Pagliero.

I looked over at him.

"How do you feel about Bobby trying to set you up as a murderer and obstructer of justice?"

"Not pleased."

Cleary began to shake, his outrage barely containable.

"These accusations are beyond the pale," he said, his voice reaching for a full boom. "What murder are you referring to?"

"My father's, you sack of shit," I said, in a voice that sounded calmer than I felt. "You killed him."

Cleary looked toward the front door, but Pagliero, slight and athletic, was there in an instant.

"Where's your proof?" asked Cleary, which prompted me to also leave my chair, walk across the room, and take the drink out of his hand. Holding it by the bottom and the rim, I dumped the whole thing in the gallon-sized baggie I'd pulled out of my back pocket.

I went back to my chair and sat down, holding the baggie aloft.

"Here."

Robert Cleary was undoubtedly a very smart man. He'd achieved a great deal in life—as a private attorney, New York City Councilman—but most important, as a prosecutor. He would realize that he and one of his brothers had left cocktail glasses, utensils, and gloves, but nobody knew about DNA in the late seventies. He'd remember all the blood flying around the men's room. He would know plenty of the Cleary brothers' DNA already had been retrieved from property rooms and little vials at the medical examiner's.

And the billion-to-one odds modern science would get it wrong.

It's not every day you get to see a prominent figure in society turn directly into a trapped rat. He looked at me, and Pagliero, and the front door, and I could nearly hear the calculations erupting in his head. He started to stand up.

"Go ahead," I told him, leaning forward in my chair. "Give it a try. Nothing would make me happier."

"Just go easy on the furniture," said Pagliero. "My wife worked hard on this room."

Cleary was still weighing his chances when my cell phone chirped. Both men looked at me as if to say, "You gotta be kidding me."

"Sorry about that," I said. "These damned things are taking over our lives."

I took out the phone and read the message from Wollencroft. Then I wrote her back and flipped the phone closed. Breaking the weird silence, I said to Cleary, "Oh, that was the NYPD. They obtained the medical records of your brother Trevor's stroke. Turns out it wasn't a stroke after all. It was brain damage caused by a severe beating. Do you want to share with Orfio why that happened?"

He didn't seem to, so I did it for him.

"You and Trevor had quite a swinging pad back in those days. Your old man kept you in easy cash, which meant lots of girls, and booze, and serious parties. And an endless supply of working stiffs to help keep the fun times going, including a grouchy French mechanic to maintain your cool car—a chick magnet I think you called it—and his girlfriend, a foxy blonde, to clean the place. I can see it happening. She's there one day, and you guys are feeling frisky, and what the hell, she can hardly speak English, and she's so hot. Come on, baby, let's party, take the day off, have a drink. She's not really into it, though, which you probably figured out somehow, but not your brother Trevor. He got swept away. He's a pretty big guy, and there was nothing Rozele could do. Except to go home and tell the French guy what he did to her. I knew that French guy better than you, because I could have told you what would happen next. I'm only surprised your brother lived. Of course, the mighty Clearys could not let this stand.

"Easy enough to find the French guy, who ate at the same place every night. So you and another brother, one of the plumbing guys, came up with a plan. Why not pretend you're a pair of Paglieros and go take care of business? You all knew each other. Went to the same church, hung out at the same civic events. Probably scratched each other's back whenever necessary. Like your father supplying Leon with getaway cars. Complete with a nice maintenance plan."

Cleary looked over at Orfio. You might be able to convert the way Orfio looked back into words, but it would fill a very large book.

"Forty years later, I show up," I said, "and your Pagliero-impersonation strategy is back in play. Only now, Trevor's one of the world's leading experts on everything Pagliero. Including close relationships with a few active thugs connected to the family. He knew who to call and how much it would cost to remove me from the situation. I kept messing up the plan by avoiding being dead."

Cleary sat in his chair with his head down, moving it side to side. Filled with regret, or working on his deniability, it was hard to say.

"What you allege happened decades ago," he said into the rug. "Who do you think would take on a case like this now?"

"I think you've met Madelyn Wollencroft."

He took a deep breath and continued to move his head around, as if trying to dislodge the unwanted realizations crowding into his brain.

Cleary looked up at Pagliero.

"You don't really believe this, do you Orfio?"

I told Cleary about the anonymous tip Wollencroft got about looking at the cops. It didn't take her long to connect Captain Frank Kelly to his father, former Councilman William J. Cleary.

"Your dad did a good job putting a lid on things," I said. "Twisting up the loyalties of a couple Irish cops who likely got a bellyful of guilt in return. One of them's still alive. He might just stonewall it, but I'm guessing he'd rather go out with an easier conscience. Doesn't really matter. Warrants are on their way to authorize collecting DNA and prints from your plumber brothers."

"You did that?" Cleary asked Orfio. "You sent the tip?"

Pagliero did what he'd learn to do best. Stay silent, with only his eyes left to convey his bottomless reserve of savagery and contempt.

As ARRANGED in advance, I left the two of them alone, giving me time to get to the Honda and beat it out of there, before Cleary had a chance to make a desperation play on the streets of Manhattan. If I hadn't been carrying precious cargo, I might have welcomed that, but better sense prevailed.

THIS TIME, when the woman who guarded the door at Saint Anthony's squawked at me through the intercom at the front gate, I said I was there to see Mr. Bonaventure, Bonnie to his friends. She buzzed me right in.

By the time I got through the front door, Flora was already on her way down. I asked the woman at the desk if I could sign up for a spot in the home in advance, seeing that I was a former resident in good standing of the Bronx. She said I'd have to prove how good my standing actually was.

Bonnie was back at his spot in the reading room. He looked the same as always, which he should have, since it'd only been a couple months from the time we first met. It just felt longer.

I asked him what he was reading. He picked up the book and looked at the cover.

"*Lady Chatterley's Lover* by D. H. Lawrence. Can't see what all the fuss was about."

"We've come a long way."

I spent the next hour telling him what had happened, how the whole thing turned out. He listened carefully, with his good ear cocked my way. He gave an occasional nod, to show me he was following the story, but otherwise offered little commentary. Until I was finished.

"I remember seeing ads for Cleary's car dealers on TV. Never met the man himself. Or his boys," he said.

"Not the kind of kids who'd come into the bar," I said.

"Did a good job of fooling me."

I shook my head.

"None of that stuff. They were smart. Enough to almost get away with it. If it hadn't been for you."

He smiled.

"So you're glad Osmund tracked you down after all," he said.

"I guess. Mostly since I got a sister out of the deal. We need all the family we can get."

"If you knew my family you might disagree."

I laughed at that, which amused him in return.

"I'm heading back east," I said. "If you ever need anything, let me know."

"Can you get me another ninety years? Didn't think so."

I almost made it out of there before he asked me, in a voice nearly too quiet to make out, "You glad?"

I turned around.

"About what?"

"That you learned what you learned. About your father."

I left without answering his question, which I felt a little bad about, but I think he understood. Some questions are too complicated to answer.

CHAPTER THIRTY-TWO

I t was really too cold to be out on the Adirondack chairs above the breakwater, but I'd been thinking about sitting there for so long, I had to do it. Amanda went along, huddled under a thick wool blanket. Eddie kept warm by aggressive and inscrutable searching along the beach and sniffing around the dune grass.

I'd been home for a few hours, and by unspoken agreement, had restricted the debriefing to, "We got them." Now that we were in our rightful place at the edge of the Little Peconic Bay, she nudged me into a fuller explanation.

So I took her through it, in some detail. As usual, she guided me along with strategic comments and questions, such as, "What made you realize it was the Cleary family and not the Paglieros?"

"Septic systems," I told her.

"Beg pardon?"

"All the plumbers I've known stop at the basement wall, where the sanitation guys take over, digging the holes, and installing holding tanks and leeching fields. The Cleary operation offered more of a soup-to-nuts solution. This anomaly stuck in my head. As I lay there underground I saw the two brothers operating backhoes and bulldozers in my mind's eye, pouring dirt over that tank we were in, and things started to fall into place. Proof that paradigms can serve both evil and good. The evil part is the human tendency to fit facts into an overall concept rather than let the facts follow their own path. Confirmation bias. But a paradigm shift can be a wonderful thing. Suddenly everything makes more sense."

"Pagliero's motives seemed mysterious because he never had any," she said.

"That's right. Why would he risk his current good citizen status with such reckless attempts on my life? Over a forty-year-old murder of a hired hand? So I kept wondering who else in the twenty-first century had so much to lose if I succeeded in my project? Who would know that opening up an old case meant modern forensics would come into play? Robert Cleary for certain. He knew Rozele and my father back in the day. As did his brothers. Something happened to her that sent my father into a rage. What if it was the Clearys who did it?"

"But not the priest," she said.

"A sin of omission or commission? We'll never know how much he actually knew at the time, but chances are he took her in to keep her both safe and silent. When I showed him my drawing of the crucifix, and told him where it was found, he probably suspected right away it belonged to one of his brothers. I'm guessing he alerted them, but who knows. I did plenty on my own to prove how close I was to getting the answer. Even if I didn't realize it at the time."

"So blood is actually thicker than water?"

"Father Cleary's god will have to sort that one out."

After a few more hours of this, she had most of the story. Everything but that thing that happened between me and Wollencroft, that we agreed hadn't happened. Amanda had never sworn fidelity, nor I in return. Neither had asked, and up until then, I had nothing to tell. What good would it serve?

I didn't know. I was only sure I was where I wanted to be forever, and that was all the certainty I required of whatever god might be managing these moral ambiguities for me.

ACKNOWLEDGMENTS

I've learned late in the game that generous experts in various fields not only keep the facts straight, they have an immense impact on the story itself. My gratitude runs deep.

Lieutenant Art Weisgerber, of the Norwalk Police Department Crime Scene Unit, and cold case luminary, made much of this book possible. As did Michelle Clark, Medicolegal Death Investigator with the Connecticut Medical Examiner's Office. Any fictional rendering pales in comparison with their accomplishments in the real world. We're all in their debt.

Bob Rooney of Mintz + Hoke, my go-to cybercrime whiz, is also a gear head of the first order. Auto repair scenes indebted to his review. The Very Rev. Jep Streit, Dean of Saint Paul's Cathedral of Boston, provided important counsel in matters ecclesiastical. My wife, Mary Farrell, and her cousin Nancy Calvert, both Bronx natives, were excellent tour guides of their old neighborhood. Eleanor Lerman helped me navigate the subways between the Bronx and the Upper West Side. Nancy Dugan, accomplished singer and short story writer, inspired the cabaret scene, complete with song list.

Paige Goettel tackled various French translations with her usual aplomb. To say nothing of her *joie de vivre*. Serge Bouliane of Tequila Communications and Marketing in Montreal added the French Canadian spin. Additional French duties were handled by Chloë Knopf. Ellen Willemin looked after my *Español*, as did Amarilis Guerra, who also advised on the Latino community in the Bronx. Harrison Colter, MD, an ER doc at Southampton Hospital, tolerated my book research while treating me for broken ribs, and a retired NYC Transit Police Officer named Sebastian Denican gave me the lowdown on Breezy Point.

If I goofed up any of their advice and counsel, it's all my fault.

As always, I'm equally indebted to presubmission readers Marjorie Drake, Jill Fletcher, Leigh Knopf, Mary Jack Wald, and Bob Willemin. And, of course, deep gratitude for Marty and Judy Shepard and their tireless Permanent Press team, notably copy editor Barbara Anderson, cover designer Lon Kirschner, and production artist Susan Ahlquist.

And many thanks to Mary Farrell, who puts up with all this, and our dogs, Jack and Charlie, who wonder why I'm hunched over the computer when I should be throwing the ball.